Lord kn⋯⋯⋯⋯⋯⋯⋯⋯⋯erena—was flustered en⋯⋯⋯⋯you frighten me? Yes, a little." She did not elaborate, but he nodded, satisfied.

"Good, for you frighten *me*, my little charmer, make of that what you will."

Serena laughed. "Well, let our charade begin! I only hope I do not lead my pretend suitor too merry a dance!"

"I shall be forever at your elbow, dancing attendance at every soirée you should happen to dream up for the Season. An excuse to be close to *my* 'intended,' you understand!"

Serena scolded herself for trembling at so lighthearted a promise. But no matter how much she scolded, she simply could not help herself. It was several moments that they gazed at each other, half with promise, half with unspoken understanding, and another half—yes, impossible in the mathematical sense but nonetheless true—held altogether with something else.

It was almost as if he had kissed her again, but this time with something more than just gloved fingers brushing over soft, much too yielding lips.

This time, the gaze between them had been like a brand, and the strangest thing was neither the earl nor Serena had moved so much as a step.

<u>BOOK YOUR PLACE ON OUR WEBSITE</u> <u>AND MAKE THE</u> <u>READING CONNECTION!</u>

We've created a customized website just for our very special readers, where you can get the inside scoop on everything that's going on with Zebra, Pinnacle and Kensington books.

When you come online, you'll have the exciting opportunity to:

- View covers of upcoming books
- Read sample chapters
- Learn about our future publishing schedule (listed by publication month *and author*)
- Find out when your favorite authors will be visiting a city near you
- Search for and order backlist books from our online catalog
- Check out author bios and background information
- Send e-mail to your favorite authors
- Meet the Kensington staff online
- Join us in weekly chats with authors, readers and other guests
- Get writing guidelines
- AND MUCH MORE!

Visit our website at
http://www.kensingtonbooks.com

LADY CARAWAY'S CLOAK

Hayley Ann Solomon

ZEBRA BOOKS
KENSINGTON PUBLISHING CORP.
http://www.kensingtonbooks.com

ZEBRA BOOKS are published by

Kensington Publishing Corp.
850 Third Avenue
New York, NY 10022

All Kensington titles, imprints and distributed lines are
available at special quantity discounts for bulk purchases
for sales promotions, premiums, fund-raising, and edu-
cational or institutional use.

Special book excerpts or customized printings can also
be created to fit specific needs. For details, write or phone
the office of the Kensington Special Sales Manager:
Kensington Publishing Corp., 850 Third Avenue, New
York, NY 10022. Attn. Special Sales Department. Phone:
1-800-221-2647.

First Printing: August 2003
10 9 8 7 6 5 4 3 2 1

Printed in the United States of America

To my family:
My magician, my artist, my gymnast, and
my handsome prince: I adore you all.

Chapter One

"The hartshorn, oh, give me the hartshorn! I fear my nerves are shattered, utterly crushed!" The Dowager Countess Caraway—Lady Fanny to her intimates—moaned a little, grinding a perfectly crisp wafer into nothing more than an unrecognizable piece of pulp. Her listeners glanced at one another and tried very hard not to roll their eyes rudely.

"Of all the impertinence! I can scarce credit it! Oh, Julia, woe is upon us! Depend upon it, the man has no sensibility at all! None! How *could* he have, when he uses us this shamefully?"

Miss Julia Waring did not reply, but her young aunt, more vigorous and lively than she, most certainly *did*.

"It is hardly shameful, ma'am, when he has given us a full ten months' grace to vacate . . ."

But Lady Caraway, once cast in the role of the oppressed, could not let such small considerations weigh with her. She closed her eyes dramatically and placed one jeweled hand against her heart.

"And us in mourning besides!"

"Half mourning," the honorable Lady Serena murmured, though she could have pointed out that though my lady's gowns were the requisite dove grays, this was more because she knew very well the color suited her. Indeed, she had long since cast off her blacks, and had fully resumed her round of social calls and recreational pursuits.

Uncharacteristically, Lady Serena held her peace. *She* still wore muted colors, though of late had softened the mourning a little, with bright sashes, or wildflowers from the moors. These she bunched into her hair on impulse, and was scolded later by her dresser, who despaired of the withering things that had been forgotten about all day. Serena was many things, but not vain, a fact that mortified both her abigail and Larson, the Countess of Caraway's fastidious dresser.

Miss Julia Waring, on the other hand . . . oh, Miss Julia was *delightful!* And she took a proper interest in her baubles and stockings and gowns. Now, however, Miss Julia was looking troubled, not surprising when her mama was wafting smelling salts in her face and insisting that she, too, must be quite overcome with shock.

"No, indeed . . . oh, Mama! I am quite perfect, I assure you! No, no, I do not need . . ." She turned her head away, causing her charming ringlets to glint in the sun. "Oh, truly, I do not need revival, I hate smelling salts, they make me cough . . ." True to her word, Miss Waring began to cough violently for one of her delicate constitution.

Lady Serena, sighing, saw that it was time to intervene.

"Madam, I must implore you not to dose Julia like this. See what an undesirable effect the salts have upon her?"

"It is not the salts that are causing her fit, but her sensibilities! Oh, dear, *dear* Julia, how are we to manage?

Cast out as we are, on the hard world, wrenched from our very home . . ."

Lady Serena bit back the retort that the dower house was anything but hard, especially since it had just been refurbished in the first style. That the bill had been sent on to the current earl was common knowledge. Only the extent of that bill was known to Serena, whose eyes had widened at the extravagance of the matter.

She had written some such thing to his lordship, but the man—himself, by all accounts, as rich as Croesus—had written back something cryptic, something caustic, but had not in any way caviled at the outrageous price. Which brought Serena back to her *own* particular problem. It was a small pickle, one which she had known would arise soon enough, one she had *meant* to scotch. . . . Oh, but she was in the basket now!

For what would his lordship say when, returning from the Americas, he should discover that the bailiff he had been corresponding with for nigh on a year was none other than herself, the Honorable Lady Serena Caraway? Would he consider himself grossly deceived or would his wicked sense of humor save her from humiliation?

She *knew* he had a wicked sense of humor—he had amused her vastly in his correspondence, one of the reasons she had continued with the deception. The man was most diverting. In all her two Seasons and her careless hostessing of my lord's larger entertainments, she had never yet met a gentleman who was not tedious or affected.

She had little expected to find such an acute mind in the incumbent earl, but she had, and had rebelled against giving up the correspondence for reasons she could only describe as absurd missishness.

Only now that the earl was returning, her cool assessments wavered and the missishness she deplored looked more, to her, like becoming modesty. Her calm management of the estate, which she had always considered capable, now appeared to her as grossly high-handed. What was more, the behavior, which would have been acceptable in a male—could not, under any circumstances, be condoned in a female.

How many times had the dowager countess railed at her about this? How many times had she positively *implored* her not to talk of farm plows? But Lady Serena had been stubborn and simply refused to listen to sense.

Worse, she had been horribly inclined to reveal her familiarity with the classics, a failing that the dowager countess still trembled at, she herself genteelly dismissing Aristotle and Hippocrates as "fusty old bores, no one knew *why* dear Lord Caraway kept so many of their books, but for the fact that the vellum covers matched so passing well with the wine-colored carpet . . ."

Serena had not paid the *slightest* heed to this voice of placid reason. Instead, she had managed to simply smile politely and nonetheless pursue her chosen studies. It was all perfectly clear to her now. She *was* stubborn and headstrong, though she had always considered herself to be merely disciplined and resolute. Now, the current Lord Caraway was coming to claim his own, and Serena felt . . . well, she did not know *how* she felt. Sadness, she supposed, that the great correspondence was at an end.

The last letter, arrived only two days back, was firmly lodged in a volume of Miss Austen's *Sense and Sensibility.* Not Pope, who was somehow too austere for the merriment the missive engendered. Oh, but he had a wit, this newest Lord Caraway! How reassured her brother would have been to know that he was not at *all* the emptyheaded simpleton he had come to fear, when despite his best efforts he had been unable to achieve an heir.

It was to this end that later in life he had married Lady Fanny, and thus blessed Serena with the most trying of sisters-in-law. Lady Fanny's daughter, however, was all that was charming, so Serena came to overlook his peculiar choice, or the fact that she was a mere four years older than her niece.

Now, however, she could no longer ignore the inevitable. Lady Caraway, casting her eyes about for the strongest footman, chose this moment to swoon, causing both him and one other unfortunate individual of the household staff to march forward and carry her up to her chambers.

"Oh! I *do* hope Mama will not fret herself into a fever!"

Alarmed, the younger of the two ladies assembled rose to her feet. She was dressed in a charming dimity, adorned with outrageous ruffles that threatened to dwarf her delicate features. Fortunately, her bonnet sat high upon her head, so her eyes were not *quite* obscured, and her sunny ringlets tumbled about her face artlessly, so you could still see glimpses of her pink cheeks and pale brows, which were puckered into a worried frown.

Serena's answer was dry, and slightly exasperated.

"Nonsense! I am persuaded Lady Caraway will recover just as soon as she finds herself alone in her chamber, without the benefit of an audience."

"Serena!" Julia shot her aunt by marriage a doubtful glance, then smiled. "Oh, I daresay you are right, but it is perfectly dreadful to *say* such a thing!"

"Perhaps if it is your *mama* of whom you speak, but since Lady Caraway is *not* my mama, I need feel no qualms. Now tell me, Julia, are you anxious about moving to the dower house?"

"Why no, not a *bit* of it! I have always found Caraway Castle a little daunting. I shall be much happier in a smaller place, though, of course, Mama . . ."

"Your mama shall be quite happy, Julia, once she has resigned herself to the fact. The current earl, I believe, shall be more than generous."

"Oh, Serena, I am certain of it! Why, he sent me a posy of flowers for my birthday and how he should have known, I can have no notion, for I am certain Lord Caraway never corresponded . . . Serena, are you quite the thing? You look shaky."

Indeed she did, for it seemed that every second she was to be reminded of her folly in pretending to be the wretched bailiff. Mr. Addington . . . oh, *why* had she not chosen a more original name? But the earl, surely, could not be expected to know that her christened name was Serena Addington Winthrop Caraway, or, indeed, anything about her at all . . . she must make plans to leave at once.

"Julia, I shall tell you a secret.,"

"A secret? What can it be? Serena! *Never* tell me the squire actually proposed?"

"Don't be such a goose, the man cannot be a day younger that forty-five! It is not I, but my perigord pie that he holds in such high esteem! I have told him time and time over that Mrs. Blakewell would make him a fine housekeeper . . ."

"Serena!"

"What?"

"You prattle! Tell me your secret!"

"Prattle? *Prattle?* Now *there* is a fine case of the pot calling the kettle black! But if you pick me some cowslips—I need them for Mrs. Murgatroyd's recipe—I shall tell all!"

"How dramatic! You shall have your cowslips, but please, please do not keep me in suspense! Mama might wake . . ." Julia faltered.

"Oh, *very* well! I am going to set up home. In London. Not in the *grand* style, you understand, but . . .

genteel. I have purchased a property in Mayfair, about a mile from the more fashionable haunts like Grosvenor Square . . ."

"Alone?" Julia gasped in astonishment. Nothing Serena could do would surprise her. Serena was so capable, so . . . clever . . . but *this!*

"No, not alone. I shall employ several servants of the first stare, and . . ."

"You deliberately misunderstand me!"

"Oh, Julia! You worry so! You cannot be so starched up as to require me to have a companion, can you?"

"Not a companion but a chaperon!"

"Now I *know* you tease! I am past my last prayers. *Way* past the first bloom of youth. The whole of Caraway knows that."

"Tush! When gentlemen line the very hallways to catch a glimpse of you!"

"Of my horses, you mean! No, Julia, you are a dear, but you cannot deny I speak the truth."

"It is not as if you have not had proposals . . ."

"But not the *right* proposals, Julia! I may seem like a radical and a bluestocking to you, but I value my independence too highly to be shackled to the first gentleman who comes my way."

"But Lord Edgington . . ."

". . . is too sober, dearest. A goodly man, but I fear I might become gloomy and out of sorts married to him. Then your aunt would become a crosspatch and I cannot think you would like that."

"Oh, now you are absurd! And try as I might I cannot think of you as my aunt, Serena! But what of Mr. Inglewood? I quite thought that *he* . . ."

"Julia, the only thing one can think of him is how good his legs look encased in their doeskins!"

"Serena!" But Julia laughed, for it was true. It was impossible to think of Mr. Inglewood's personality when his thighs, uncomfortably stretched into the tightest of unmentionables, practically begged to be remarked upon.

"He *is* very handsome . . ."

"But sadly uneducated despite the best efforts of Cambridge, I am afraid."

"Are you always so fastidious?"

"Always. It was a sad trial to my dear brother Spencer, who seemed to think my dowry and noble blood must make me respectable to *any* young man, and was therefore doubly annoyed with me for being so choosy. I had the pick, you see, of London's eligibles, yet I was so indecorous as to turn not one, but all, down."

"Are you perfectly certain that was wise, dear?" Julia's ringlets fell into her eyes doubtfully.

"Not *perfectly* certain, but tolerably." Serena looked amused.

"I daresay I might have succumbed to Lord Linklater, but unfortunately his odes always made me chortle, which somehow seemed to profoundly displease him. He gave up after the third sonnet to my winged stature, whatever that might mean. He was not, I recall, pleased."

"No, indeed. But he is to be married to Miss Peterson. It was in the *Tatler* and I daresay the *Gazette* only yesterday. Do you not feel a little regretful?"

"Not a jot of it! Miss Peterson will suit him far better than I, though I trust you do not take offense, Julia, dear, when I tell you I find this trend of conversation quite tiresome!"

Julia looked guilty. *Especially* since she had been conniving with dear Mrs. McNichols, whose acquaintance she had made in Bath. Well, it made perfect sense, really, when Serena needed to marry and *she* had a son who sounded all that was respectable, not to mention handsome, amiable and suitable. It had not struck Miss Waring that this son might have ideas of his own, or if it *had,* the issue seemed only trifling, for it was but to set eyes on Serena than to fall in love.

Serena had poise and style and all the attributes Miss Julia Waring admired decidedly, but lacked in abundance herself. Now, however, she adopted a soothing tack, for she thought the topic must be depressing for her friend and scolded herself for introducing so painful a conversation.

"I shall say no more, then, dearest! Tell me about this house."

"Oh, it is pleasant, not at all out of the ordinary way, but it shall suit me very well, I believe, for the stables are in excellent order and I shall be able to remove all but a couple of the bay horses to my London address."

"Shall you not be dreadfully lonely?"

"No, for doubtless I shall still receive my fair share of invitations, and though the salons are not large, I can open two up to form a quite respectable reception room. Do not look so anxious, Julia!"

Miss Waring smiled. "I shall not, for it sounds like the greatest of good fun and I envy you your freedom, Serena!"

The wistfulness in her tone was poignant to her aunt.

"You shall visit me often and though I do not aspire to your dizzy heights of elegance, I fancy we shall make a pleasant enough stir."

Julia laughed. "You are funning again! Only I *shall* miss you! I have become quite accustomed to your plain-speaking and good sense! You are more like a sister to me than an aunt by marriage."

"Well, just because you are at the dower house and I in London does not mean we shall lose touch. Indeed, I am perfectly certain I can cajole your mama into a Season . . ."

Miss Waring's curls shook dolefully. "Mama says her

health is too frail, and her finances . . . Serena, I should not say this, but Mama is clutch-fisted!"

"She is, but she has no call to be. Spencer left her very well off, you know, and the current earl . . ." Serena bit her tongue.

The current earl would not thank her for divulging the full extent of his generosity. Moreover, if she had not been deceiving him for a twelvemonth, she would know nothing whatsoever of these financial arrangements. She held her peace, but could not help remarking, rather sharply, that Lady Caraway could afford a Season for her daughter.

"Perhaps." Julia looked cast down, then smiled brilliantly. "Serena! *You* could sponsor me!"

"I?'

"*Yes*, for you are forever telling me what a matron you are. And *I* could accompany you and lend you countenance . . ."

At which, the Lady Serena arched her brow so high that Julia giggled. "Well, it is better than jauntering all about London without a companion! Oh, Serena, I would be so good! *Not* a sore trial to you at all, and though I might break a few hearts, I shall *try* not to get into any scandals or waltz before I have permission, or flirt with the Prince of Wales though he is so fat I cannot see why I would be tempted . . . or . . ."

"Stop, child!" A dimple played about the corner of Lady Serena's mouth.

"I never realized there were so many hazards involved in a young lady's first Season. You quite terrify me!"

"Oh, Serena! Nothing terrifies you! Oh, please say I may join you in London! It will be such . . . *ripping* good fun."

"Not if Lady Caraway hears you. She would wash your mouth out with soap for using such cant."

"Tsha! Mama would more likely faint and make me feel guilty for a month or more. Oh, please, Serena! Please, please, please!"

"Very well. I shall speak to Lady Caraway, but no promises, mind!"

As it was, it took Serena a week to approach Lady Caraway with Julia's scheme. Truth to tell, she had some such in her mind when purchasing the little house, for up until now, Lady Caraway had shown no signs of dislodging either herself—or her daughter—from Caraway Castle, never mind bending her mind to the problem of a Season.

"Well!" she said. "Well, well . . . I would never have thought it, but Julia has always been an undutiful chit . . ."

"Put that hartshorn down at once!" Serena's tone was so commanding that she did not know who was more surprised—the dowager or herself. But the hartshorn was duly laid down upon the occasional table, and only a small ivory fan was produced in its stead.

This the dowager fanned herself with vigorously, obviously feeling *very* ill used, but Serena made no comment, concentrating, instead, on her persuasive skills. At the end of her well-rehearsed recital, my lady was regarding her speculatively, for while Lady Serena was wild and independent to a fault, there was no doubt some small grain of sense in what she said.

Much of this small grain related to financial considerations, for though the dowager countess was left very well-off indeed, she could not rid herself of the notion that she was in dire straits, a fact that was confirmed each time she donned the Caraway jewels and realized, rather mournfully, that they were no longer hers.

Oh, if *only* she had borne Lord Caraway a son! Oh, if *only* they did not have to kow-tow to some trumped-up upstart from the Americas! Serena closed her ears firmly and helped herself to a fresh Valencia orange. She refused to criticize the new earl—whom she secretly admired quite enormously—and hoped her silence would have a dampening effect upon her sister-in-law.

It did, for the countess would not waste displays of sensibility on her unfeeling and ungrateful relations. She merely waved Serena feebly away, and announced, in failing accents, that she required her maid.

Serena, obliging, rang for Redmond, but smiled a little as she reached the door. The countess was behaving exactly as she had predicted. She had just stepped onto the slightly worn carpets of the second corridor when she was summoned back by the tinkling of my lady's bell.

"Serena!"

"Yes, ma'am?" Serena closed the door to allow for privacy.

"You will procure the necessary vouchers for Almack's?"

"Of *course,* Lady Caraway. Sally Jersey was a friend of my father's."

"Hmph! Opinionated hussy! I remember . . . well, it shall not do to gossip and I daresay I am the very soul of discretion . . ."

"Oh, *naturally.*" Serena's eyes were alight with irony, but Lady Caraway saw nothing amiss in what she said. Slightly mollified, she reached for her vinaigrette—never far from her side—and inquired about arrangements for modistes and other London essentials.

What she was *really* inquiring about, in her roundabout way, was who was to be footing the inevitably large bill, and Serena managed to very eloquently inform her that the entire matter would be squarely her own concern. "For you *must* see, ma'am, that I am very fond of Julia, not to mention anxious for a young companion."

"Indeed, yes, for you are a sad scatterbrain, Serena, and although I hesitate to have to inform you, you are now almost entirely on the shelf. Yes, I *quite* see how young companionship may serve to bolster your sagging spirits . . ."

Serena smiled sweetly and swallowed a rather cutting retort.

"My dear, she may go, for I am not an unnatural parent, and if she chooses to go pleasuring rather than to minister to my ailing nerves . . ."

"*Redmond* shall minister to your ailing nerves. And here she is. Redmond, I fancy your mistress has sore need of one of your tonics. She looks frail."

Since Lady Caraway looked nothing of the sort, Redmond regarded Serena suspiciously and pursed her lips.

She had *never* liked her ladyship, and the sooner Lady Serena removed herself off to London the better. Despite Serena's precautions, Redmond had had her ear pressed to the gilt-embossed keyhole, I am afraid.

Fortunately, Serena seemed blithely unaware of her dagger-looks and happily removed herself from the salon.

Lady Caraway was left looking at nothing but Redmond and a dish of long, skillfully peeled rind. She waved both away, her rings glittering bold in the sunlight.

Chapter Two

A smile lightened the features of Robin, Lord Caraway. His long, black hair may have been unfashionable in length, but the vivid crimson of the ribbon that bound it was of the finest quality, making even the most discerning of critics nod grudgingly in approval. After all, when one was as handsome as Robin—not to mention as rich—one could afford to defy the conventions. Even Amelia Stanbury, who knew every pattern card to perfection, and who could recite her *Debrett's* and her Charlotte Gilford's books of etiquette with unwavering certainty, agreed that it would be a shame indeed to take a scissors to those long, lustrous locks.

Of course, all these considerations were made under the cover of a great deal of giggling and blushing and twirling of silk-tasseled parasols, for naturally young ladies of quality did not discuss gentlemen at all, no matter *how* fine their attributes.

Fortunately, Robin was oblivious to these ruminations, or he might have seen fit to crop his shoulder-length mane posthaste. Instead, he merely adjusted his ribbon and did not so much as seek a mirror to inspect the result. He was no dandy, though his boots were fashioned most elegantly for comfort, and no one could possibly quiz him on the cut of his coat, or on the whiteness of his freshly-starched cravats. It was just, one supposed, that he did not suffer trinkets—or fools—gladly.

He refused, in the roundest of turns, to invigorate himself with scented pomades, or to brandish a quizzing glass, or even to allow a seal or two to dangle from his waistcoat. It was considered, in some circles, a trifle unfair that he should be so damnably handsome. He bore his good looks with a shocking ill will, disposing at an early age of the necessity for not only daily fittings with his tailor, but also with the indispensable services of a valet.

It was perhaps just as well for him that he had not stayed in London to hear the endless lists of complaints laid at his door, but had sailed to the Americas instead, where he had made a fortune in such commodities as sugar and rye. There were whispers that he had also spent some of this time as a privateer, or even more dramatically, as a pirate, but these were whispers only, and could in no way be verified but for the very fine state of his cellar, and for his immensely proficient use of the short sword.

Since he did not generally engage in duels, and since his cellars might, after all, have been legitimately come by, society merely called him a rogue, and ensured that he was always the first to be invited to any social gathering that happened to arise.

Sadly, he more often than not chose to decline, and when he did not, was most indiscriminate with his favors, a source of great annoyance to matchmaking mamas who would have preferred their daughters to be singled out more properly. Instead, almost every maiden in the room became afflicted with a strange and improper malady—dreamy giggles and distressing inattention to other more likely suitors. Still, he was so engaging a gentleman, and so rich, the invitations continued to flow.

"Daydreaming?" Captain Adam McNichols sallied into the room without knocking. He grinned and pointed at an inviting decanter half filled with a sublime, reddish gold liquid.

"Ah, port! The very thing!"

"My dear fellow, it is just gone ten o'clock!"

Adam filled himself a glass of the precious liquid. "I know, but really, Robin, one simply *cannot* pass by your cellars. It is a crime that one man alone should own such bounty!"

Robin suppressed a grin. "I am *not* alone, it seems."

But Captain McNichols had a talent for ignoring the most cutting of comments and was now happily engaged in tilting the glass to the sunlight. "Excellent vintage!"

"Yes. Adam, I do not wish to seem . . . you know . . . *inhospitable* . . . but did you barge into my private chambers merely to praise my wines?"

"No. Of course not! *Shoddy* thing that would be!"

"Ah." The whisper of a smile, but again, lost on his young companion.

"Truth is . . ."

"Rolled up?"

"Gracious, what a suggestion! As a matter of fact . . . oh hang it, Robin! I don't perfectly know how you guess these things. It is really most unnerving! Have no fear, though, I shall be as right as a trivet in no time!"

"That is what I fear."

Adam had the grace to color.

"Well, if you must know, it is the Fansham woman . . ."

A twinkle of amusement lit Robin's eyes. "Harpy, you mean!"

"Yes, but you must admit she has the most extraordinary . . ."

"Proportions?" asked Robin helpfully.

"You laugh, but yes! That is *precisely* what I mean. Well, she wanted a bracelet of diamonds and I was hardly listening to a word, for I had my mind on Mrs. Minchin's macaroons—she promised to bake me a plateful and I swear, Robin, they are the very best . . . well, I digress—at all events, I thought I could stand the ticket, but galloping good gracious, you can have no *notion* of the cost of these things!"

"What, macaroons? You can procure some perfectly acceptable ones from my cook for nothing at all."

Captain McNichols brightened. "Can I just? I shall hold you to that, my fine sir, though you deliberately misunderstand me . . . I mean the diamonds. I was never more dumbfounded than when presented with the bill! You can have no *notion*, Robin! No notion at all!"

Lord Caraway smiled. If there was one thing he *did* know, it was just that. He had bought several such himself, and for women far more beautiful than the Fansham one.

"Let it be a lesson to you, cub!"

"Oh, *pray*, do not start moralizing!"

"I? Hardly! That would be rather like the pot calling the kettle black. Draw on my banker in the morning."

"I would rather not, unless you hold it against my land or my bonds. You have been too good already . . ."

"Fustian. Now . . . I trust, by the look on your furrowed brow, that you have some *other* pressing matter to impart?"

"Yes! I mean . . . No! Not, that is, if you would prefer me to call later . . ."

Robin grinned. It was the sort of engaging smile that instantly put men at ease, and sent ladies into the type of trancelike ecstasy that required either a high dose of smelling salts or a chaise longue upon which to elegantly swoon. "Don't be such a cork-brain, Adam. I cannot possibly permit you to call later when you are bursting with . . . good God, I know not what! News, I suppose, but you cannot possibly expect me to survive the suspense. Tell all now, I pray you, if you have finished with my port."

"What? Ah, beg pardon! I shall replace the stopper at once, I should not have left it so, but in truth, Robin, I am distracted."

"So I see. Here. Let me help you. You are butterfingered, too."

"I have had a letter from Mama. It came with the last packet."

"Then I must congratulate you."

"Congratulate? How in the world did you know what the letter contains . . . ? Oh! I see, you are roasting me. You mean congratulations that my mother wrote to me at all."

"Indeed."

"Well, it is not very kind of you, though I dare swear you will change your mind when you hear what news I have."

"Let me hear it as we ride. Much as I am loath to continue this state of unparalleled suspense, my horse is being brought from the stables as we speak. See, there he is now."

Robin indicated the windows of his extensive home. Far below, a dappled stallion was being walked by one of the stable hands. He looked frisky, but his bearing was everything a man could require of such a beast.

Adam's gaze followed that of his friend's.

"He is a prime one. I wish you would sell him to me."

"You shall have him upon my deathbed and then, alone. Do hurry up, will you? I have a sudden compulsion for speed."

With which words Robin strode down his pristine hallway, grabbed at his riding crop, then proceeded to advance down his highly polished mahogany steps three at a time.

He did not seem to notice the stares of his butler, or the fluttering lashes of two undermaids and a housekeeper, all armed with such weapons as feather dusters and floor polishes.

Captain Adam McNichols, watching him, wondered for the umpteenth time how it came to be that such a man as he, so vigorous, so unbounded by conventions, so ready to run, rather than walk in a stately fashion, had been saddled with the ancient Earldom of Caraway. It seemed that the gods were having their joke. He wondered, rather fleetingly, at whose expense.

The day was dappled with bright sunshine and a few tiny white clouds drifted in the sky. Robin felt the wind at his back and drove his stallion to greater lengths than ever before. In truth, he was restless, his wanderlust—always a demon—grasping at him once more. It was time to move on, time, he supposed, to assume the mantle that had been flung upon his unwilling shoulders.

Not that he did not see the funnier side of it—him, being cast as an earl when once he had been a common pirate on the deep blue seas. Well, not *common* perhaps. *Never* common. That smile flickered in his eyes again, and his lips, almost unconsciously, curved into a quick grin. He may not ever have been common, but he had been a pirate nonetheless, though the riches went to England, and certain invaluable packets were wrested from the French. Oh, how he longed for those days now as he drove Pan onward, east, toward the morning sun.

Behind him, Adam thundered to catch up. Robin spurred his mount faster yet, over a thicket which he effortlessly cleared and across a small area of flatland that led, he knew, to the sun-bleached cliffs. On the horizon, he could see *The Albatross,* anchored out at sea, its great white canvas sails flapping lazily in the sea breeze.

A small crew would be sweeping the decks, checking the mainsails, inexpertly stitching any small tears that were discovered, painting the masts with a fresh black coat of paint, and no doubt imbibing—moderately, he hoped—the casks of rum and apple cider he had stocked just after his return to shore. They would be whistling, he knew, several ditties unfit for ladies' ears, but merry nonetheless.

Robin began to hum. His eyes meticulously scanned the waters, dancing with sunlight, then rested with a smile upon the trusty skiff bobbing against its moorings. Close to shore, just a small adjustment of breeches and he could wade to it without getting wet. For a moment, he was tempted, but that would mean scrambling down the cliffs, and though Adam would not mind in the least, the horses would doubtless object.

So my lord contented himself with a loud, penetrating whistle and a long, lingering wave across the coastline. He could see nothing of his men, but there was always the chance that *they* could see him, especially if bold Lem was playing with his spyglass again.

He patted Pan, then thrust his hands into his pockets, watching with a smile as Adam, far below, could be seen galloping helter-skelter up the steady slope toward him. His fingers curled yet again over a crisp unopened missive, waxed, strangely enough, in his own, unfamiliar seal.

The Caraway seal of England, and Lord only knew how Addington, as a mere bailiff, was authorized to use it. Not that he minded in the least—he was not such a nip-farthing as that—it only added yet another mystery to the already mounting mysteries that were, at the moment, tantalizing his curiosity.

He pulled out the letter, glancing curiously at the

delicate strokes and the soft, calligraphic twirls that he had come to recognize across the *C*'s and *E*'s. Then, seeing Adam catch up, he stuffed the letter back into his greatcoat and waited, a smile just curling about the tips of his very fine masculine mouth. A shocking habit, stuffing his pockets with wafers, but then he was not at the mercy of valets and tailors, and therefore did not have to suffer their black looks at such sacrilege.

Still, the wafer was burning a hole in his pocket. It amused him to think how eager he was to read it. It promised of a day eased, a little, of the usual constraints and conventions. His reward for meticulously overseeing his business prospects—a wearying but necessary business—and promising to attend not one, but two, society functions in the evening. He grimaced at the prospect, for American ladies were even more eager than their English counterparts to attach themselves to his person—and slightly less timid.

Interesting, but dangerous, for the slightest slip could have him leg-shackled in a minute, a circumstance he was anxious to avoid for a while yet.

He supposed, now that he had acceded to the title, that he would have to think of matrimony before long. It was amazing that Addington—who lost no time in delicately hinting at *all* his responsibilities and steering him blithely in the right path, should have been reticent about mentioning *this* aspect of his duties. Indeed, it was astonishing, for since taking up his correspondence with Robin, the estate manager had pulled no punches and had been surprisingly forthright in his suggestions. It was precisely this candor that Robin appreciated—and the obvious humor behind the carefully penned lines.

Mr. Addington's letters were always welcome. They were a place where the wryness of the earl's humor could be mirrored, faraway, in an understanding mind.

He had never, ever, looked forward to his mail as he had begun to these ten months past.

Not even a *woman* had held his attention for quite so long, and there had been plenty, indeed, of these. But *this* writer had no buxom features or inviting lips, *this* writer did not scribble languidly of passion, or boldly of promises. Indeed this writer was not even a woman at all.

Puzzling, for the hand was so delicate, the sheet so neat, he could have sworn . . . but he was being ridiculous. Men could write just as neatly, particularly so if they were entrusted with the management of whole estates. . . .

Not for the first time Robin wondered about the writer, and how such a clear-thinking person should have come to be the bailiff of Caraway.

True, bailiffs were uncommonly good with issues of tenancy and stock and even fencing, now that crop rotation was coming into vogue, but usually they were less educated than their masters, and *usually* maintained a subordinate role. This one, however, though not pushy, precisely, was nonetheless conversant with more than one would expect from a simple bailiff . . . a second son perhaps?

Certainly, he must have been educated at Eton, then Oxford, full of interesting notions, keen assessments, and a dry, half-confessed love of the land that was no less real because it was understated. Most particularly, however, the man had a fine sense of the ridiculous. Even now, a smile hovered on Robin's lips as he remembered one or two preposterous comments penned quickly in the last of the epistles. Almost, the man made him long for home, for the England of his childhood . . . .

Certainly, the correspondence had quickened his interest in this damned inheritance, something he had not foreseen. Caraway was up until recently hardly much more than an odd memory to him, and his sudden elevated title still made him laugh more than just a trifle.

It was really one of those strange and extraordinary quirks of fate. But the bailiff, with his wry humor, and his insightful caricatures of all the residents, made him see otherwise. He was quite caught up in the follies of the residents, from Mrs. Broom, with her awe-inspiring turbans and her selective deafness, to the dowager countess herself, with her die-away airs, and her propensity to swoon into every available male arm. Really, it was reprehensible comment for a bailiff, but so funny my lord could not find it in him to depress Mr. Addington's pretensions.

Not pretensions. *Exuberance,* more like. He had naturally been everything that was respectful. Certainly he had been everything that was *helpful,* advising on tenants and occupancies and particulars of planting, advertising for milkmaids, keeping the accounts . . . which reminded him, he had not seen any account with respect to Mr. Addington's *own* wages. He must look into the matter.

Pan, growing restless, moved away from the cliffs. Robin gave him his head, then found himself leaping effortlessly across a hedge of honeysuckle. He laughed.

"Little varmint!" Then, taking tighter control of the reins, he thundered over a stile and over yet another hedge, this time of a green plant the earl could not identify. Pan was just settling into a light canter, again, when hooves behind him caused the horse to slow. Or perhaps it was his light and languid pressure upon the ribbons.

Adam, breathless, had just caught up.

"Pull up, Robin! By God, I could swear you were half your age!"

"I am not precisely decrepit, Adam, though I must infer you were complimenting my indubitable skill."

"*Confounding,* not complimenting! I am breathless and you meant me to be so!"

"Only to show you that you do *not* want Juno! Not even on my deathbed. Now tell me this news at once, before I have to knock it out of you!"

"Mama wants me wed . . ."

At this dire pronouncement, Robin did nothing so gratifying as to look shocked. Instead, his eyes twinkled with slightly sympathetic amusement.

"Not terribly astonishing. *All* mamas want their sons wed."

"No. You do not understand. She wants me wed within the twelvemonth."

If Captain McNichols had said *"dead"* in a twelve-month, he could not have looked more indignant. His best friend and mentor was so villainous as to actually chuckle.

"A little abrupt, perhaps, but one must allow for such foibles."

"Robin! You do not understand! She wants me to wed Lady Serena Caraway!"

"Ah."

"Why 'ah'? in that famous, inscrutable way of yours?"

" 'Ah' as you put it, because you begin to interest me a little."

"Well, I don't quite see why—you can hardly know the female—very likely straight out of the schoolroom and cross-eyed into the bargain. If Mama likes her . . ."

'Not cross-eyed. Tall, if I recall."

"You *know* her?"

"The coincidence overwhelms me. I believe she was my late cousin's sister."

"Not the Earl of Caraway's?"

"*I* am the Earl of Caraway! And no, don't guffaw in that undignified manner though I quite see why you should want to . . . ! But in essence, yes. Lady Serena is a cousin of sorts . . . The late earl's sister."

"But, Robin, she must be in her *dotage!*"

"Not so. Older than you, perhaps, but only by a fraction. Serena was the last born of the fifth earl's fledglings. Born prodigious late, too—too late for his wife, who died in childbirth. Spencer, my cousin, succeeded to the title quite shortly after her birth and raised her at Caraway."

"But Spencer married, did he not?"

"Yes, when *he* was in his dotage! No doubt keen to raise a blood heir. Must have stuck in his gullet, the vision of any one of our scion succeeding. Well, I cannot say I entirely blame him. We have always been a faintly *disreputable* branch of the family tree, you know."

Adam chuckled.

"I can't think why! It is not so *very* disreputable to be a pirate!"

He achieved, with this remark, a faint, enigmatic smile. "Privateer, Adam! Privateer! And with your sword skills, disreputable is the *very* word I would use!"

"You tease me, just because I am not so swift on my feet as you, and refuse to assay those dangerous lunges and twists you are so fond of."

"Those lunges and twists saved our lives a few times."

"True. Sometimes I wish . . ."

"Times have changed, Adam." The tone was gentle, now, as if to a child.

"I wish they hadn't. I wish you were still plain Robin Red-Ribbon and I . . . I . . . a boatswain again!"

"But we are not. I am Robin, Lord Caraway and you are the very Honorable Captain Adam McNichols. We grow old, you and I."

"It is not fair!"

"Indeed. Now canter with me to those posts and you

may beg my consent to the match. I assure you, it is as good as any."

Adam ignored the last comment, but pounced upon the first.

"*You?* What in tarnation's name do *you* have to do with it?"

"Everything, I imagine, since I am now the head of this illustrious family."

"God! I was forgetting! But I don't *want* to marry her! That is my *point,* Robin! Mama has no business poking her nose in my affairs."

"How inelegantly put. *Not,* I fear, the best way to approach me."

"I am *not* approaching you."

"Ah, well, in that case, what are you in such a pother about? Come with me this evening to Lila Gingham's soirée and forget all about the chit."

"Mama has probably raised the poor girl's expectations."

"Then you shall have to strangle her."

"Lady Serena?'

"No, you fool, your mama! A meddlesome creature, if I recall."

Adam grinned. "Yes, but she bakes the best jam tarts in all of London."

"True. A virtue one cannot lightly overlook. No, indeed . . ."

Robin turned Pan around musingly, his eyes flickering, once more, to the shore.

"If you have no interest in the Lady Serena, tell her yourself. Look. I have some business in France, now the blockade is over. Accompany me for old time's sake on *The Albatross*—she is ready to sail—then return with me to London. I have a notion I need to set my affairs in order."

"The prodigal earl returning?"

Robin grinned. "Something like that. I have been . . . eh . . . reminded of my duties. I would be remiss to leave it any longer, more's the pity."

"Who has had the confounded impertinence to remind you of your duties?" This was said with burning indignation, though it was but yesterday that Captain McNichols himself had been guilty of the same. Robin swallowed his amusement.

"Would you believe the Caraway bailiff? His letter is burning a hole in my pocket as we speak."

Adam stared. "The bailiff! Now I know you are funning! Burning a hole in your pocket indeed! More likely burning merrily in the grate!"

"You wrong me, Adam, you wrong me. Would you believe I find my bailiff . . . intriguing?"

Captain McNichols shook his head sorrowfully.

"Mad in the head, that is what you are, Master Robin!"

"*Lord* Robin, if you are going to stand on points. And, my dear Adam, I begin to think you might be right. I *am* going mad. I certainly seem to enjoy my regular estate reports more than the weekly *Tatler!*"

"Then let us repair to England at once. I never thought to say it, Robin, but you must sorely be in need of a bit of town bronze."

"And a bit of muslin!"

Adam chuckled. "As if you were deficient in *that* area! Sometimes, Robin, I envy you your easy good looks. And your . . . air. It is not imperious at all, yet people seem to tumble over themselves to please you. It is most disconcerting, besides being damnably unfair."

"You will cease talking nonsense, if you please."

"Very well, but mark my words if every woman in London does not fall over herself to catch you."

"I am not a *hare*. I shall not be caught. Now *do* give

over looking so glum! By the by, if you *should* want Lady Serena, you have my blessing. I suppose I shall have to dower her . . ."

But Lord Robin's words were lost on the wind. Captain McNichols, in very fine form, had led his mount into a gallop. He wanted to hear no more words about matrimony, especially when they so closely concerned himself.

Chapter Three

The *Albatross* glided smoothly into port, the unfamiliar ensign of Lord Robin's unicorn and hart flying lazily in the breeze. If it raised a few brows, he was far too busy at the helm to notice it, or even to care. Possibly it was the bare soles of his feet that was causing the most comment at the docks, but he had been too long from society to really do much more than smile in amusement.

One blushing young maiden had the misfortune of meeting his eyes just as he examined the lead line for depth, making the swift decision to berth ashore rather than use the skiff. To her, he offered a cheery wave and a slight kiss of his gloved fingers. The gesture was wasted, for though the lady's color changed rather gratifyingly, his actions had the effect of causing her to turn away sharply and to jab the brim of her parasol into the beaver of a passerby, causing her further embarrassment.

Robin's eyes twinkled wickedly as he watched her go, then he cast his mind to other matters, like the safe bestowal of his goods, paying off the various officials who awaited his pleasure, finding Adam in the sudden mill

of people, purchasing a chaise and four—an extravagance
Captain McNichols gasped at, for there must surely be
some such conveyance already housed in the Caraway
stables—and other last-minute excitements that drove
pretty young ladies quite out of his head.

At last, when he was once again properly shod and all
that was respectable, he accepted a ride in Adam's conveyance, as his own newly purchased one required several refinements that were not quite ready—and the
services of a blacksmith besides.

Adam's chaise was fitted with burgundy squabs and a
decanter of port that he might have found satisfying,
had it not been very early on in the day and Robin's
nerves, for some strange reason, squeamish. He was
filled with a certain misgiving, for it was a strange thing
to leave a country a rogue and return a respectable lord.

Not that he had ever *truly* been a rogue, but society
dealt in appearances, and certainly by all appearances,
he had been wickedly roguish. He would not be surprised even *now* if ladies trembled to see him, or the
odd high stickler chose to cut him for the faults of his
youth. Did he care? Not a jot. Or not a very *large* jot, at
all events.

Despite these doubts, Robin denied himself the pleasure of Adam's reunion into the bosom of his family.
Though the young man had served him with both
courage and resourcefulness, it was not necessary to exchange dreary commonplaces with what was obviously a
doting mama, despite her skill with jam confections.

So, just short of Strawberry Hill, which was on the
outskirts of London rather than in the more fashionable area of Mayfair, Captain McNichols bade the Earl
of Caraway a reluctant farewell. Not before he had tried,
though, for the seventeenth time, to assure Robin of his
welcome. Robin, who was heartily sick of the town
chaise—badly sprung, and worse for wear, considering

the large ruts in the cobbled flag-paths that needed attention—shook his head firmly .

He further underlined his intentions by stepping down without so much as a glance at the tiger, who was just about to attend to the steps. As a result, he nearly trod on the poor boy's fingers, but by dint of swift reflexes, avoided such a calamity and rewarded the urchin with a silvery coin that seemed to greatly gratify the little fellow.

"Go! I shall walk to Caraway. It is but fifteen miles or so as the crow flies, and though I admit I am no crow, it shall not take me much more than the morning. Truth is, I feel sadly in need of exercise and the fresh air should clear my addled brains. Besides, much as I am rather attached to you, I cry craven at having to be present when you tell your mama you have overset her wedding plans. I know what females are like, and I take leave to inform you I would as soon be on a storm-blown sea than at Strawberry Hill."

From inside the coach, Adam made a comical gesture of dismay.

" Good point. So would I. I only hope Mama has not gone so far as to actually *propose* on my behalf!"

"Then you shall just have to *unpropose*. You cannot be held to account for your mama's actions. I am sure Lady Serena will be perfectly understanding—good God, *relieved,* even, when she sees your ugly countenance!"

But Captain McNichols prided himself upon his handsome features, so the teasing comment merely cast him into a further gloom—he rather feared the lady would like him too well by half. Robin, amused, doffed his marvelously fashioned beaver hat rather carelessly and waved.

"Adieu, you coxcomb! I am off to claim what is left of Caraway Castle. By all accounts the dower house, at least, has undergone the most hideous transformation. All lilac carpets and great gorgon head furniture, gilded in gold, with lion's paw feet and Chinese silks in the receiving rooms . . ."

"God!" Captain McNichols laughed. "I hope for *your* sake the castle is in better repair."

"It is. Thanks, I believe, to the bailiff, though he says little on this score. If the castle has been spared the dowager's renovating, then I owe him a greater debt than his last quarter's wage."

"And I am sure you shall pay it handsomely. You were never a clutch-fist, Robin."

The earl laughed. "On that note of high opinion, I shall leave you, cub. Good luck with your mama and do not allow yourself to be fleeced by any Captain Sharp!"

"Robin! I should call you out for such a slur on my character!"

"I don't fight children, Adam. You are a mere babe in the wood, though I admit your sword arm is coming along nicely. Take a few lessons with gentleman Jack— he shall admit you if you plead a bit and send him my compliments."

"What, the Earl of Caraway? He can hardly be acquainted with you!"

"No, you gudgeon! But plain Robin Red-Ribbon, of *The Albatross,* should gain you instant admittance! But not a word, mind, of what that Robin has become."

"My lips are sealed on that score, and you know it."

Robin's eyes twinkled. "So sober, my Adam! Of *course* you are not a gabble-monger. How can you think I think it?"

"I don't, only you . . . oh! You are teasing me again."

"Indeed, but I shall leave before you have thought up a suitable revenge. Tool along up that archway and I shall salute you from the shade of this courtyard."

Captain McNichols laughed and did exactly that.

* * *

Lord Robin found it rather strange, ambling first down the town cobbles with here and there a narrow archway filled with urchins and smiths and people too busy to stop their business to stare at his relative finery, to country lanes he had not thought to see again, and certainly not in such circumstances as these.

Much had changed—the willow trees, mere saplings when he had been a boy, grew in full force along the riverbanks, their leaves sweeping at the water's edge with pleasing grace. Here and there a sheep grazed, which was new and really rather curious, also the fencing, which had never been so necessary before. Still, much remained unchanged, the winding paths uphill to Caraway, the gamekeeper's hut, the stone crofters' lodges, and even the wrinkled old men who smoked tobacco and nodded wisely as he passed. The sense of familiarity overwhelmed him as he had not expected.

He had always known he was Spencer's heir, but had somehow cast the matter to one side like an old and insignificant glove. It just had not seemed possible that the earl, fastidious in all things, should not produce for himself an heir of the blood. His late marriage had not surprised Robin—or grieved him—in the least. He considered it to be the strangest of all whimsies that he should inherit the title and the crumbling pile of stones that was the castle. After all, he had forged a very different life for himself for many years now, and was perfectly satisfied with the outcome.

If a part of him longed a little for these familiar green fields, he told himself firmly that it was simply the contrast from the long days at sea and the giddy life of the Americas. He was not one to become fanciful! Still, his step was light as he muddied his elegant riding boots and allowed his baggage and tiger and coachman and other accoutrements of wealth and title to linger upon the road, somewhere between the harbor and Mayfair and Caraway itself.

His own tiger was a feisty little thing, more than capable of fending for himself, and if his possessions took several days—and a less dusty path—to make their arrival at the castle, he would not be the one to complain. At least he had procured for himself the best of all coaches, so there would be no delays caused by axle changes or wheels cast adrift upon the great southbound road.

At last, when he had jumped two stiles, tramped something above fourteen miles, splashed through an unexpected stream, frightened the life out of several sheep—and muddied his fine lawn shirt, he found himself within sight of the castle. Not much had changed, but for the higher hedges around the imposing flagstone carriageway, and the cheerful vines that crept along stone walls—honeysuckle, he suspected, and grapes. He picked a few, tasting with enjoyment the sweet, juicy flavor of sun-ripened fruit. Almost ripe, but not quite.

"May I help you, sir?"

Inquiring eyes met him calmly. Delightful eyes, really, for though they tried to hide their twinkle of amusement, they failed dismally. Lord Robin for the first time reflected on the picture he must present and licked his fingers—ungloved—and smiled ruefully.

"Not unless you have a large kerchief. Mine is beyond despair."

"Here. Take mine. It is not large, but it will serve."

"How kind you are! Do you always treat strangers thus?"

"Only the ones who steal our fruit! Good day, sir!"

"Wait!"

The lady stopped.

"Your name?"

"This is a most improper forum for introductions, sir!"

"Are you always so decorous?"

"I strive to be." Serena firmly discounted from her mind the highly improper correspondence she was currently engaging in. The stranger could know nothing of that. Besides, she told herself, *that* was an aberration. She was usually *everything* that was proper and decorous. She furthered her point to stop herself from laughing—the gentleman before her was making a most dramatic gesture of anguish.

"The very fabric of our society is built upon order and decorum, sir."

"Then I am doomed. I am hopelessly *improper.*"

Now why did she suspect the rogue was speaking no more than the truth? She hardly even *knew* him! Worse, why was her *own* heart behaving in a suddenly dramatic manner of its own? It was all this talk of impropriety, she felt sure. No, the man must not be encouraged, otherwise she would have to suffer the indignity of smothering a laugh.

Or worse. She did not dwell on the worse, for it sent her pulses racing most annoyingly for a confirmed spinster like herself.

"If you are so improper, then it is well we are not introduced." The words were severe, but still that twinkle gave her away.

"Hoist by my own petard!" But the gentleman seemed unrepentant. Serena hesitated, frowning just slightly. A strange thought had just occurred to her.

"Are you traveling far, sir?"

"Only as far as the castle gates."

The lady frowned, puzzled.

'We are not expecting guests. Do you bear messages of some kind? My Great-Aunt Matilda . . . ?"

"Good God! I have been mistaken for many things but never, I think, for a common errand boy!"

"Nobody said anything about *common,* sir, though I

perceive I have made an error. Intriguing. You do not bear messages and you are not an invited guest. You stea—sample our Caraway grapes and your destination is the castle."

Lord Robin bowed with a flourish, though his hat, it must be said, was decidedly damp.

"You are all that is kind, my lady. You adroitly changed the word 'steal' to 'sample.' Very adept."

"Not so adept if you noticed," came the quick response.

"I feel, somehow, that I should notice *everything* about you."

"I feel, somehow, that you are a rogue. I must leave you, sir, and wish you well. The servants' entrance is around that clay pillar. I suggest, though it may not be your custom to do so, that you use it."

"I do not *wish* for the servants' entrance."

"You do, if you want to avoid a severe fit of the hysterics. The dowager's sensibilities are frail, I am afraid, and not up to your cavalier attire."

"What? Muddy boots and a dampened shirt? *Surely* her ladyship is not so frail as that?"

He was regarded with a quizzical and slightly amused countenance.

"It is not my place or indeed *custom* to malign the dowager countess. I will wager you a guinea, however, that if you present yourself to her in that garb your mission—whatever that might be—will be rendered perfectly pointless."

My lord was just about to argue the point, when he remembered certain harassed references to her ladyship from his bailiff's missives. Perhaps the lady was wise to be cautious. Though he had every right to walk up the stone steps and dramatically announce his arrival, he revised his intentions with a sigh.

"Very well, then. I shall not disturb her ladyship's

peace. I shall simply bask in the afternoon sunshine until my shirt is dried, my hat less damp and my boots a trifle less muddy. I trust it is not a tragedy if I use your handkerchief?"

Lady Serena dimpled. "It depends upon your viewpoint, sir. If *I* were the handkerchief I might consider it a tragedy. I was not made for such uses."

"But think! Would it not prefer mud to . . . well, for want of a more delicate way of putting it, mucus?"

"Sir, you shock me! *This* handkerchief was not designed for such lowly purposes!"

"No?" Lord Robin's eyes gleamed.

"No, for you must understand it complements two of my town dresses perfectly, being made up, you will note, of mulled satin, and edged with the finest of Bordeaux lace."

"How vexing. You have just convinced me that my boots will have to remain muddy. A conundrum, for how I am to avoid her ladyship's intriguing display of hysterics I am at a loss to discover."

"You are funning me! You must have taken rooms in town."

"No, I bypassed Worthington and walked from the outskirts of London as the crow flies. If I had kept to the roads I would be hours from here yet."

"No wonder you are so muddy! It is a wonder you are not collapsing from exhaustion."

"I have been accustomed to worse, my lady—and the day is so sunny."

Serena smiled. His use of her title did not strike her as strange, for she was accustomed to being addressed in this manner and hardly gave it a moment's consideration.

"You are lucky. It usually rains this time of year. What of your baggage, sir? I cannot believe you have none."

"Oh, fear not! I have not descended upon Caraway

without so much as tooth powder or a change of linen. Though I must warn you, my dear, that I cannot—I simply cannot—engage to wear the padded shoulders and nipped-in waists that are *de rigeur* hereabouts. My attire is sadly simple."

"Simple, but not, I assure you sir, sad."

"Indeed?" Here an amused brow raised at the involuntary remark, for it was not generally the custom for young ladies to openly admire a gentleman's garb.

Serena refused to blush. She was not, after all, a green girl—nor was she so missish as to pretend she was. Though she might have felt a slight qualm, she ignored it and allowed the twinkle in her eye to brighten.

Unbeknownst to her, the very *lack* of a blush endeared her to him instantly. Robin *much* preferred plain speaking and honest admiration to simpering any day—besides which, if truth be told, he was flattered. Quite extraordinary really, for someone who seldom cared a whit what others thought of him or any of the outfits he chose. Which led him, of course, to the required explanation.

"My baggage is probably ten miles from London at the very least and I have no wish to accept the hospitality of my dearest friend, who at this moment is probably having at least one female rail at him like a fishwife."

"How very distressing. I *quite* understand your reluctance, sir." Serena's eyes danced, but she experienced the most peculiar quickening of her pulses, almost as if they, too, danced. She could not understand why,

"Do you?" My lord's tone was suddenly soft. He *was* reluctant to head back to Strawberry Hill, but his hesitation had less to do with Captain McNichols's parent than with a certain intriguing young lady. Even her grave, dark skirts patently failed to dim her inner light.

Serena's heart stopped for a moment. Well, it *felt* like it had stopped, though she knew this must be nonsense. She was breathing, after all, though her smile was slightly more tremulous than she could wish for. She wondered if she could have mistaken the man's meaning. But no, she thought not, for he was looking at her with a degree of warmth that was not quite . . . proper. Oh, bother proper! She had never been a high-stickler in her life, why should she begin now?

She smiled.

"If you are really set on the castle, Mrs. Dumpley's muffins are not to be missed, You could dry out in the kitchens—there is always a large fire burning in one of the gates. It should take no time at all, for though you are damp, you are not actually *soaked,* and though your boots are muddied, they are nevertheless very fine. We have an excellent man who could black them at all events."

"*We* have?" Robin regarded her keenly. "You must be mistress of the castle then. Either the dowager countess—which I know you are not—or you must be the Lady Serena Caraway! There is no need for introductions, after all, my dear lady, for we met several years since."

Lady Serena regarded the newcomer keenly. Then she shook her head slowly, though a puzzled frown slightly furrowed her high, intelligent brow. "Several years since I was not out."

"I rest my case. You were not. We met, quite accidentally, at the fishpond. It was on the occasion of one of my rare visits to Caraway. I don't know who was more in disgrace at the time—you or I—but I nevertheless believe it was my pleasure to rescue you from a drowning."

"From a . . ." Lady Serena looked puzzled. "Good God! You are . . . Robin, Lord Caraway! I did not look for you to return so quickly!"

"Ten months—no, closer to eleven—is hardly *quick,* Lady Serena."

"Yes, but . . ." Serena held her tongue. She had almost revealed her knowledge of the earl's most recent intentions. Indeed, his missive to her was burned into her consciousness and occupying almost every thought of her day. She must not make a slip like that again. She changed course, to distract his quick wit from her hopelessly obvious gaffe.

"It was not a drowning you rescued me from, Lord Caraway, but a scolding! I can swim like an eel, you know, but I had no business being out by the ponds when guests were by. I would doubtless have received the most dreadful tongue-lashing had you not intervened."

"Then I am most glad that I did. Now, about this bootblack . . . will he not object to blacking the boots of a perfect stranger? One, moreover, who has arrived unannounced without a stick of baggage?"

"Oh, in the ordinary way he would—he has a very high notion of what is fitting, has Hanks, but I could wheedle him. It is no doubt very bad for me, but I fear the servants spoil me dreadfully."

"Because you wheedle?"

"Only when I have to. You may stop laughing sir, wheedling is a very necessary art and I am told that in a female it is perfectly entrancing."

"Vexing, more like! " But Lord Robin was smiling.

Chapter Four

Captain McNichols had barely had a chance to remove his beaver and exchange pleasantries with Gifford, the trusty manservant in whose able hands rested the task of keeping his mother and three lively sisters in order, when he was accosted by not one but *two* of these same sisters. His mama followed close behind.

Mrs. McNichols, of course, did not precisely prance around his coat sleeves, nor did she pull playfully at his immaculately wrought cravat like his *sisters* but she *did* call him imperiously to her side and demand a kiss. This, just as if he were a boy in coattails which, naturally, was the manner in which she viewed him still.

Captain Adam McNichols, who was nothing if not kindhearted, suffered these ministrations gladly and even rather fondly commented on his sister Louisa's hair—arranged in a way that he was told, was "all the rig." He allowed himself to be drawn into the green salon, and he even suffered, without a murmur, the sweet orgeat that was proffered him from Gifford's salver. Not a complaint did he make, though he thought with longing of Lord Robin's amply stocked cellars.

He also observed (with a slight inward groan) that there appeared to be nothing so cheering on offer at Strawberry Hill. He really must make haste to rectify that circumstance. Still, he was an admirable sort of fellow and he suffered gladly the inquisition that followed, understanding that though his sisters shouted two at a time and his mama tapped impatiently with her silver-topped cane, it was only their great joy at seeing him again that caused them to behave so rashly, and to upset the tea things in their excitement.

Still, there was no harm done, as Lucy the serving maid was still in their employ, and after an excited little bob of her own, cleaned the ensuing mix of china and milk and polished silver salvers without the least bit of fuss.

Captain McNichols rather wished the *orgeat* had shared the same fate, but he was an unlucky devil—or so he thought—and thus remained with his half-drunk glass quite intact.

For what seemed an interminable amount of time he parried questions about *The Albatross*—not for the world would he divulge its true function upon the high seas—and he had the satisfaction of boasting about his life in the Americas without actually divulging much about opera dancers and other such unsuitable luminaries.

His mama smiled upon him dotingly and his siblings regarded him cautiously, if patronizingly. When the discussion inevitably came round to the latest gossip in London, especially the romantic exploits of Robin Red-Ribbon and his crew, who were now famous for their privateering exploits—and more specifically for foiling the French at every turn, Adam merely smiled politely and agreed that it all sounded "too exciting for words."

But he managed a polite yawn at that moment, and deftly changed the subject, confirming his sister's worst fears that he was really a bit of a slow-top. Captain Mc-Nichols, if truth be told, was a pattern card of patience and reticence for a man bursting with stories and anecdotes that would have caused his mama's straight white hair to curl instantly. But he had sworn an oath to Robin, and he, like his crew, would rather die than break it.

He drew the line, however, at being called "baby" and positively glowered when Ermentrude—the oldest of his siblings—teased him over his pronounced lack of beard, despite his best efforts at achieving a vaguely piratical effect.

"Hush," said his mama, eyeing him keenly and demanding, with a sweep of her arm and a tinkle of a great many jeweled bracelets, "do not tease him so! Can you not see he is weary still from the voyage? And why he should not think to introduce to us the young Earl of Caraway, of whom we have heard so much over the last few months, one cannot even *begin* to imagine!"

"Mama, he was in haste!"

"Hmph! Well, I cannot fathom what his hurry was since he has dawdled nigh on a twelvemonth to make his appearance. Society is agog, I can tell you that. Now on the subject . . . I have made the acquaintance of Lady Serena Caraway, your young friend's cousin, I think it is, though I can never quite be sure if it is once or twice removed, though I rather suspect . . . oh, Louisa, dear . . . do be a dear and leave us to have a comfortable coze! I have something very particular to say to your brother . . . now you, too, Ermentrude, and don't scowl, so, I won't have it, it is very bad for the complexion as you are well aware. I shall not permit you to have frown lines before you are thirty. No, that is worse. Scowling is markedly worse, is it not, Adam, dear? Now you mark my words . . ." But the ladies did not remain to mark Mrs. McNichols's words. Indeed, they escaped most thankfully to the sewing room, there to make speculative remarks about their brothers' health and marital prospects. Sad to say, despite the room's obvious function, no sewing was taken up whatsoever.

In quite another room, in quite another place, a great flurry of stitching was being undertaken, for it must be said that while Miss Julia Waring was not a dab hand with the decoction of potions, nor a bruising rider (unlike the able Lady Serena), she sewed quite exquisitely and was even now engaged in the hemming of a wondrous morning gown of shimmering pink, crusted with tiny seed pearls and lined, inside and even on the overdress, in silver.

She was perfectly content with her lot, humming a sweet, melodious tune and watching the window outside as her hands flew effortlessly over her work. Mama, once again, had the sick ache and though she sympathized, she was nevertheless young enough and pretty enough to be extremely excited about the prospects of her presentation in London.

Oh, the balls! The crossing of the hallowed portals of Almack's! Unlike other young ladies of her age, she suffered none of the anxieties and paroxysms of fear in this regard that she might have—Serena had promised to procure her vouchers and she was perfectly certain that this would transpire.

The Lady Serena, she knew, was sublimely competent. It also helped, of course, that she was on foremost terms with all of the great patronesses of the age. Even the Princess Esterhaczy had once graced Caraway with her presence, though naturally not as often as the likes of Sally Jersey, whose husband had been on intimate terms with the late earl.

No, Miss Julia Waring was not at all concerned about her entrance into society, only that she might not have quite so many dance partners as she might. But such fears were all perfectly natural, and did not in the least blight her overall sense of anticipation. She was excited, as all young maidens are at that particular age and stage in their lives.

Her head was full of dreams of dashing young men, who would look into her eyes, whisk her across dance floors, fight for her favors (but only in the most gentlemanly fashion and if they dueled over her, naturally no one would actually get hurt, save perhaps for a dashing scar or two). The minutes passed into hours but Miss Waring hardly noticed, so absorbed was she in her happy, absurdly nonsensical thoughts.

It was only when the dinner gong struck and there was still no sign of Serena, that she cast aside her stitchery. All but the bodice was now complete and *that*, she thought, she might leave to a seamstress. She ventured out into the gardens. There was *still* no sign of Serena, but she did not worry unduly. Her aunt—no, she could not think of Serena as her aunt!—was often late, caught up in estate business and such.

It was a wonder to her how much Serena knew, and what an interest she took. It was admirable, for sure, but certainly more a man's work than a lady's. Still, Serena was no ordinary lady and Julia could not help but feel thankful for that. She might not suffer spasms at the thought of Udolpho in a *Castle of Otranto,* or share any of her enthusiasms for the Minerva Press novels, but she was truly the best—the very best—friend a young lady could have. And she had the added cachet of taking her to London! Miss Waring wanted to hop on her delicately slippered feet but she restrained herself, not wishing her mama to have an apoplexy if she happened to cast her eye out of one of the tall, lead glass windows above her head.

* * *

Captain Adam McNichols, in the meanwhile, was wishing—politely, of course—his *own* mama to damnation. Or, if not to damnation then to perdition at the very least, for it appeared, from her conversation, that she had proposed on his behalf.

It seemed incredible, but apparently Mrs. McNichols—who naturally only wanted the very best for her handsome and eligible offspring—had decided that Lady Serena was not only a diamond of the first water, but also wasted in spinsterhood.

Apparently it was Adam's first task to rescue her from this ignoble state—a state that his mama deplored, and could only believe that *Serena* deplored, despite her maidenly protestations to the contrary. After all, as Miss Julia Waring confided, Serena had even considered taking to mob caps! It was *unthinkable* with such a wealth of lustrous copper hair. Short, but that could be remedied, of course. No, it was all perfectly clear. Adam simply *must* rescue her from her impending doom.

"No, no"—she held up her hand imperiously. "Before you protest, Adam dear, it is not purely pity on my part, else naturally I would be marrying you off to *all* the spinsters of the neighborhood and that, of course, can not be—" Adam was slightly gratified to hear this pronouncement, but not much, for his beloved mama continued.

"No," she insisted, "Lady Serena's *own* perfection makes the match so necessary. Oh, she's kind and heavenly and a beauty and perfect in every way, save for the occasional lapses into discourse more suitable to males. But doubtless you could soothe the bluestocking from her nature—I know how persuasive you can be with females!"

Mrs. McNichols knew nothing of the sort, for Adam had advanced his influence with and knowledge of females considerably since he had set sail on *The Albatross* three years before. Still, his mama could know nothing of this—to his secret relief—so he remained silent on this score, and chose instead to rail at her with regard to her preposterous matchmaking activities.

"Mama, how *could* you speak for me?"

"If I did not, *you* certainly would not have, and indeed, my dear, you will only thank me for it, for Lady Serena is a model of propriety and goodness, quite apart from being able to produce absolutely the most soothing balm for chilblains I have ever come across . . ."

"Mama! If it is chilblains you want a cure for, I can direct you to any number of country doctors who could provide you with your needs. I tell you, I do not require a wife!"

"You are pulling straws with me, son, you *know* I only mentioned the chilblains as a small aside. Lady Serena is everything you could want in a wife, Adam, besides being of the very first family and possessing a dowry that would quite make you stare! I have taken the liberty of procuring for you a special license, which is no small thing, let me tell you, besides the cost of a new roof for the church . . . now where did I put it? Oh dear me, how perfectly silly I am! It is right here with my correspondence. Take it, Adam, before I am such a scatterbrain I forget . . ." Mrs. McNichols thrust the parchment on poor Adam, who felt doom was now perilously upon him unless he made a firm and urgent stand at once.

"And did this paragon accept me, Mama? I am merely curious, you understand!"

"Of *course* not, what have I been telling you? She is the very model of propriety, Adam! She could not accept such a proposal from anyone other than yourself, though naturally she no longer requires parental permission—which is fortunate, since both her parents are long deceased and it was the late earl who was her guardian, but this is all besides the point . . ."

"For the first time I perceive you speak some sense, Mama!"

But Adam's newfound wryness was quite lost on the doting Mrs. McNichols, who in throwing her loving arms about his person, quite destroyed the elegant line of his cravat and cried that she had known how it would be, and that she'd felt all along that it was simply a matter of time before Adam could be brought to her viewpoint.

Upon which Adam, good-natured as he was, compressed his lips firmly and perceived grimly that if it was not his unfortunate duty to actually *marry* the female, it was at least common civility to *speak* with her and apologize for his mother's supreme forwardness.

So he agreed to make all haste to Caraway—in the morning, of course, after he'd had the benefit of an excellent sleep in the featherbed that had been kept specially for his use. He was assured that his dear old bear Griffin was still warming the sheets for him, though he had but recently been patched, owing to the circumstance of some of his stuffing leaking.

Whereupon, with a sigh, Captain McNichols thanked his mama and confirmed that yes, he did indeed remember his childhood toy and that yes, yes, he was thankful that he had been so restored.

He also muttered a heap of piratical epithets into his toast that would have shocked his mama and even his elder sisters, but *that,* he thought, was a liberty he deserved. Griffin indeed!

"Could that be a gentleman?" Miss Waring rather thought so as she guiltily ignored the third sound of the gong—honestly she did not know why they still bothered, for with her mother's sick aches and Serena's jauntering about the countryside the covers were always being held back anyway—and peered across the marbled pillars of the gazebo.

Yes, she had been perfectly correct, it *was* a gentleman, though strangely damp and not quite . . . Julia tried to find the word. He looked wild, and masculine, and highly improper . . . though why he should, with such fine boots and a lawn shirt that fitted as though it were molded to his very body . . . Julia blushed, for she had not *seen* so fine a body before, nor such perfectly fitting breeches . . . gracious! He was positively indecent, though he must have begun the day with immaculate grace.

Miss Waring had a seamstress's eye, for she was very fond of needlework, and could see that though the gentleman seemed quite larger than life, his clothes—despite their deplorable, muddied state—were most exquisitely styled and stitched. A gentleman, then, despite alarming appearances.

Lady Serena, slightly to his right—looked very fine herself, in her black velvet riding habit, though why she would not have military style epaulettes when they were all the rage . . . was she blushing? No, of course not. *Nor* was she batting her pretty lashes to show her fine eyes to advantage . . . Julia peered a little more daringly round the pillar. She gasped. Serena, in the company of such a paragon, was actually *glaring*.

Miss Waring tiptoed to get a better view. Yes, her eyes had not been deceptive. Lady Serena looked cross. She was scowling. Very fiercely, too, and the gentleman—heavenly, oh, heavenly—was that a ribbon he sported? It was. Oh, those long locks, soft as silk . . . but he looked frightfully annoyed. Gracious, it looked as though he were going to *shake* Serena. He *was!* He was shaking her! Should she step out and defend Serena? Whatever could they be talking about?

Miss Waring breathed a sigh of relief when Serena slapped him. "Oh, dear," she could not help thinking, "I wonder whoever he can be?"

Positively *mad* with indecision, Miss Waring was spared the necessity of taking any step at all by the Caraway footman, who at that moment appeared, soft-footed at her side, and respectfully murmured that the dowager awaited her company in the breakfast room, she having arrived but five minutes since, and mindful of the first remove which might spoil if further delayed.

Miss Waring needed no extra telling, for she was both excellent-natured and rather timid—she had no wish for one of her mama's famous scolds.

Chapter Five

Serena's heart fluttered traitorously. She knew she was in more trouble now than she had ever been in her life, never mind the small incident of the pond. Good gracious, if his lordship should even *suspect*... And yes, he *was* as damnably handsome as she had imagined, and his smile *was* as intriguing as she had pictured.... She had better advance her plan and remove herself from the household at once, before she lost every shred of her usual common sense. Before she was unmasked in front of this man who had no business to be as attractive as he was... before...

"Lady Serena! Are you well?"

"Perfectly, thank you! Just wool-gathering, I fear. If you are the Earl of Caraway, I must welcome you at once, my lord, and naturally you shall make your entrance through the grand hallways. I cannot think what can have overcome me to make any other suggestion."

The earl grimaced wryly. "You have just been at pains to tell me. And on the basis of what you *have* just said, I think the back entrance plan is the most sensible. I have no wish to endure the dowager's vapors in a damp shirt."

"But you cannot . . . this is absurd, my lord! You cannot enter your own home through the back door. It is unthinkable!"

"Unthinkable or not, I can, and shall. I have it on the best authority that the dowager wishes to throttle me anyway. I do not wish to be on a back foot when I first renew my acquaintance with her."

"But who can have been carrying tales about the dowager?" asked Serena, forgetting for a moment her own rich and lively accounts in the letters she had been blithely penning. "I assure you, the countess is everything that is civil when guests are about."

My lord's lips twitched. He was a master at reading between the lines. "That may be so, but I nevertheless have the most impeccable sources! Now do be a dear and allow me to enter the portals of my own home in whatever manner I desire."

"The servants will think it mighty strange in you, sir!"

"I shall take that risk, I think, Lady Serena. Unless . . . good Lord, why did I not think on this before? You shall escort me, if you will, to the bailiff's residence. He will overlook my dubious attire until my baggage arrives. I have certain matters to discuss with him, in any event. It is the perfect scheme!"

Lady Serena paled almost perceptibly, but Lord Robin, accustomed as he was to young ladies paling in his presence—or alternately flushing a rosy red, one would never determine which was likely to occur—did not immediately see anything amiss.

"The—the bailiff, my lord?" Serena, for once, was at a loss for sensible words.

"Indeed, yes! Your Mr. Addington. I have had some most helpful correspondence from him. He is the very man to take pity on me in my present predicament. Does he take the south cottage lodgings?"

"Yes! No!"

"Now what does that mean, I wonder? Yes he does, or no, he does not?" Robin looked amused rather than impatient.

Serena gazed at him wildly, causing a faint furrow of interest to cross his features. He could discern no real reason for the lady's sudden confusion. But then he had seen it time and time again . . . even the most sensible of females succumbed to moments of dizziness.

He could not think why, for he was not overly vain, and though he *did* know he had an unaccountable effect on womankind, he had not, up until now, noticed the symptoms in the fair lady Serena. He stood by patiently, though, whilst she gathered her wits.

As she did so, he surprised himself by having the sudden impulse to kiss her. He wondered what her reaction would be. Then he frowned, reminding himself that he was no longer Robin Red-Ribbon, captain of *The Albatross,* but a fusty old peer of the realm.

Peers did *not* kiss gentlewomen unless they were betrothed. Which brought him, of course, to the conundrum of Adam. *This* was the lady Adam's mama had so set her heart upon. An excellent choice, so why, then, did he feel it so keenly?

Why did he so instinctively disapprove? Why was he so set on throwing a spanner in this particular spoke? He could not say. But he suddenly felt the matter fiercely. How flippant he had been when he had granted Adam his consent—and how serious he would be when he withdrew it. Not that Adam needed any further urging, but he would attend to the affair all the same.

"My lord—" Serena struggled with the lie, for it was not in her nature to be dishonest.

"Yes?" Robin, brought back from his musings, *still* found he wanted to kiss the tip of her nose. It was really perfectly charming and a damnable temptation, being so close, as it was, to his own countenance. He was—despite his excellent physique—built on the slight side, so that, Serena being tall, he was confronted rather too closely with the tip of her nose and her vaguely uptilted lips. Horrifying, really, for one so accustomed to feminine charms. He schooled himself not to obey his impulses. Impulses, he knew, led to nowhere but trouble.

"Mr. Addington has left our employ."

"He has done *what?*" The tone was uncharacteristically sharp.

Lady Serena colored, but ignored the annoyance evident upon my lord's features.

"He left about a week ago."

"How so? I had no *notion* that this was his intention!"

"No, indeed, but nevertheless, it is so. I have placed an advertisement in the *Gazette* for his replacement. I hope that is acceptable, my lord."

"No, it is *not* acceptable!" Robin tried not to glower at the Lady Serena, but failed. It was quite unaccountable, really, how much he had been looking forward to making his bailiff's acquaintance. Indeed, he felt he knew him already. The correspondence that had passed between them was of so intimate a quality that he could almost picture Gabriel Addington, though he had not, obviously, ever had a portrait or miniature. Still, the man's mind had been so incisive, penetrating and humorous that he had positively *longed* to make his acquaintance.

"What is his direction, pray?"

Serena gulped. It was hard to make up a good Banbury tale when the recipient was glowering at you balefully—and most unfairly, in her opinion.

"I do not rightly know, my lord. London, I would have assumed, though that is no sure thing, for I believe he had a sister in Bath . . ." Serena frantically summoned up this imaginary sibling as interested eyes burned straight through her skin. Or so, of course, it felt.

"You shall furnish me with this sister's directions directly."

Oh, how imperious! Serena bristled suddenly, though she knew it was she herself at fault, and drew herself up just a fraction straighter. Her lovely eyes could not quite meet those of the Earl of Caraway, but no one could possibly find fault either with her bearing or with the dismissive gesture of her prettily gloved hand.

"There is no need, my lord. Though Mr. Addington was dismissed, it was not, I assure you, without a character. I feel sure you will agree that there is therefore no further need . . ."

But she may just as well have held her breath. My lord's demeanor, increasingly stern, was now positively incredulous.

"Dismissed? Gabriel Addington was *dismissed?* " Robin tried not to roar, but truly, he failed utterly.

Serena, both panicked and annoyed by his attitude, did not have a moment to be glad that his lordship should react so. Clearly, he had looked forward to meeting the man she had fabricated with the light-hearted tilt of her pen. She should have been gratified—in other, less heated circumstances she might have been—but for now, she was only terrified of exposure.

"I cannot see what consequence this may have! He was, after all, merely a servant . . ."

"I, my lady, do not treat servants so abominably!"

Neither did Serena, but it could not help her case to say so, so she altered her tone to match his and practically shouted that it was none of her concern, and the matter was far beyond the point since Mr. Addington was gone—long gone at that, and there was no way of recalling him.

"That is what *you* think, my lady! As of this instant, no orders are to be carried out on these premises without my express permission! Mr. Addington, as it happens, was worth his weight in gold, though you might not even be aware that he has not been paid so much as a brass farthing since he has started to do the household accounts! You did not, I trust, reimburse him for a year's worth of unstinting service to this estate?"

Serena shook her head grimly, for how was she to lie when the books were neatly inscribed in her own hand, perfectly balanced and ascribing nothing whatsoever to the fictional bailiff? Oh why, oh why had she made him up? It was an unforgivable thing to have done. She was mortified, but more so because the Earl of Caraway was looking singularly unamused, all hint of his previous charming demeanor vanished as the morning dew on a sultry afternoon.

She stiffened her back in response, her color heightened in anger—though whether at herself or at him she had no idea—and murmured tightly that naturally since he had now bothered to return, control of the estates would devolve entirely to him.

"Good! For I intend to reinstate Mr. Addington—you can have no notion, Lady Serena, how invaluable he has been to me throughout these months—and I intend, too, that he be paid adequately for the sound advice he has rendered me, not to *mention* active work!"

"Good Lord, you can naturally have no understanding of such matters, but apart from his incisive mind and ready wit, he has advised me almost entirely on the suitable crop rotations for these parts, not to mention other farming innovations like the introduction of these sheep. Scoff not! It is *these* sheep, Lady Serena, that will supply you with wool for the winter and the tenants with work spinning and weaving. I am practically self-sufficient, thanks to Mr. Addington's achievements! I cannot impress upon you enough how much I value his services!"

"You have made your point, my lord." Serena's tone was dry, but her eyes were traitorously wet, for while she could not help but be desperately pleased at the high esteem in which my lord held the fictional Mr. Addington, it did not help her situation one whit. As a matter of fact, it made it all the more precarious and desperate.

Lord Robin, slightly ashamed at making Serena tremble so, spoke in softer tones. He quashed the sudden impulse to put his arms about her and soothe away the tears that moistened her lashes ever so slightly, for he was not a hard-hearted fellow. Truly, he was aware of his own shortcomings, one of which was a temper swift to ignite, but equally swift to diminish into ashy embers.

He could kiss her, of course; her lips were suitably parted and it would be no small thing to close the gap between them, but he thought not. He was, after all, still very angry, though he understood that she may have erred in ignorance rather than out of spite. Besides, though she offered a tempting prospect, it would not do to arouse any expectations. She was not, like the absent Gabriel Addington, a servant to be trifled with at a whim, but rather, the daughter and sister of an English earl. Robin therefore exercised outstanding restraint, considering it was more in his style to steal a kiss than not, and merely offered her back her own kerchief.

"I am not going to cry, my lord!"

"Excellent, for I loathe and despise watering pots, which is frankly why I wanted your Mr. Addington in the first place. It was to escape the hysterics of the dowager countess, if you rightly recall."

"Indeed. I am sorry I am not able to help you. "

"It is a truce then, for I forgive you. Now tell me, little Miss Stubborn, what onward direction were you given for Mr. Addington, for I cannot believe he left without so much as a backward glance."

Serena nearly confessed, for he was looking at her keenly, and she wondered which would be more mortifying—to tell him who she was, after all his high praise—or to maintain the stupid fiction. All in all, the fiction won, for what possible explanation could she have for her outrageous behavior?

Now he might merely think her hen-witted—if she told him the truth, he would think her unconscionably forward. Not an easy choice—she wondered, really, why his good opinion mattered so much. Then she swallowed hard.

"My lord, there was none, I tell you. Best forget all about him. Doubtless he will send in his bill in due course." And he *would,* thought Serena grimly. She would demand payment simply to put an end to the matter, and then she would never, ever again deal in half-truths and lies so long as she lived.

"You expect me to believe that?" Robin's tolerance was tested just that little bit more with this unexpected defiance in the face of all his calm explanations.

"He cannot have vanished into thin air. You must, my dear lady, have kept his onward address! You told me only a moment ago you agreed to furnish him with references and not cast him off without a character."

"I said no such thing! Merely that he was not cast off without a character, as you put it. He was provided with perfectly good references, if you must know."

"Lady Serena, I do not wish to belabor the point, but

he must have left an address in case mail was forwarded to him in error . . . oh, in case of a *hundred* instances I can think of!"

Serena squirmed under his gaze. She wished they could regain their easy camaraderie. Oh, why had she not escaped to London sooner?

"If he did, I cannot think what I have done with it." The lie stuck in Serena's throat, but truly, she could not think of *any* excuse likely to fob off the earl in such a penetrating mood.

"Then think, Lady Serena, before I shake you."

His tone was dangerously low, his head—very handsome, as she noted even as she swallowed—much closer to hers than was strictly comfortable.

"You threaten me."

"Be pleased I only threaten a *shaking*, Lady Serena."

"You are insufferable."

"So I have been told. Now think! Do you or do you not have an onward direction? It really is very important to me."

"I tell you, I do not."

What else could she possibly say? It was the truth, after all. Which was how, quite naturally, the Honorable Lady Serena came to be shaken—but not with all of Robin's strength—and how he, as a perfectly natural consequence, came to be slapped in the shocking manner witnessed by Miss Waring in the garden.

There was a moment's silence as Serena—sensible, responsible Serena—recovered both from the novel sensation of a man's hands upon her shoulders—and from the stinging she felt through her gloves. In a flash, she knew which had been worse. Her slap, undoubtedly; for the shaking, though outrageous and mortifying and seriously annoying, had nevertheless also been oddly pleasurable, a matter she would ponder later in the privacy of her chamber. The slap, however, had been a very real response and really far too harsh for the crime. Or so she thought, scrupulously just even in the most trying of circumstances.

"I'm *so* sorry. My abominable temper! I did not intend you to sting *quite* so much."

My lord's eyebrows rose a fraction. Then, rather against his will, a sudden rueful smile lit his forbidding eyes. "How *much* was it meant to sting? I am merely curious, you understand."

"Only a little. Not enough for your cheek to be streaked. I am afraid I do not know my own strength. It was very bad of me."

"Indeed, but then, you were provoked."

"But naturally! I would not dream of doing such a thing were I not. You were trifling with me."

"I have hardly *begun* to trifle with you but we shall discuss that when my shirt is not damp and my cheek not so abominably abused."

Serena could not think what he might mean. That odd smile remained, so he hardly looked menacing, but she wondered, all the same.

"I *have* said I was sorry."

"No, it is *I* who am sorry. No matter what the provocation, I had no right to treat you thus. I have a damnable temper and am far too used to giving orders."

"We are both at fault then. I am sorry about Mr. Addington. If I had his direction I would give it to you at once."

"That is all I can ask, I suppose, though I do not hide that his absence is a severe disappointment to me. At all events, I shall further make my inquiries in London. He is bound to have registered with an agency. Cry truce, for the moment?"

"We seem to be doing that rather too often, my lord. I had not expected to brangle with you so."

"Had you expected to be docile?"

"Oh, perfectly! You can have no notion. Your smooth running of the estate is a testament to your excellent good sense. I thought we would be in perfect accord." And that, since Robin had been palpably taking every scrap of Serena's wisdom for nigh on a year, was the truth.

Chapter Six

Lord Robin, confronted with the prospect of entering through the backstairs or through his own front entrance, opted for the more conventional route.

Serena, desperate to preserve their tenuous amity, and unable—she thought—to endure the sight of him warming his shirt in the kitchens—convinced him that the dowager's tantrums would be as nothing to her own if he did not assume his rightful place immediately.

Robin, tired of the farcical position in which he had been placed, and anxious to sample the fine wines he was certain were laid down for him in the cellars—put up an opposition that was merely feeble and allowed himself to be outsmarted by the magnificent creature he had so unexpectedly stumbled upon.

Clearly, Mr. Addington had failed him, for apart from a couple of glancing references to Lady Serena's sojourn at his estate, the man had exercised none of his quick wit and incisive mind in describing her. Her presence, therefore, was something of a shock to him, for though he had been prepared for meeting the delightful Miss Julia and her less-than-delightful mama, he had not expected to meet anyone as witty, beautiful—and frankly, elegant, as Lady Serena. In short, he had not expected to have his feelings so suddenly—and brutally—involved.

If he had, certainly he would have spent the night in London—even at Strawberry Hill for all its faults—rather than make a fool of himself outside his very own castle. Yes, he *had* been a fool—a fool not to kiss her and a fool to shake her as he had. Now, despite the quaint truce between them she surely, held him in disgust. Or if not *disgust,* precisely, then certainly not awe or trust. He was a perfect fool, really.

Two minutes later, he was confirmed in this opinion, for the dowager was indeed succumbing to a fit of the hysterics. The butler, never before confronted with so much excitement in having the unprecedented task of announcing the prodigal earl, did so in loud, stentorian tones that could have been heard across a ballroom, never mind a small breakfast chamber.

Lady Caraway shot the earl a poisonous glance of fury, then called at once for her vinaigrette before simply swooning in her seat. Poor Miss Waring—seated at the furthest end from the table in the hopes of avoiding her mama's wrath—could do nothing save apologize in a fluster and upturn her chair in her haste to be of assistance.

The earl, cursing his fate and rather wishing he had remained either on *The Albatross*—or better yet, at his comfortable estate across the seas—gallantly came to the rescue and plucked the moaning dowager from the tablecloth as if she were no more than a mere featherweight, which anyone with the slightest brain could see she was not.

He seated her upon the squabs of the nearby window seat then drew the curtains, whether against the glare of the sun or the gilded wallpaper that lined the room from ceiling to floor one could not quite discern.

Julia, making frantic signals to her aunt, could nevertheless not manage to catch her eye. She was practically dying of curiosity, having witnessed the whole fantastic scene outside and wondering intensely at its outcome. But Lady Serena, for once, seemed oblivious to her plight, insisting, instead, on dishing out large quantities of deboned estate duck onto Robin's plate.

But he found himself entirely without appetite and with no recourse to any port whatsoever, the redoubtable butler having made off with the decanter in his excitement.

It was left to Serena to ring for the housekeeper and ask her to prepare my lord's chambers. From the manner in which that female paid heed to Serena's instructions, Robin inferred that it was *she* who had long since had the running and management of the house. This was a fact he found puzzling, given Mr. Addington's serious omission with respect to mentioning her in those most enlightening of all missives.

For the life of him, he could not think *why* the bailiff had been so reticent in writing of Serena, but he meant to find out, if it was the last thing he did.

Serena, wishing to coax just that sort of thought from his head, offered to show him the grounds of Castle Caraway—which had undergone extensive alterations since he had last visited—and also the layout of the first floor, though naturally not the chambers on the third floor.

"I am relieved to see that it is only the breakfast chamber that has been redone in gold."

Serena's eyes twinkled in quick appreciation. "Yes, and it is a marvel that you returned when you did, for her ladyship has entirely finished redecorating the dower house and wishes to wreak the same sort of transformation upon the castle."

"Then it is not a moment too soon that I have made

my reentry into civilized life. Tell me, do the portraits of your family still hang in the library?"

"No, they were removed to the picture gallery when my brother was still alive. He said he hated staring at the crusty faces of his ancestors when he was trying to read a simple book. Would you like to see them? Some are very fine. The last, I think, was done by Gainsborough."

"A very fine artist. I should like that, indeed."

"Come, then, it is not so very far, though we shall have to go around that colonnade, I think. Two of the rooms have been shut up for repairs."

"Ah, yes, the repairs." He had the estimates for these in his pockets, but he did not mention as much to Serena, who was at last catching her niece's eye and trying to convey some message or other rather unsuccessfully. All that happened was that Miss Waring began to giggle nervously at the sight of Serena's arched brows, and Serena herself gave up signaling in the blackest of despairs. Oh, it was impossible, simply impossible!

What she was *trying* to convey to Julia was that she must stay, under all circumstances, and act as chaperon. But naturally, Julia, agog for intrigue, thought she meant the precise opposite.

This simple comedy of errors resulted in Julia slipping away on the flimsiest of excuses, leaving Serena tongue-tied, staring at the forbidding face of the second earl and his multitudinous progeny.

At which point Robin—for he *was* Robin Red-Ribbon after all, and not much used to being a fusty old peer of the realm—seized his evident opportunity and kissed her just precisely as he wished, in front of at least four of his noble predecessors. He did not, to his surprise, earn himself another of Serena's notorious slaps. Instead, to his amazement—and complete undoing— he found the lady unusually compliant in the circumstances. Not only compliant but also a little complicit, for it was *her* hand, not his, that stole gently round his neck. Naturally it was then but a small step for him to reposition himself so that his own hand found a more amenable spot—right round the neat stitching about her trim, elegantly clad waist. It was a salutory and most satisfactory experience. Robin, much inclined to prolong the matter, promptly did so.

Serena, her head lost to all reason, found her body most distressingly pliant, and she knew that even if she wanted to run away, she could not, for her legs were like trifle and her heart was beating louder than the ormolu clock upon the shelf. She was brought to her senses not by her own maidenly shock, but by a deep, throaty chuckle at her side. Robin, finished, for the moment, with his exploratory pursuits—very satisfactory if not at all appropriate—could hardly contain his sudden mirth.

"What is so funny, my lord?"

"*You* are, my lady! And no, before you slap me simply as a matter of form, I must tell you that my intentions are strictly honorable. How honorable are yours, I wonder?"

But Serena was not in the mood to be quizzical, for her heart was beating faster than it ever had in her life before, and all she could think of was that if Lord Robin discovered he was kissing his bailiff he could not be best pleased.

She was feeling very guilty indeed, and it was easier to pin her guilt on her previous crime than to dwell upon her current one—a most unmaidenly desire to carry on kissing. That was precisely what the honorable Lady Serena wanted most in the world, though she could not fathom why at all. Or she could—given his fine stature, teasing eyes, wide smile, and sensuous lips—but she found it easier by far not to admit as much to herself. She was, after all, both sensible and maidenly. There was no doubt about it—the whole of Caraway knew it—*she* knew it; she cast the knowledge about her like a cloak, protecting her from all the whims and fancies and wiles and paroxysms of the gentler sex.

Lady Caraway's cloak, it had once been called by a half-laughing, half-serious suitor who had just suffered a gentle but firm rebuff. Lord Robin had just seriously tugged at the cloak, and the thought was both exhilarating and frightening, for it challenged all she believed about herself and her own inner desires and logic.

"I endeavor always to be honorable, my lord, which is why I have arranged almost immediately to leave for London. You cannot imagine that it would be suitable for me to remain at Caraway while you are in residence."

"Poppycock! This is your home and has been since you were born. If anyone is the intruder, it is I."

"In theory I must agree, for I am bluestocking enough to question why estates must default to the male heir."

Robin looked amused. "You would prefer to be mistress of this estate?"

"Why should I not when it is *I* who knows it best?"

"There is more to an estate than finding the best picnic spots and hiding places."

"*Indeed.* And if you are suggesting that *that* is where my knowledge begins and ends I hold you at strong fault, sir."

"I stand corrected. Perhaps you will help me with my crop rotations, then. I am sowing rye in the northern field . . ."

"You mock me, my lord. And it is not rye you are sowing, but barley."

Robin's eyes looked suddenly alert. He did not make the mistake of showing his interest, however. Rather, he displayed a sudden—if extremely false—fascination in the mix of hues Gainsborough used in the execution of the portrait of the fourth earl. As he was scrutinizing an area that could be regarded as turquoise, he murmured that he was certain it had been rye but he could very well be mistaken, for the southern boundary was certain to be fallow and the rye he had just purchased might have been intended for *that* field, after all.

"But you decided *against* rye! I remember, for I discussed the issue with the merchant at the time, and the price was prohibitive. You decided to plant tea experimentally in the southern square, despite the fact that the climate cannot generally sustain such a crop. That is why we tried the shelters . . . my lord, you *must* remember it. The planting was completed only two weeks ago. You cannot have forgotten that—it was *your* suggestion!"

"Mine?" His eyebrows were raised in lazy surprise, though those vivid blue eyes were now more than simply alert—they were riveted.

Fortunately Serena, still trying to recover from the assault upon her senses—and from her errant thoughts that made her desire the whole sorry incident to reccur—did not notice in the least. "Yes. It was a *very* good idea, though I worry so much about the cold. It has not been so fine as I had hoped but with the shelters . . ." Her voice broke off midsentence as she realized what she was revealing.

But my lord now seemed interested in the textured execution of the fourth earl's nose and hardly seemed to be paying her the slightest attention at all, which both relieved her, angered her, and puzzled her.

Lord Caraway had always displayed the most remarkable interest in crop rotation theories throughout the entire course of their correspondence. Could this man, she wondered, be an impostor? The thought flashed through her mind but was dismissed at once. How *could* he be, when he so exactly matched her recollection of him?

Oh, undoubtedly he had filled out a little since they had last met, and his hair was longer, and he had a certain indefinable arrogance about him that had not been there before, but it was, surely, the same man who had fished her out of the pond all those years ago?

She chose to firmly ignore the thought that she had not immediately recognized him a few hours earlier. How *could* she have, when she had supposed him safely across the seas, not ambling about the grounds of the Caraway estates? It was reasonable that she had not immediately jumped to the conclusion that he was the breathlessly awaited earl and the sole cause of her immediate troubles.

If it were not for him, after all, she would not now be leaving the home she had lived in all of her life. Neither would she be lying through her teeth about a nonexistent Mr. Addington and making up stories about his siblings in Bath. The situation was preposterous! And when he looked at her so, beneath hooded lashes of dark, silken velvet—or so it seemed—she could hardly think at all.

Unbeknownst to her, beneath those hooded lashes, Lord Robin was regarding her with an interest not derived entirely from his own manly desires, which he had already established she aroused within him. No, his look was speculative indeed, for though he thought furiously, he did not believe he had spoken to anyone about his plans for barley in the northern field, nor did he think the delightful Lady Serena could have the faintest interest—or knowledge—about the planting of tea, which she did. Not only did she have a knowledge of it, it appeared that she was overseeing the process. Curious, rather curious. However, he held his peace.

Serena, anxious to cover any gaffe that she might have made, began to chatter about the portraits, until Robin, with a tolerant air, murmured that he had rather enough of the ancestors for his first morning.

"Oh! Would you like to see the second floor? It is drafty I am afraid, but the library is situated on it and I think my brother made an excellent job of refurbishing the place, although naturally the rest of the castle is in hopeless disrepair. Gaming debts, you know." Serena made a disapproving face and walked on so quickly that brave Robin Red-Ribbon, formerly of *The Albatross,* almost had to run to catch up.

"Wait!"

Serena stopped, rather breathless. She was certain it was from her pace rather than from the peculiar sensation she had suffered from all morning. How traitorous her mind was being! It was not, after all, as if she were a green girl. She had been kissed before, though naturally without quite as much ardor or . . . no! She would think on it no further—it was merely unsettling. Her biggest problem was to prevent Lord Caraway from suspecting either the loss of her composure, or worse, her ill-kept secret. Ill-kept, because she had thrice nearly revealed herself today. Fortunately, she was positive he had noticed not a thing. She could not, however, rely on his being either blind or stupid much longer. She suspected he was shrewder than he would have the world believe.

"Am I too fast for you?"

My lord's eyes twinkled. *"You* answer *me* that, lady Serena! *Are* you too fast?"

Serena colored. "Now you are absurd, sir. You deliberately misunderstand me and most ungentlemanly you are, too. I shall slow my pace to match your own. No, better yet, I shall leave you to your own devices. Doubtless you can find your way around without the guidance of an ignorant female. Take the winding stairways—they bypass the main ballrooms and lead you far faster to the living areas. The library is unmistakable. The handle on the door is a lion etched in brass."

"How fanciful! The work, I infer, of the dowager?" His eyes twinkled, for even now he could remember the numerous pronouncements Mr. Addington had made on the countess's love of the Gothic, the thematic, and the simply bizarre.

Serena laughed. "No, the handle is too classical, I'm afraid. Not at all in her style. But here, my dear sir, I must love you and leave you."

The eyebrow raised at this was quizzical in the extreme. "Must you? I mean, naturally you must love me, but is it really quite essential that you leave me?"

Serena's eyes held answering laughter despite her reservations. "Utterly, sir, if you propose to outwit me at every turn of speech. As for loving you, it would, I suspect, be an extremely foolhardy thing to do."

"Oh, quite definitely. But such a small consideration as that would not stop you, would it?"

"Not if I really *did* love you."

"Then I can hope?"

"You are absurd, my lord! You forget you are in England, land of the gossipmongers. Your antics are in the *Tatler* at regular intervals, I assure you."

"How intriguing! *What* antics, if I might make so bold as to be interested in my own concerns?"

Serena flushed. She did not care to quote him all his inamoratas as outlined by the *Caraway Crier,* the *Tatler* and the *Morning Post.* Generally, she did not stoop to reading gossip, but his name always seemed to just jump at her off the page—it was really quite extraordinary.

"If you do not know, it is not my place to tell you."

"Oh, Miss Prim and Proper! Perhaps I should just compound my sin again and kiss the truth from you."

"You would not dare! At all events, *there* is Miss Waring. I can see her now."

"Where? I do not see her at all."

"But I *do.* Julia! *Julia!*" Craven, Lady Serena drew down a glass pane and yelled down to the prettily clad young lady in the topiary gardens below. She was rewarded for her efforts by a shy wave, which Serena immediately announced was a summons.

"Come, my lord, we must go at once. Julia needs us."

Robin, his eyes alight with ill-concealed amusement, allowed himself to be bullied down the staircase once again. After all, he reasoned, the topiary gardens must surely be a welcome relief from the ancestors. Serena seemed to have forgotten her intentions to desert him. Yes, following on Lady Serena's heels was definitely the better option, and he rather enjoyed Lady Serena Caraway's rear view as she made her hurried escape right past him. If her sleeve happened to brush, for the fraction of an instant, with his own, none but the most uncharitable would say that she noticed.

Chapter Seven

"What the devil are *you* doing here?" Lord Robin, rather the worse for a sleepless night pondering the various charms of a certain young lady resident in his castle, positively bit his bosom bow's head off.

"I say, Robin, you are being mighty uncivil this morning! I rode over here just as fast as I could escape Mama, which was no small feat, I can tell you! By the bye, I believe I passed your baggage carriage along the route, for I took the roads—much safer, you see, with my town chaise. Mind if I help myself to this . . . What *is* this?"

"It is a salmon mousse, of sorts. Not at all, do sit down and make yourself perfectly at home."

Captain McNichols grinned. "You *are* out of sorts! I cannot for the life of me think why—it is not *every* day one takes possession of a castle. It looks in fine nick, too—"

"Then you must be blind! It is freezing and the plaster is cracking off most of the sills—"

"Oh, grumpy, grumpy! Nothing that a good mason cannot fix. You must employ a French chef, Robin—This mousse is magnificent."

A gurgle of delight met this pronouncement. Not from Robin, who seemed unusually wrapped up in his thoughts, but from a pretty young maiden who did not fit Mrs. McNichols's description of his projected bride one iota. *This* maiden was all rosebuds and pink muslin and shiny curls. Her vivacious eyes nonetheless seemed awed by the sight of two fine gentlemen at the breakfast table.

Captain McNichols rose at once, but the pleasant, lighthearted creature waved him to sit almost immediately and commented that she could not help but overhear his admiration for the mousse.

"I made it, you know, for Serena is forever telling me that it is imperative for the lady of the house to know more than her housekeeper, though how in the world she thinks I am going to *ever* know more than Mrs. Dumpley, I cannot think, for it is an age she has been at Caraway, and had the running of it even before Mama married the previous earl . . . Oh! My tongue is running away with me again!" This, as she tentatively took her place at the furthest end of the table from the gentlemen, she still being a little shy at finding such unusual breakfast guests at Caraway.

Captain McNichols increased her confusion by passing her the tray of fresh buns, completely bypassing the hovering footman. His eyes were bright, as they flickered across to Robin.

"Yes, but it is such a *delightful* tongue, is it not?" asked his lordship promptly, his previous bad temper momentarily forgotten in this easy flirtation. Truth to say, flirtation came as naturally to him as breathing. He acquired, for his pains, a firm kick in the shins from Captain McNichols, who was staring at Julia—for naturally, it was she—as if quite transfixed.

Miss Waring, singular among ladies in that she was perfectly immune to Robin's charms—being a little in

awe of him, and also several years younger—retorted
that he was talking a great deal of nonsense and that
she was sorry to have interrupted their meal. "We plan
on removing to the dower house today, my lord. It has
been ready this age but Mama . . . well, Mama . . ."

"Has not been equally ready?"

Julia nodded at the earl's quick understanding. "It is
hard to leave one's home, sir. Mama is very attached to
the castle."

Lord Robin thought it politic at this point not to point
out that by all accounts the lady was more attached to
her status than to the dilapidated eaves themselves. He
was just nobly swallowing a particularly wry response
when his thoughts were mirrored almost precisely by a
second female voice.

Lady Serena, having cast aside her blacks for a sunny
periwinkle blue, languidly entered the room. Her eyes
sought Robin's almost instinctively, then looked away almost *equally* instinctively. It was ignoble of him to return her glance with one of his own! One, moreover,
that made her knees feel like jelly—which they weren't,
being both strong and elegant—and her heart race
within her breast, a sensation she found decidedly uncomfortable, not to mention wholly annoying.

She had not reached *her* ripe age just to start behaving like any green ninnyhammer just out of the nurs-
ery! She had enjoyed a certain pleasant interlude with
the new earl and must on no account read anything
more into the matter. She was certain *he* would not,
though he was being extremely unchivalrous in regarding her with such a meaningful expression and such
amusement in those bold, dark blue eyes! Honestly, if
she had him to herself again, she would be inclined to
strike him once more to wipe that smirk off his face.
Look what ignoble thoughts he engendered! It was really, she thought in annoyance, the outside of enough.

Turning quite pointedly from his offending countenance, she addressed her next remark to Julia. It was *this* remark that had so exactly matched Lord Robin's private thoughts. "The dowager countess will *never* feel herself ready, Julia! It is a sad fact that she stands on her dignity far too much to care to remove to the dower house. She must be made to face the fact and at once, for I am perfectly certain his lordship does not want to be troubled by a household of womenfolk at his breakfast each morning."

"You make the notion not unattractive."

But Serena ignored this murmured remark, not feeling it worthy of a reply, since Lord Robin was determined to be disagreeably flirtatious this morning and it was her firm intention to quash such a dangerous practice if she could help it.

Far from being either deterred or depressed by this cold response, Robin turned his charms on Miss Julia, which infuriated Serena all the more, certainly not because she was feeling any twangs of envy, but because she disapproved of his indiscriminate use of his undoubted charms. It was well enough for her, perhaps, but Julia was a most impressionable child and it simply would not do.

But Julia, confronted with her first real male attention, did not seem to see the matter in the same sensible light at all. After all the necessary introductions had been made, she blushed, and giggled, and confided all manner of nonsensical things to her male audience, including the fact that Serena was an outstanding gardener, an excellent rider, and a dab hand with the accounts, which *she* was not, being so featherbrained as to not know one column of figures from another.

None of these gentlemen seemed to hold her at any real fault for this, though Serena wanted to throw a pillow in her dear niece's face to stem the sudden flow of chatter. Next she would be mentioning how Serena had taken over the estate books and transformed Caraway from a ramshackle liability to a profitable venture! She did not, for Julia knew nothing of the accounts, but there was still ample reason to throw a pillow in her direction to stem the lively flow. Robin, Serena noticed, looked enraptured.

In the event, by dint of breathing deeply and asking herself why in the world she was so perturbed, Serena restrained her mischievous impulse and contented herself with pouring a scalding hot cup of tea. This she calmly drank, not wincing in the slightest, and wholly ignoring the look of amusement on Lord Robin's face. He seemed to read her thoughts, that man! She must keep them shuttered, else he would suspect the truth—that she was not what she claimed to be—and she would very likely die of mortification.

"Isn't that wonderful, Serena!"

"Isn't *what* wonderful, Julia?"

"Serena, I can swear you have not heard one word in six this morning! I am *guaranteed* not to be a wallflower at my first entrance to Almack's, for both Lord Caraway *and* Captain McNichols have secured my hand for the opening dances!" Julia sounded genuinely overjoyed, not at all coy or missish, a fact that made Serena regret her first impulses. Julia was a dear, it was not fair becoming angry with her for what was, after all, a very minor offense. If Serena did not fear exposure, Julia's chatter would not be a problem.

"How lovely!"

It was pointless, Serena thought, to point out that Julia, with her bright golden curls and delightfully open nature, had never *been* in any danger of wallflower status. On the contrary, more like a honeypot to starving bears.

"*You* could never be a wallflower, Miss Waring. It defies belief!"

So: Lord Caraway had wrested the thought from her head and turned it into a prettily turned compliment. She wondered why she felt so out of sorts about it, for Julia was behaving very prettily and dimpling quite adorably as she always did when she was pleased.

"Oh, no, you can have no *notion* of how I have dreaded being left without partners! It must be so mortifying to be dressed in one's very best, with the orchestra playing something quite jolly, and not being able to join in. It happened to one of the Appleby sisters, though I cannot understand why, for Delia was dressed to the rig just *exactly* as if she had stepped out of a fashion magazine, which I am sure she might have done, for she was forever being fitted in London, and you *know* what modistes there are like!"

My lord nodded seriously, which, sad to say, encouraged Miss Waring all the more, for she had quite forgotten her shyness in the great barrage of compliments she had been receiving. Captain McNichols, not to be outdone, took her hand and announced that he would slay any man not sensible enough to *immediately* be struck by Miss Waring's worth.

"Then I shall not lack for any partners, sir!"

"No, indeed! We shall have to fight our way through the throngs, won't we, Robin?"

Robin dutifully conceded that they would, but his eyes were full of mirth as he glanced sideways at Serena.

"A conquest, methinks."

"You are very bad, my lord! You are not to trifle with her."

"And why not, pray? She looks no worse for trifling. Indeed, she looked a trifle peaked last night and now she is flushed with health."

"Flushed with flattery, you mean! And I take leave

to tell you, sir, it was my syrup of negus that put the color back in her cheeks, not any flirtatious wiles of yours."

But Robin only laughed, and said he'd *suspected* all along that Miss Waring's assessment of her talents had been true.

"What can you mean?"

"Only that if you make syrups you are a capable nurse, housekeeper, and gardener."

"Well, I am!"

"As good with accounts and figures?" The tone was sharp and the eyes, dark with something indefinable and probing, scrutinized her face carefully.

Now it was Serena's turn to flush, for she had no wish for him to puzzle together any of the pieces leading to her folly.

"That is a man's job, my lord. I'm not a man!"

"No, indeed, I am more aware of that fact than I quite like to be, Lady Serena. Periwinkle blue suits you. Have you ever been out to sea?"

The subject change startled Serena. "In a boat?"

"Naturally, that is generally the way, I believe."

Serena ignored the amused sarcasm. "No, for until Napoleon was defeated it was never thought wise, then my brother died and naturally . . . well, there were things to attend to at Caraway."

"Like dismissing the bailiff?"

Oh, not that again! Sparks flashed in Serena's eyes, but she managed to answer quite placidly. "If you must revert to that tired topic, my lord, then yes. Like dismissing the bailiff."

"But you never did, did you?"

Shock registered on Serena's face. It was not pretty, in the way of Miss Waring, but it was nonetheless quite out of the ordinary. Classical, almost. She was unaware of how the sunlight through the French windows lighted her cheekbones and added a lustrous reddish shine to her cropped, coppery hair.

"What *can* you mean?" But Robin, for once, held his tongue. Serena, extremely uncomfortable under his scrutiny, tried to press him, but he shook his head firmly and even was so bold as to place a finger upon her lips, a fact that made the dowager countess—who had just made her grand entrance—quite heave with outraged indignation.

"*Lord* Caraway!" She tapped her cane on the floor several times for effect and drew out her quizzing glass.

"Madam?" Robin casually withdrew his hand, leaving Serena breathless, Captain McNichols amused, Julia hopeful—for she had had a sudden *wonderful* notion—and the countess glowering.

"I *hope* that is not the type of behavior you learnt in the Americas, sir! Here in England we treat our ladies with respect, we cherish their sensibilities, we do not—not—"

"Not *what,* ma'am?" asked Robin mildly as he nodded for some more coffee.

"We do not mishandle our lady folk, sir! My husband would turn in his very grave if he knew . . . oh, Serena! If you should suffer any harm . . . and my little Julia! Oh, it is all too much! Who would have thought we would have to bear such treatment under our very roof . . . My smelling salts, if you please!"

For once, Serena obliged, thinking it was best to suffer great whiffs of vinaigrette being waved in her face than the paroxysms of amusement that Robin shot her way. It was too bad that he seemed to understand her so well, or to share her view of the ridiculous. So she ministered to the countess, while Julia worriedly excused herself and left the breakfast room in search of the redoubtable Redmond, the countess's personal maid.

The countess, at the center of the scene she was now

causing, shot a look of loathing at the incumbent earl and raised her eyebrows haughtily at the sight of Captain McNichols, who was rather wishing himself back at Strawberry Hill.

"And who might *you* be, pray?"

"I am Captain McNichols, ma'am,"

"I have heard of you. Your mother wants to marry you off to Serena and a damned impertinence I thought it, since Serena is not past her last prayers, mind you!"

Serena, the first to know of such matters, looked startled.

"Good God! Can you be . . . are you . . . I mean, my good sir, are you Captain McNichols of Strawberry Hill? I am afraid I never quite made the connection when we were introduced."

Captain McNichols, feeling suddenly trapped, nodded rather miserably.

Serena laughed. "I have made the acquaintance of your mama several times! She is such a sweet lady, but I do believe she has taken some wild notion into her head that we might suit. I am afraid I have merely nodded and smiled politely, thinking you were perfectly safe across the seas."

"I returned on *The Albatross* last night. Lord Caraway and I are friends."

"Then you were not safe at all! My dear sir, I am most dreadfully afraid your mama might think me an excellent bride, but I assure you we shall not suit."

Captain McNichols who had been thinking so all morning, but for very different reasons, now flushed and mumbled and muttered, rather heroically, that Serena was too harsh on herself, and that indeed she was exceptionally beautiful, just as Mrs. McNichols had described . . . .

The countess, now looking speculatively at the pair, waved aside Redmond, who had entered the room fast on Julia's heels, and ignored, for once, the sal volatile cast in her direction. She was thinking swiftly, as all mamas did, especially one so ambitious as to have bagged an earl *herself.* Too bad he had died so prematurely. But that was an old complaint, nothing near as important as the ruminations now formulating in her mind . . . by George! It was the very thing.

Serena could wed this Captain McNichols chap, for though he looked all very fine in his smart uniform, he was not at all suitable for her Julia, who should marry a peer at the very least. And speaking of peers, why ever not this Robin character himself? With a haircut and the services of a decent tailor like Weston, miracles could be performed. She would not be so unfeeling as to marry Julia off to a barbarian, but the man appeared to have some redeeming qualities . . . .

So lost was she in her speculation that she failed to hear Serena's muttered expostulations or Captain Mc-Nichols's praise—tangled, as it was, with an earnest desire to free himself from any perceived obligation. In the midst of all this, Robin's eyes were dancing, and Miss Waring's color was surprisingly high, for she had just been smitten with those first innocent but nonetheless intense pangs of first love.

Her mama, eyeing her through her reverie, accepted the smelling salts at last, wafted them elegantly about her person, and noted that the silly creature—for so, regrettably, she thought of Julia—looked all pink and fluttery. She was delighted, for it did not occur to her that Miss Waring's affection might be misplaced. The earl, besides being an extraordinarily fine figure of a man— she had to concede that—was also far higher in rank than Captain McNichols and therefore the most obvious choice for any young maiden, no matter how henwitted she might be.

Alas, poor Julia did not seem to share her insights.

The sal volatile seemed to restore the dowager's flagging spirits. It helped, no doubt, that she regarded her daughter as a biddable thing, and that she felt much cheered by the notion of herself remaining on as the chatelaine at Caraway.

Doubtless Robin—who stood quite obviously in the need of guidance—mark his current deplorable attire—would welcome her experience. Who, after all, was better fitted to hostess balls and evening soirées? They could open up the London town house, remove all the Holland covers, emerge from this dreary mourning . . . . She could not help but wonder why she had not thought on the matter before.

Well, naturally she had been too weak, what with the shock of Caraway's death, and the knowledge that she was to be evicted—yes, evicted—from the ancestral home . . . but she had better act now before the chance slipped from her grip. These things did not just happen, they took planning—careful, calculated, cunning planning as she well knew. She clapped her hands together loudly,

"Very prettily put, Captain McNichols. I am sure you and Serena will make an excellent match of it. Redmond, call the butler, if you please. I am certain the cellars can spare some of his lordship's vintage best for the occasion, for though I do not imbibe *much,* I *do* feel that on occasions such as these it would be ungenerous to be stinting." The countess rang her bell so that it pealed through the breakfast chamber and several house staff appeared at once, as a result.

Before Serena could stop her, she was making a betrothal announcement in glad tones, whilst the house staff—such as had the good fortune of being near the landing when the bell had rung—all sank into little bobs and bows and murmurings. Captain McNichols, now decidedly green, shot an anguished glance at the earl but Robin, more amused than shocked, was laughing too much to be any aid at all.

"No, no, Serena, do not gawk at me so, it is most unbecoming. No, not another word if you please! Captain McNichols, my foot is suffering from the gout. Would you be so kind as to take a turn with me in the gardens? I sometimes find exercise to be beneficial."

She had outmaneuvered poor Adam before ever the champagne had arrived. Serena, pacing angrily up and down the Aubusson carpet, had a full hour and fifteen minutes to wait before she could vent her wrath upon her least favorite sister by law.

Chapter Eight

Robin, Lord Caraway, had stopped laughing. This because the Lady Serena had threatened to do him an injury if he did not.

"It is singularly unamusing, sir! And I *do* think you might have helped rather than laughed!"

"What might I have done? If you had only firmly set your foot down instead of leading poor Adam on . . ."

"Are you *mad*? What in the world can have made you think I was encouraging his suit?"

"You smiled at him brilliantly, you had no business wearing that periwinkle blue if you do not want every man not in his dotage to fall at your feet . . ."

"You are not in your dotage!"

"Don't tempt me, Lady Caraway. I rest my case and if Miss Waring were not present I would show you just how."

"Oh." Serena swallowed back a quick retort, for she was flushing at just how much she wished her niece were *not* present. Then she caught herself up short and waved away the champagne and fluted glasses that had just made their appearance.

"No, no, Mrs. Dumpley, I am afraid there has been a

misunderstanding . . . no, no, I am not betrothed . . . no, no, not at all, but when I see how disappointed you look I almost feel quite guilty! Oh, very well, set the glasses down on the sideboard. I am sure Captain McNichols will require a restorative drink when he returns."

"Undoubtedly." The voice behind her was wry. It was also far too masculine for its own good, and brimful of an amusement that made *her* want to laugh as well.

Mrs. Dumpley bobbed and fussed about the table, *dying* of curiosity, but far too well trained an upper servant to ask any questions. As she later told those elevated members of the household who were in her confidence, "If that gentleman be the new earl, well, there would be a regular to-doing in the neighborhood, for if he were not fine to the ninepence—not but what his shirt could not do with some hot irons—there weren't nobody what was."

Then Delia Simmonds, the second housemaid, told everyone within hearing that he was a "proper dish 'e was, and that it set her to wishin' . . ." but no one heard what it set her to wishing, for she was ordered very sternly to be mopping the scullery floors, not dithering her day away with idle—not to mention sinful— thoughts. Still, even Mrs. Dumpley gave a loud sigh as she bit into yesterday's jam tarts and pondered his lordship's smile. All of this was for later, however. At *this* moment Miss Waring, slightly pale, inquired about the strange turn of events.

"Serena, I can *swear* I have never heard of Captain McNichols before this morning! When can you have met him, I wonder, for though I rack my brains I can think of no time . . . *wait!* Was it when I ran into Hookham's and you had the sick ache and . . ."

"No, no! You run on ahead of yourself, Julia! Besides, it was *you* who had the sick ache, not I. I met not him, but his mama. Do you not recall dear Mrs. McNichols from Bath?"

"Gracious, yes! She spoke of a son and I *did* say . . . oh, my goodness, Serena, this is all *my* fault!"

"A Cheltenham tragedy, I perceive, " murmured Robin, but was ignored by his audience of two unchaperoned maidens.

"Don't be nonsensical, Julia! How can this . . . . misunderstanding possibly bear on you?"

"I am afraid I encouraged her in the notion, Serena! You know how fond I am of you, and you were looking down in the mops in Bath, and when she happened to mention a son . . ."

"Julia, I could strangle you! I don't know whether to be more mortified that you pushed me forward, or that you thought me in the mops!"

"Neither, for I hate it when you are angry and oh, *pray*, Serena, don't frown so . . ."

"Yes, it *quite* mars your countenance."

"I shall quite mar *your* countenance if you do not stop being so frivolous, my lord!"

At which Miss Waring looked shocked, and the earl amused.

"Touché! I stand admonished. Shall we go rescue our dear Captain McNichols, or shall we let him suffer a little while longer?"

"Oh, you are a beast!"

"To let him suffer, or to suggest that he *shall?* "

"Both, for it cannot be so very bad being betrothed to me!"

"I shall have to try it, sometime, then tell you the results."

"Now you are absurd again." But Julia, who knew Serena better than most very good friends, noticed a telltale blush upon her friend's face that had not been there a second ago. It led her to some immediate and rather curious conclusions, but she was too well-bred to quiz Serena in such company, so she stored up her

questions for later. Whether the gentleman *also* noticed
Serena's animated color was a moot point, but suffice it
to say that the young lady under scrutiny now felt the
strong need for some air.

"I shall go search them out at once. You wait here!"

The tone was imperious, hasty, and addressed, quite
clearly, to the gentleman, whom she wanted to flee with
urgency.

The answer was languid, and again, faintly amused.
"But I cannot stay. You forget, the infant."

"I am *not* an infant!" Julia was indignant, for it was
quite obvious that his lordship was referring to herself.

"No? Then all the *more* reason for a chaperon! Tell
your aunt that she must stay, to protect your morals."

"Protect my *morals?*" Julia, pretty to a ninepence but
quite beyond the earl's humor, looked more than a little ruffled.

"Do not looked shocked, Julia dear. That was a slip of
the tongue. His lordship doubtless meant I must stay to
protect *his* morals. You, quite naturally, are beyond re-
proach."

Lord Robin flicked Serena an appreciative glance,
but addressed Julia quite seriously. "Whatever the case,
a pretty little snip like you is in need of a chaperone if
the conventions are to be met. I have a much better
plan. Lady Serena and *I* shall seek them out, leaving *you*
in no danger at all."

Serena shot the earl a suspicious glance but bit back
the obvious retort. If she asked how safe *she* would be
with him, his eyes would only twinkle at her dangerously, his stance would be mocking, and he would
know—oh yes, she was positive he would *know* how very
much she liked the danger. So she remained uncharacteristically silent, hesitated a moment, then nodded.

"Come then, for I have it on the best authority I am
an apt leader and therefore quite beyond the need for

such nonsense as chaperonage. Julia, if your mama returns, *do* put her right about this muddle before poor Captain McNichols quite sinks with mortification!"

It was useless for Julia to point out that she could never sway her mama, so she nodded obediently and prayed fervently that it would be Serena who found her first. "Shall I wait here, in the breakfast room?"

"Yes, for Lady Caraway has not yet broken her fast and doubtless she will return here, rather than to the receiving rooms. You may read my copy of the *Gazette* to stave off boredom."

"Oh, no! I assure you, I shall not be bored!" The lovely Julia was filled with the first blossoming of true love, and felt perfectly capable, therefore, of dreaming away her entire morning.

"Good! Then we shall take a brisk walk to the topiary garden, for your mama is very proud of it, and will doubtless wish to display its worth to the captain."

"What about the ice house? She is very proud of that too!"

"Yes, but she can hardly take a stroll to the ice house. Captain McNichols will think it very peculiar of her."

"Then the gazebo?"

"That is at the other end of the South Park. Your mama would surely not leave us stranded with the earl for so very long a time?"

But even as she said it, Serena knew she would. If the dowager countess wanted something, despite her die-away airs, she would achieve it ruthlessly. But what could she possibly want?

To keep Captain McNichols from Julia? To convince him that he really *had* intended a proposal? Or was it more subtle yet? Serena had the strangest feeling Lady Caraway's impulsive behavior had something to do with the earl.

Her attitude had changed abruptly. Serena wished she knew why.

"Oh, very well, then, we will try the South Park. Ready, your lordship?"

Robin smiled. It was enough to break the hearts of the steeliest of maidens, never mind just one. Serena swallowed hard, and kept her tone light and slightly caustic as she led the way.

"I only hope we have not just been sent on a wild-goose chase. They are probably nowhere *near* the South Park!"

"I rather hope they are not."

His meaning was too transparent, even to Serena. She said nothing, as they wound their way down the main staircase in full view of the underbutler and at least two housemaids, but when they were finally alone, she took leave to give him a fine trimming, which served only to amuse him the more.

But there was more than amusement, which puzzled Robin as much as it did Serena. There was something quite intangible between them, some sixth sense that suggested they had met before, if not in person, then certainly in spirit.

Serena felt it, too, for she scolded him as if she had known him her whole life, rather than a few short days. She supposed it must be the intimate nature of the correspondence between them that set her at ease. She could see beyond the long hair and the creased shirt— beyond, even, the Caraway title, to the incisive mind and the quick humor she knew he possessed. They were kindred spirits. *She* knew it, but *he* was hampered from the immediate truth by not knowing the source of those invaluable letters. For an instant, when he stopped, half holding his hands to her, she nearly told him.

The moment was lost, however, by the arrival of the long-awaited baggage coach and a varmint of a tiger with the foulest vocabulary and the cheekiest grin Serena had ever seen.

"You should wash his mouth out!"

"I have, but do you know, he only grins and says it is 'better than a whippin' what old guv would 'ave dished out not, but what 'e taught me them words 'issef, 'e did, but for cheek an' such.' "

Serena cast her head back and laughed. "You are an excellent mimic, my lord."

"Only because you are an excellent audience. Serena. Tell me, why do I feel I have known you forever?"

"Because you have."

"That is not what I meant and you know it. Being a distant relative and having access to the estate once in a blue moon is not the same as . . . it is the strangest sensation. I could swear I know your mind!"

"Serena! *Lady* Serena!" The shrill voice of the dowager countess wafted from the balcony above.

Serena tilted her neck and shaded her eyes from the sun. Yes, she feared as much. The dowager was looking severely displeased. Julia, flustered, stood behind her, making helpless gestures. There was no sign of Captain McNichols, but Robin guessed he must be inside, making well-earned inroads into Caraway's best champagne. The morning—spent mostly with the dowager—must have ranked, for him, as supremely hideous.

Feeling a little guilty at permitting his friend to so suffer, Robin murmured that he owned a seafaring vessel and that they could both easily run away to sea.

"To avoid the dowager? Coward! We must rescue poor Captain McNichols before he hangs himself!"

"At the notion of his betrothal? He is a lucky man."

"And you, my dear sir, are a frivolous one!" But Serena could not help feeling her spirit lighten quite nonsensically at his smile, and the flirtatious implication.

Above them, on the balcony, the dowager was having spasms, for she did not like the way Serena was pushing herself forward, nor the way the earl seemed totally duped by her charms. It would not do at all! As for Julia! Well, if she knew no better she would say she was making calf's eyes at this captain . . . this Captain Nobody! But naturally, it could not be . . . it must not be . . . Julia would not be so foolish . . . .

"Julia, his lordship is approaching. You look faint. Fan yourself."

"But, Mama, I am not faint at all!"

"Then *become* so, I pray you! Your fan is the height of fashion, for I bought it myself, and the pink so becomes you . . . Julia, do you hear a word I say?"

But Julia did not, for she was staring at Captain McNichols, who looked very dapper indeed in his smart regimentals, and who was opening her fan out gently, mouthing that it was, indeed, pretty. So Miss Waring, a little bewildered, fanned herself most becomingly and had a perfectly delightful flush upon her cheeks when the earl finally made his languid entrance.

"Caraway! How *good* you are to come so quickly! I cannot think *what* overcame our Serena to behave so hoydenishly. Serena, my love, I *know* you are used to having the run of the household, but *can* you not remember when decorum is important?"

Her victim, who did not spar with people unworthy of her wit, bit back a scathing retort and smiled benignly at the captain.

"Captain, I hope you have been put out of your misery."

The captain, who hoped so, too, but could not very well, in present company, *say* so, murmured that he could not fathom what Serena was alluding to.

"Ah, the *best* of good manners!" Serena smiled kindly upon him. "But tell me, sir, are we not in perfect accord that we do not suit?"

The look of relief on Adam's face defied good manners. Robin, who had surprised himself by feeling a slight pang of anxiety on this score, breathed a small sigh of satisfaction. He had thought not, but could not for the life of him think why Adam should prefer little Miss Ringlets to the more intelligent—and yes, it could not be disputed—beautiful—Lady Serena. Some imp of mischief beset him, though, for instead of aiding his friend, he added to his notable confusion. He took from the table the fluted glass that Adam had discarded just moments before.

"To your betrothal, I believe." The amused voice of his best friend could not be mistaken. Captain McNichols could at that moment gladly have floored him with his fists, friend or no.

"Yes, yes, we shall drink a toast!" shrilled Lady Caraway. "Now where are those servants when you need them? Ring the bell, Julia dear!"

But Julia, for once, was obstinate. "Mama, he doesn't *wish* to marry Serena."

"What nonsense is this? It is all settled. We have been talking of it this half hour at least." Which was only partially true, for while Lady *Caraway* had certainly been talking, Adam had not been permitted a word in edgewise.

"It is by no means settled, my lady. Far from it. I shall not be marrying Captain McNichols—or anyone else in the near future, so do not think upon it again."

"Serena, you are a very contrary child! If your brother were alive . . ."

"He is not, and I must beg you to save your quarrel with me for later. I am perfectly certain we do not want the gentlemen to pass out from boredom."

At which, Lady Caraway once more needed the aid of her vinaigrette, once more washed her hands of Serena, and once more forbade Julia to be allowed to make her come-out under such poor chaperonage.

Lord Caraway, after paying off the coachmen and murmuring orders to the underbutler with respect to the stowage of his luggage, added wicked fuel to the fire by murmuring that he, for one, was not bored at all, but rather, entertained.

Which bought for him a kick in the shins from Captain McNichols, who was surprisingly swift despite his stockier build, and a chuckle from his cousin, or half cousin, or whoever Serena was—he could never quite figure it out. Well, a chuckle, then a scold, for he was being quite outrageous, really, in annoying the dowager further.

"Oh, that I should live to be so ill used!" bemoaned the dowager. Then, remembering that it was not salubrious to her scheme to alienate the earl, she changed tack and berated Serena instead.

Serena was firm. "Ma'am, if you do not wish Julia to be chaperoned by myself, that is your prerogative, but I must insist that she still have her Season. There is no reason for her to languish at Caraway when she is of an age to make her court appearance."

"You forget, Serena, that I am impoverished, destitute! I cannot afford such frivolities for Julia."

"Can you not?" The voice behind Serena was like velvet, but Serena, sensitive to such things, felt the steel behind his tone. Oh, it was a fine kettle of fish! Now *Serena* was amused, for she knew perfectly well just how much Robin, Lord Caraway, had kept the dowager in funds. "Destitute" was a somewhat ill-chosen word in his august company.

Lady Caraway was cornered, for too late, she had remembered the very same thing. She had forgotten, in her annoyance, the source of her extremely comfortable annuity. "We shall discuss this later!" she announced, seizing her cane and looking at the potted plant as though she were contemplating attacking it.

"No, my lady, we shall discuss it now, for I cannot believe, after all these gentlemen have had to endure today, they cannot endure this one last discussion."

"It is not fitting!"

"But it is, since I am the head of this . . . did I nearly say ramshackle? How silly of me! I meant to say . . . remark-able . . . family."

"Oh, I *knew* he would push himself forward!" groaned the Dowager Lady Caraway, wholly forgetting that but a moment ago she was fawning over him quite shamefully.

Robin grinned. He did not consider permitting the lady to live rent-free in his home for nigh on eleven months an indication of his forwardness. Neither, it seems, did Serena, for she seemed more shocked by the lady's denouncement than himself.

"Lady Caraway, you forget yourself! When I *think* how his lordship has been tolerant, how much he has paid of his *own* fortune to restore the dowager house—for I can promise you that it was not the depleted *Caraway* fortune that permitted those excesses . . ." Her voice trailed off at the sharp glance the earl cast her way. She had nearly exposed herself again. Too much knowledge, she realized ruefully, could be dangerous.

Fortunately, the dowager countess prevented his eyes from boring too deeply into her own by fainting. This, naturally into the arms of poor Captain McNichols, who had gallantly stepped forward to shield Julia from the dead weight of her mama.

He might have laughed—especially if he had caught Robin's eye—but the situation was too dire. Miss Julia was near tears and he wanted nothing so much as to kiss them away like the soft dewdrops on roses that they were. How fanciful he was becoming! But oh, those dreamy eyes, he could get lost in them, and when she smiled at him, and murmured her thank yous . . . oh, he no longer felt like the right-hand mate of a famous privateer.

The dowager moaned a little in his arms. Serena caustically remarked that perhaps they should dash a pail of water over her face to revive her, at which my lady awakened instantly—with fluttering eyelashes of course—and complained that she had never been so ill-used in her life and would pack up her things directly for the dower house, for it was plain where she was not wanted, and so on, and so on, until Captain McNichols thought his arms were going to break off.

He was strong, but not so strong as to hold the dowager long enough to sustain another of her tirades. So he placed her feet gingerly on the floor and hoped she would not swoon again. She did not, having recovered both the use of her feet and the use of her lungs. This she used rather volubly, but when it came to scolding Julia, who appeared rather used to such treatment and surprisingly unflustered, the captain would bear no more.

"Ma'am!" he thundered. "I will not have you speak so poorly of Miss Waring!"

For which he received a dire glare and the threat that if he thought he might have the slightest chance of courting Miss Waring rather than Lady Serena, he was really very much mistaken. Julia paled at this, for it was clear her heart had been perfectly smitten from the outset.

And the captain? His response was unreadable. But that arrested look had suddenly appeared in the eyes of Robin, Lord Caraway. It was fortunate for Serena's peace of mind that she did not notice it at all.

Chapter Nine

The preparations for Serena's departure took no time at all, for she had been preparing for a week at least prior to Lord Robin's sudden return to his estate. To make matters simpler, Serena had bought, from the previous owner, much of the furniture that now stood awaiting her arrival under Holland covers. It would be but a simple matter to whip them off, dust scrupulously— for this she had engaged the services of several house staff who even now awaited her orders—and move in.

There would be none of the usual frenetic hoisting of furniture through the upper French windows, none of the cavalcade of carriages arriving with kitchenware and linen and harpsichords—all these had already quietly and efficiently been installed, along with other essential instruments, a French chef—for Serena meant to entertain at least on a small scale—and sufficient candelabras with white wax candles to last, if not a lifetime, then a Season at least.

So it remained only for Serena's personal effects to be packed—this was done in record time, for Serena's taste was simplicity itself and she had none of the woes of worrying about feathered bonnets and muffs that might be crushed, or even which multitude of under-dresses to take and which to discard—all Serena's were exquisitely stitched, but very similar in style and hue. She had been in mourning for her brother Spencer up until now, and so had had no real need for much more.

Now, as she glanced at herself in the large, gilded mirror that had been hers since she had been in swad-dling cloths, she felt an odd twinge of dissatisfaction. It had nothing whatsoever to do with the fact that Lord Caraway admired periwinkle blue and that none of her gowns were that color save the one she had worn nearly a week ago, and which now awaited pressing and the re-furbishment of a bit of lace. No, she told herself, Lord Caraway had nothing to do with it at all, but she simply *must* have her wardrobe updated in London. It was no good bringing Julia out if she looked like a regular crow. She'd scare away the suitors before they ever dared *approach* poor Julia.

And no, she would *not* don a mob cap as she'd in-tended. Her cropped copper locks would provide the perfect foil to Julia's long, bright ringlets. No, indeed, Lord Caraway had nothing whatsoever to do with the matter. Still, as she threw in a sunflower silk ribbon she had never thought to wear again, its color being too frivolous by far for an old maid, Robin's mysterious smile persisted in haunting her most damnably.

Lord Caraway, in the meanwhile, unaware of the tur-moil he was causing, buried himself in the estate for all the world as though he had been born to it, rather than having had it thrust upon him. In two days, he had rid-den the length and breadth of the property, inveigled himself into the affections of his tenants, and had had several interesting conversations with the gardeners, the small leaseholders, and the parish priest, all of which gave him the impression that Serena had had a *lot* more to do with the estate than he had first given her credit for, though naturally he had realized from the start that the smooth running of Castle Caraway itself had been due virtually entirely to her efforts.

But *this* was another matter. Apparently Gregory Mitchens had Serena to thank for the leak that had been stopped in his roof, and Mrs. Morrison's smoky coal range had been repaired by dint of the ordering of a chimney sweep.

"And you would not believe what 'e found up me chimney, me lord, that you won't," the woman said archly. "It were no wonder it be smokin' and all, but 'er ladyship like, she said that be awful dangerous, for what wiv all the dry tinder an' all, the 'ole 'ouse could go up in a shake, like wot 'appened wiv Jimmy Tarradale wot lives on Lord Netherfield's land, an' she gave me a 'ole farthing, she did, to 'ave the chimney swept."

Lord Robin, happy to compound Serena's bounty with some of his own, added another farthing to the one already given and suggested this one be for a chicken in the stew pot. His popularity was instant, for there was no greater chatterbox than Mrs. Morrison, and you can be sure that curiosity about the new master of Caraway was rampant among his tenants, all of whom had been rumormongering and wondering and guessing about him since the days of the *old* lord, when his name had not been permitted a mention.

A few coins judiciously administered had unleashed other tongues, and most of them, he thought in bewilderment, made virtually no mention of Mr. Addington, and rather a great deal about Serena herself. In fact, when it came down to it, no one knew much about

Addington at all, except some of the older crofters, who muttered vaguely that they supposed " 'e 'ad 'loped off."

If Robin had thought carefully, he would have realized that the crofters had responded to his casual questioning about "the bailiff" rather than about "Addington," who no one would have known at all. Fortunately for Serena, he was not, at this point, thinking too clearly, so it was not until much later that he began to doubt the fabrication Serena had taken such care to produce.

It still was puzzling, though, that although everyone could remember the time mistress Serena had arrived with a rattle "for baby Ned, wot was born out of wedlock to Nanny Briggs and nearly went to the foundling home save for Mistress Serena argumenting most fiercely with the preacher"—nobody correspondingly spoke of Mr. Addington, who had made so many of the recommendations that had improved their lives.

Lord Robin, casting his mind back to one of those improvements, now asked Johnson, a farmhand, how the new well was performing.

"The well, me lord? It is the best thing wot ever 'appened to this place, it is! There ain't no roundaboutation about it—the new well is a thousand times better than the old 'un, wot is crumblin' in ruins and soilin' the water-like, not to mention near dry, for whatever anyone may tell yer, that was no place to site a well an' oi don't know what the old lord was thinkin' of, bless me boots!"

"So the new well is a definite improvement?" There was a smile in Robin's voice, for the question was really rhetorical, given the enthusiasm of the small crowd gathered respectfully about him.

"Indeed it is, aye an' that be for sure, for there ain't now but a smidgeon of disease around here, what with the clean water an' all."

"Very good." Lord Caraway nodded in agreement. "And the irrigation?"

"Oh, much better, me lord, since 'er ladyship showed us them newfangled ways. We 'ave some spring crops, we do, and that don't never 'appen before, Caraway wot 'avin' a later 'arvest than most. Reckon there will be summer crops too, wot with the tea and all."

Robin then made a complete inspection of these said crops, and noted how neatly the rows had been sown, and how promising the first green buds appeared to be.

"Outstanding," he commented, more to himself than to his listeners, but his words were met with rapt applause and again that strange, puzzling plaudit that it was all her ladyship's doing. He let this pass, thinking that perhaps Addington had preferred to work quietly, and that Lady Serena, pretty and sympathetic, might have unwittingly claimed credit that was not strictly her due.

But when it came to the magnificent hall that stood proudly on the far east of his estate, he owned himself dumbfounded. Addington had written to him about something of the kind. If he recalled correctly, his permission had been required, though not his funds. It seemed that though the clubhouse was being built, the expenditure was not going to be offset against his inheritance.

All he'd had to do was to sign consent for the use of the land, which naturally he had done, as above all things, he trusted Addington's judgment. He'd expected to see a modest barn-type structure, not something as palatial as this, with *Caraway* scribed beautifully above the carved, hinged door, and a stairway leading upstairs to a series of neat, well-swept rooms, modestly furnished and all serving very specific functions.

In the first, babies were tucked up neatly in wooden

frames that served as cots. Some crawled across the floor—their knees protected by sea grass matting—and others were dandled gently upon ancient laps. The largest room was a kitchen area, with a modern coal range and a huge fire burning merrily in the grate. There were baskets of clothes and sewing things and swatches of material, all in differing stages of design.

He was given to understand that nobody went cold at Caraway, for material to clothe themselves was provided for—green, he noted, Caraway colors—and the old ladies, too frail to work the fields, were happy to sew and chat and gossip among themselves in the meeting house. Another well had been installed, and a series of outhouses . . . the whole structure was elaborate, with ornate winding stairs carved by "old man Howick, simple-like, but always whittlin' at somethin, and why not them stairs, says Lady Serena loik, and blow me down wiv a feather, a mighty fine job 'e 'ad been doin' ever since, and wot wiv 'im bein' paid an' all for 'is toim . . ."

There were endless stories like this, all incomprehensible to Robin, who knew nothing of the matter, but who began to suspect strongly that if it were not *his* personal funds that had been sunk into the enterprise, it must have been Serena's. But why had Addington not informed him of the magnitude of the project? He would have been glad to have funded it, for a worthier cause he could hardly have dreamed up himself.

As he shook hand after hand, and accepted curtsy after smiling curtsy, he resolved plainly that Serena must not only be reimbursed, she must be forced to tell him the full extent of her expenses. The welfare of his tenants was, after all, his entire responsibility.

For the next week, he busied himself with discovering just how much he was indebted to that meddlesome young lady. Clearly her own brother had never had the welfare of Caraway so much at heart.

He fully intended to pay her back every penny he owed her. To this end, he buried himself in his books, ignored her often entreating looks, the hardest thing he had ever forced himself to do in his life, denied himself some rather more obvious pleasures in the form of two milkmaids, three under housemaids, two young ladies who should certainly have known better, and the lovely lady Serena herself, whose lips practically begged to be kissed despite appearing disapproving every time he chanced to catch her eye. A week of severe self-sacrifice, then, but enlightening. Very enlightening indeed!

Serena was eager to leave Caraway. In the midst of her own hasty preparation, the dowager had decided— portentously—to at last dislodge herself from her boudoir in the castle and establish her new domain in the garish—but excessively comfortable—dower house.

These arrangements served to overshadow everyone else's. They seemed, moreover, to be shrouded in high melodrama, the like of which the village of Caraway had never seen before. Small wonder the earl had buried himself in estate work and was literally nowhere to be seen in the days following his arrival, save, perhaps, for a polite and hasty breakfast. To all pleas and hints and toadeating charm he seemed quite invincible, much to the dowager's annoyance and Serena's private amusement.

Captain McNichols, by the same token, had long since returned to Strawberry Hill, but not before he had extracted a promise from Julia for the first quadrille of the Season. He also, in perfect form, requested Serena's hand, which she duly promised, but begged him to phrase differently.

"Not your hand, sir! I have already refused that, and very relieved you were too!"

Which caused everyone to laugh but the dowager,

who scowled and muttered several nasty epithets which no one could quite hear, under her breath.

The only thing marring Miss Waring's perfect happiness at the prospect of being led across the floor—she dreamed of the time when she had procured the necessary permissions for a waltz—was her mama's continued and absolute abhorrence of poor Captain McNichols.

She refused, when asked, to concede that he was a fine figure of a man, that he was the very pink of the *ton*—Serena found him a little *too* much so, but she had not the heart to malign him for so small an offense—or more importantly, that he was perfectly, perfectly eligible. He was not a lord, but his blood was good, and through his mama was related to at least two of the finest lineages in the land.

But Lady Caraway persisted in her silly dreams and announced with vigor that if Julia was so bird-witted as to pay him the smallest attention she could kiss her Season good-bye.

Serena, excessively annoyed by this high-handedness, bit her tongue with difficulty. Her sister-in-law was displaying a mortifying snobbishness in refusing to acknowledge the captain's excellent qualities. Worse, she was repulsively self-ingratiating with the new earl, who seemed to take her unwelcome civilities in his stride.

On the occasions when she was being particularly mortifying, Serena's eyes would fly to his face, but she could never quite divine whether it was amusement or something quite different that flashed through his glance as she did so. She chose not to dwell on the matter, for the something else was . . . unsettling. His lordship's thoughts were none of her concern and if they made her tremble, it was no one else's business but her own.

She would be glad to leave Caraway once and for all.

She had lived her whole life under the shadow first of the earl, her father, then under the earl, her brother. Spencer had never held her under a tight rein, and she had never, of course, been under the thumb of the current dowager, but this was not for want of the countess trying.

Serena closed her mind to the hours and years she had put into the Caraway estate. Not her duties, but her life. She had been present at the birth of countless babies, at the funerals of innumerable laborers, she had helped shear the first wool, lamb the first lambs, pick the first fruits, produce the first wines, decoct the first herbal remedies . . . oh, the list was endless. She was part of Caraway, and Caraway, she supposed, was a part of her.

The era had ended and the sooner she could progress with the new one, the better it would be. So it was with great relief that she heard by the next post that her establishment was now quite ready and that the advance baggage—including voluminous trunks containing Julia's new gowns, court dress, pumps, bonnets, and assorted fans had all been safely bestowed.

It was left only to say farewell to the dowager and arrange the town leg of the trip, which was not overly long, considering that Caraway was already situated not so very far from London itself.

Lord Caraway took his handsome head out of the estate books long enough to offer his own carriage for the trip, an expense Serena would not countenance, but which he insisted upon as head of the family.

Serena might have been annoyed at his high-handedness, but it was done with such a charming smile and such a sense of the ridiculous—that he should be head of a family he hardly knew—that she conceded almost at once, and thanked him very prettily indeed. Then, all

matters satisfactorily concluded, she took down her
fishing rod and prepared to spend her very last day in
the childhood home of her past.

This was necessarily a lonely business, for Julia re-
coiled at the idea of snaring "a poor fish," and Spencer,
who used to be Serena's companion in the past, was
now no longer the Earl of Caraway. But the day was
mild, there were plenty of strawberries for the picking,
and Serena was perfectly content with her own company.
Lost in thought, she was startled when a familiar-look-
ing boot appeared in front of her nose.

"Might I offer a possible solution to your dilemma?"

The boot shifted slightly, affording Serena an excellent view of a muscled calf and an equally muscled
thigh. Robin, Lord Caraway, looking particularly dapper, of course, in doeskin breeches that emphasized his
lean proportions all too perfectly for Serena's maidenly
countenance. Worse, he was rigged to the nines in a velvet riding jacket of brilliant blue, almost an exact match
of those memorable eyes.

He might not have aspired to the height of fashion,
but no one surely could guess as much. He might not
particularly care whether his cravat fell à la waterfall or
à la Seville, but whichever way it happened to fall, it
looked entrancing.

Serena rested her rod upon the rocks, clamped it
down with a chiseled stone, and lifted her brows.
They arched copper in the sunlight. Her bonnet, of
course, was nowhere to be seen, though through the
undergrowth my lord caught a faint hint of trailing
ribbon.

"My dilemma?" she repeated vaguely. Her heart was
beating wildly at this sudden encounter.

"Good God, girl, have you not heard? The whole establishment is in a spin, in the very grip of drama itself
and you are reeling in fish!"

Serena smiled, rightly judging that since he looked neither panicked nor earnest, but rather plain mischievous, Julia had not contracted the plague, the castle was not ablaze, and the dilemma, therefore, was of the non-calamitous description.

"Not reeling in, sadly. I keep forgetting it was the northern boundary that we stocked."

"We?" Robin regarded her face keenly.

"I mean *you*, what a careless slip of the tongue! Forgive me, I have been used to the running of Caraway."

Robin *did* forgive her, but he regarded her thoughtfully. If recollection served, it was only he and Addington who had known about the decision to restock the northern boundary at the expense of this pleasant pond. It was on Addington's suggestion, actually, for he said there was less chance of poachers depleting the fish if the locations were switched. A trivial matter, really, but one Serena should not—*could* not—have been privy to. Interesting—yet another piece in a maze of puzzles he seemed to be amassing this last week. The sooner he located the missing bailiff, the better it would be. He reserved these thoughts, however—who wouldn't, when confronted with a dazzling beauty in an isolated spot with an entire pleasant morning to while away?

"May I sit down?"

"You will muddy your . . . you will be muddied." His lordship's eyes twinkled. He could swear the honorable Lady Serena had been about to commit the most heinous offense of referring to his unmentionables. A delightful color was rising to her cheeks even now. Adorable! Best pretend, of course, not to have noticed.

"I have suffered worse. At least *this* time I have a fresh change of clothes. You, by the by, are muddied."

"Yes, shocking is it not? But I set no store by such a sad fact, for this is a very old muslin. The organza sleeves are ripped, too, if you observe closely, which I do pray you will not. I do not regard it at all."

"You do it an injustice. I, *au contraire, shall* regard it." And so my lord did, gravely, as he raised her from her perch and twirled her about gently.

Serena felt a heat surge through her that was almost pain it was so strongly felt. And that, just at the simplest of touches! It was astonishing what Robin, Lord Caraway, could so carelessly achieve when the most ardent of her suitors had so dismally failed. *This* was the spark she had always dreamed of, had believed was possible, had refused to compromise for, had . . . But it was useless to reflect on such thoughts when it was obvious the earl was bored to tears at Caraway and regarded her merely as a helpful diversion.

"Yes." He brought her thoughts back to the present. "Slightly faded, definitely muddy, extraordinarily beautiful."

"The dress?"

"Certainly not! You!"

"I am *not* slightly faded!"

"You are, if your sister-in-law is to be believed! She has been causing a scene like none other this morning."

Serena frowned. "Dare I ask, or shall I just hammer myself over the head?"

"On no account! Ask, by all means!"

"Well?"

"Apparently she has heard that Adam—Captain McNichols, you know—has marked Miss Waring's dance card not once—which she declares would be forward enough—but twice."

"A hideous crime!" Serena's eyes lit up with laughter even as she groaned.

"Indeed."

'But surely, my lord, his dastardly deed has not given rise to any more extraordinary commotion than usual?"

"No, but the sin is compounded by the fact that he is not seeking your hand."

"How mortifying. Am I in disgrace?"

"I fear so. I, however, am her ladyship's great comfort and rock to lean upon in these days of dire distress. Apparently I am in favor."

"You would have to be blind as a bat not to notice. It is mortifying. The strange thing is, she could hardly utter your name this twelvemonth without choking."

"Ah." There was a moment of wry silence. "Do you think it is my personality, my dashing air, or my exquisite sense of taste that has altered her opinion?"

Serena was quick to retort. "More like your exquisite title and ownership of Castle Caraway, but I quibble! Do not, I pray you, permit me to deflate your hopes."

"Not hopes, my dear—worst fears. But come! I have a solution to offer."

Serena steadfastly ignored the "my dear" that caught so at her heartstrings and eyed him sideways.

"But what is the puzzle? Lady Caraway is not unknown for her spasms. There must surely be more."

"There is. She has forbidden Julia to undertake the journey under your aegis. Worse, she is threatening to attend the London Season herself."

Serena dusted herself off. "Good God, this *is* a crisis. Julia . . ."

". . . is weeping in the conservatory. I *did* try to kiss her out of her doldrums, but she looked more frightened than grateful, I fear."

"You are an unconscionable rogue! Of *course* she did! Gentlemen don't just go around kissing whomsoever they please." Serena was shocked at the sudden surge of jealousy she felt despite his careless, teasing manner.

"I must go to her at once, then talk some sense into the countess."

"The *dowager* countess."

"You quibble again."

"I do not—the matter is really rather pertinent to me, for the Countess of Caraway, you know, would be my *wife.*"

Serena laughed. "Horrors, yes. We would not wish to confuse you. I shall refer to her as dowager in future, though naturally her ladyship despises that appellation. But if Julia is distressed, I must go at once!"

Lord Robin grabbed at the long organza sleeve. Well, it was not a "grab," precisely, but it served to halt Serena in her tracks and have the subsidiary effect of causing her cheeks to flush, a circumstance she certainly hoped the earl did not notice. He did, but his hand remained upon her as he earnestly entreated her to alter course.

"It will not serve, you know, for all her tears will merely dampen your already sadly damp gown. She will come round and when she does, she will not thank you for catching her behaving like a watering pot. Besides, she will probably only have wicked things to say about me!"

"Which undoubtedly you deserve."

"No, for when I mean to be wicked it will be with more persuasion than I used on poor Miss Waring."

Serena avoided his eyes, for really, he was far too entrancing to think on what he might possibly mean by that roguish comment, and she did not wish him to gain the satisfaction of seeing her in the slightest bit intrigued.

Robin, having overset her completely—though fortunately she had not revealed as much—now released her from his light grasp, but immediately compounded his sin by taking her hands and turning up her palms, and playing, a little, with his fingers upon her wrists. He seemed not to notice the heat generated between them, but Serena did. She pulled away sharply, seeming ruffled, but other than a tiny upturn of his lips, he gave no sign that he knew he had won this particular battle.

"Serena! Listen a moment! I have been struck by one of my unusually cunning notions."

"Which is . . . ?" Serena asked demurely, for the look he was regarding her with was causing her pulses to behave most peculiarly for a confirmed old maid like herself. He did nothing to help with his lazy smile, which seemed to penetrate into her very being. A smile like that should really not be permitted unless in the presence of dozens of chaperons and several twittering gossips. Serena nearly told him so, then stopped herself just in time as he gestured to a seat beside him on the rocks.

"Sit by me, my angel, and I shall tell you. " Serena had no time to digest the endearment or puzzle out how he could use it so carelessly and casually, for he was leaning forward in sudden boyish eagerness.

"Gracious galloping great heavens, of all the rare starts! There is a fish upon your line. No, no, I am not joking. See? Pull it in, quick!"

She did, with a triumphant ease that amused him and expended her energies most satisfactorily. It also, of course, *quite* explained her flushed cheeks and shining eyes, though not, naturally, her trembling knees, which she chose to ignore.

"Shall I gut it or do we simply throw it back?"

"Gut it by all means, if you can!"

Which challenge Robin, with quizzical amusement, found himself quite unable to resist. Thus it was that the Honorable Lady Serena, far from having a day's quiet introspection, found herself in a most interesting position—alone, unchaperoned, and perfectly at ease— though a little breathless—with both an earl and a fish. A singularly wriggly one it was, too.

From Lord Robin's point of view—though naturally

he did not voice this errant thought—it was more than just the *fish* the lady had hooked. He did not know whether to be rueful, wriggly, or damned well satisfied. Time, he supposed, would have to tell.

Chapter Ten

It must not be thought that Captain McNichols was idle in this time, either. After disappointing his mama a thousandfold by not entertaining the notion of marriage to the lovely lady Serena—no, he argued, not even though her hair was a perfectly delicious shade of copper and she knew every decoction possible for the cure of ague—he redeemed himself a modicum.

Whilst it was a mere smidgen—for Mrs. McNichols had been quite set on Serena—it was sufficient to allow him a small amount of peace in his own home. He let it be known that whilst the Lady Serena was *not* his choice, it was not the institution of marriage *per se* that he was averse to.

This seemed to greatly cheer his family—though why his sisters should care he frankly could not conceive— and led him to be invited to a bevy of ballrooms he would rather have done without. So much for that rare bit of peace in his home! Now, of course, he was dragged from soirée to soirée, from excursion to excursion until he thought he might very well make his escape back across the seas, if not to America, then to the shores of France at the very least.

Only the anticipation of one day spotting Julia, languishing delicately like a wallflower against one of the silk-lined trellises, made him soldier on bravely. Not that she wanted to *languish,* despite all her claims, but he *had* promised to be foremost in his attentions to her and so he would be, if only she would make her town appearance!

This matter, unknown to him, had now reached a stumbling block. The dowager had scathingly denounced Redmond for not resupplying Caraway with smelling salts, which was unfair, for the merchant had sent up a supply not two days ago, but the countess's use of the substance had increased dramatically over the days following the earl's fateful return; and she had closeted herself in her room with a hot brick upon her bed and announced that Julia was to remain to minister to her.

Miss Waring, after her tears in the conservatory, had dutifully dried her eyes and ordered her trunks to be unpacked, for she was not so dreadful a child as to disobey her parent and possibly cause more spasms to ensue.

No amount of persuasion by Serena could shake her, for she was feeling guilty at having been so selfish. If her mama did not want her to have her Season, she would remain at Caraway, though she did rather wistfully comment that perhaps a small excursion could be arranged. Serena did not know who she wanted to shake more—Julia, for being so damnably compliant, or her mama for being so unscrupulously manipulative. In the event, after much contemplation, she decided that the earl's cunning scheme, as he cheerfully put it, might just serve.

To wit, the earl suggested that if he remained at Caraway, poor Miss Waring would be stuck at Caraway too. If, however, he took up residence in London, it followed as the night the day that Julia would be sent on her Season after all.

"But what of Captain McNichols?" Serena objected very reasonably. "He cannot well be denied our door, yet I am perfectly certain the dowager would have it so."

"Aha! But *here* is the beauty of my little contrivance," the earl had said, grinning as he skinned the fish—no longer wriggling—with masterful disregard for his attire. "Adam will be courting you, for it is obvious that that is what your sister-in-law has in mind."

"But *why?* I cannot conceive . . ."

The earl could, but he held his peace. It was becoming perfectly clear to him that the entire estate of Caraway had been run virtually single-handedly by Serena. It was impossible to have spent a week working on the account books, talking to the tenants, and generally observing what herbs had been planted and where without seeing Serena's touch.

How it came to be that the bailiff had practically never uttered her name *still* was a puzzle but one he was perfectly confident of solving. The dowager, however, must have been well aware of Serena's contribution and threatened by it. She probably ascribed her own lukewarm reception by the villagers as Serena's doing. To boot, she wanted Serena off Caraway and marriage was the best way of achieving this.

She must have quite despaired every time Serena had refused a suitor. His conjecture happened to be perfectly true, for Spencer, Serena's brother, had long suffered the countess's complaints in this regard. Fortunately, though he could not understand Serena's stubbornness himself, he had always defended her choices.

Now, Adam, handsome—the earl smiled—conceited little sprig!—and available, was the dowager's last straw, so to speak. She was furious that her quick attempt to seal a proposal had gone awry, but she still cherished hopes. It was but to nurture these hopes, and Adam's welcome would be confirmed.

"You mean," said Serena, staring, "that I am to encourage Captain McNichols's attentions?"

"Very likely I will slay him if you ever do, but you can pretend, my dear Serena, you can *pretend*."

Serena ignored the latter part of this utterance and regarded him keenly. "Why would you slay him?"

But Robin only raised his eyebrows and smiled knowingly, and a wave of contentment swept over Serena from the tips of her boots to the top of her short, cropped hair.

"Why would Captain McNichols consent to such a scheme? It is using him shamefully, is it not?"

"Not when he can be close to Julia. You surely cannot have missed his preference in that direction."

"It is calf love. He is young yet."

"Not so young as he doesn't know his mind—*or* maiden!"

"I collect he is not entirely . . . green?"

The earl's eyes lit up appreciatively. He reflected for a moment on the Fansham woman and several other similar such, and shook his head. "Not green, precisely, no. But surely, Lady Serena, you are treading on thin ice here? As head of the family I really must warn you that you should have no knowledge of such matters."

"Alas, I am beyond redemption! Do not, I pray you, try to reform me."

Robin privately thought it would be a great shame if anyone did, for he much approved of Serena's forthrightness. Certainly it made a difference from every silly young maiden he had encountered, who felt it necessary to swoon if ever he overstepped the invisible mark, or to cackle coyly, which he abhorred all the more.

"Do you think he means marriage?"

"I do not think he knows *what* he means yet, but certainly he deserves the chance to explore the possibility. I do not, by my observations, believe Miss Waring is entirely averse to the notion."

"Good Lord, no! I think it has been madness and moonshine with her from the first moment that she saw him. But I am not certain that it is not just a function of her first encounter with a personable gentleman."

"Second."

"Beg pardon?" Serena looked startled.

"I believe she first encountered *me,* strictly speaking."

Serena laughed. "I said *personable,* sir."

"You are a baggage!"

"So I have been told, I assure you a dozen times or more. It is a trial."

"Allow me to pity you. Here, have a piece of your fish. It is badly scorched, but tasty."

"We shall have the gamekeeper descend on us soon."

"We shall not, for I paid him off handsomely."

"What?" Serena looked both amused and shocked, if such a combination can be imagined.

Robin smiled smugly. "He is a very good fellow. Made his acquaintance about three hours ago. As soon as he mentioned that he had seen you heading for the pond, I took immediate precautions. He appeared gratified."

"You shouldn't have to bribe your own staff! Halswell is a very good man!"

"Doubtless. But he will be better yet with a half sovereign in his pocket and I really, really wanted to speak with you. Alone."

Serena wanted to retort that he had had an entire week and not availed himself much of that opportunity, but held her peace. It would not do to look as though she were dangling after him, which decidedly she was *not.*

The fish was good, causing her to comment idly that he had been right—bass *was* better than trout, under the right conditions. It was lucky that some had been left after the restocking. If poachers were dealt with firmly, the pond should regenerate, quite *apart* from the northern boundary stock. Robin nodded, but shot her a most piercing glance that would have caused her to startle had she but seen it. Fortunately, she was too concerned with licking her lips to realize she had committed a serious strategical error.

None but Addington and the earl knew that bass was being cultivated, just as none but he and the bailiff had known about the stocking of the northern boundary. There was some link between Serena and the mysterious Addington, and he hoped to goodness it was not a romantic one! His fingers clenched at the very thought. Surprising that he, who had been perfectly happy in his bachelor ways, who had defied any woman to ever really change that sentiment, found himself regarding Serena, perfectly naturally, as part of his future. He wondered what she would say about Robin Red-Ribbon and did her the justice of thinking she would approve. Well, time enough there would be for private confessions, if only he could convince her of his plan!

It was a very cunning plan, actually, for in Serena feigning an interest in Adam, and he feigning an interest in Julia—for such was *quite* necessary for the dowager's peace of mind—he had an excellent excuse to haunt Lady Serena's establishment and get to know her more intimately than if he had been merely the titular head of family at Caraway.

The gossips could wag all that they liked, but if they thought his interest was in Julia, they would leave Serena in peace. He *wanted* that peace for her, most fiercely. And he wanted more than that, but he was prepared to step slowly. Marriage was not a step that he had contemplated overmuch, and it was not one he was prepared to leap into unprepared. Serena was utterly dif-

ferent from the females he was accustomed to. He
wanted the chance to understand both how, and why.

"It all seems so . . . underhanded."

"You value honesty so much?"

Serena nodded, though she could not help thinking
of her own tangle of lies. She wished again she had told
the earl sooner. It seemed worse, now, that she hadn't.

"Even a white lie like this, that can harm nobody?
Without it, Julia shall remain here and I shall have no
excuse at all to shirk my responsibilities at Caraway. People
will think it very odd in me. They won't, if I am known
to be dangling after pretty Miss Waring."

"You could dangle after *me*." Serena was half laughing
as she said it, but could have bit her tongue for making
such a ridiculous—not to mention entirely immodest—
suggestion.

Robin grinned, his white teeth wholly too sparkling
for Lady Serena's tranquillity of mind. Really, the man
had no business to be so handsome. It was bad enough
that he was educated, liberal, and endowed with an
acuteness of mind that Serena found both tantalizing
and discomforting. If it were not for the chasm that lay
between them—namely, one huge lie—Serena might
even have felt moved to flirt. Well, just a little. It was,
after all, every young lady's right and Serena had been
most circumspect in the past.

She did not permit herself to think beyond light flirtation, for naturally the man was—well, if not a rake precisely, then very close. She could tell by that wicked
smile and that illuminating twinkle that exuded more
than just self-confidence . . . it was treacherously hypno-
tizing—and she was perfectly certain he knew it. Shame-
less!

Was the remark worthy of the kiss he had just planted
on his fingertips then gently wiped across her lips, from
left to right, then back again? Serena could hardly ana-

lyze this problem as she strove not to do something entirely irrational like fling herself into his arms or swoon like the tiresome dowager. Whilst she was battling with the annoying beating of her heart that suddenly seemed perfectly deafening in the smoky stillness, he answered her question quietly, but with something subtle between them that compounded Serena's confusion.

"Dangling after you—though undoubtedly perfectly delightful"—here the smile widened quite unbearably—"would nonetheless be too close to home. I might get burnt, like this poor fish here."

He did *not* say he had already been burned, but his look might just as well have. Serena felt that strange tightening sensation in her lungs, almost as though she could not breathe. He allowed the intensity of the moment just a second to linger before turning to more deflating reasons, like the dowager not countenancing such a courtship and returning to London herself.

"For I *think*," said the earl, "that we are all unanimous in our dislike of such a course!"

Serena smiled her agreement, but frowned a little at his reasoning.

"She would not do that—return to London, I mean, for she abhors unnecessary expense and though my establishment is genteel, it does not have all the comforts of the dower house, let alone Castle Caraway. She would have to reside with Lady Bowbeck, her bosom friend, though in truth they are like poisonous asps and I doubt the one would do the other any genuine good turn."

"A hotel?"

"Only the finest and that would again put her purse strings to unnecessary exertion. No, she would more likely insist Julia return to Caraway."

"Impossible for Adam, who is becoming quite annoying in his conversation. Everything is 'Miss Waring' this and 'Do you think Miss Waring' that until I cannot help retorting that he should ask her himself!"

"And he cannot do that at Caraway."

"Not with the dowager glaring at him and very likely showing him to the door!"

"Then London it shall be, sir. Do not frighten Julia in your attentions."

"Frighten her? Do I frighten *you?*"

There was a moment's hesitation. He *did* frighten her, but not in the manner he was meaning. He frightened her because he challenged all her perceptions about herself, he awoke something within her that was dormant and that she had never expected—well, only in childish daydreams—to be revived. He frightened her because he disrupted the pleasant life she had mapped out for herself and left her craving for something a good deal more.

Something that was very likely impossible for a hundred good reasons, but something that had nevertheless shaken her inner being to the core. She did not think he could shake Julia in quite the same way, or frighten her for *those* reasons. His general manner, however—altogether too charming—might fluster her, or keep her tongue-tied.

Lord knew—she herself—calm, capable Serena—was flustered enough. She answered his question honestly, for he was cocking his head to one side rather quizzically. His question had not been rhetorical.

"Frighten me? Yes, a little." She did not elaborate, but he nodded, satisfied.

"Good, for you frighten *me,* my little charmer, make of that what you will. As for Julia, I will be the very soul of circumspection. I *can* be, you know."

Serena laughed. "Well, let the games begin! I only hope I do not lead poor Captain McNichols *too* merry a dance!"

"I hate to deflate your consequence, but I very much doubt he shall notice. Besides, *I* shall be forever at your elbow, dancing attendance at every soirée you should happen to dream up for the Season. An excuse to be close to Julia, you understand!"

Serena scolded herself for trembling at so lighthearted a promise. But no matter how much she scolded, she simply could not help herself. It was several moments that they gazed at each other, half with promise, half with unspoken understanding, and another half—yes, impossible in the mathematical sense but nonetheless true—held altogether by something else.

It was almost as if he had kissed her again, but this time with something more than just gloved fingers brushing over soft, altogether too yielding lips. This time, the gaze between them had been like a brand, and the strangest thing was neither the earl nor Serena had moved so much as a step.

We'd Like to Invite You to Subscribe to Zebra's Regency Romance Book Club and Send You 4 Free Books as Your Introduction! (Worth $19.96!)

If you're a Regency lover, imagine the joy of getting **4 FREE Zebra Regency Romances** and then the chance to have these lovely stories delivered to your home each month at the lowest price available! Well, that's our offer to you and here's how you benefit by becoming a Regency Romance subscriber:

- *4 FREE Introductory Regency Romances are delivered to your doorstep (you only pay for shipping & handling)*

- *4 BRAND NEW Regencies are then delivered each month (usually before they're available in bookstores)*

- *Subscribers save almost $4.00 off the cover price every month*

- *You also receive a FREE monthly newsletter, which features author profiles, discounts, subscriber benefits, book previews and more*

- *There's no risks or obligations…in other words, you can cancel whenever you wish with no questions asked*

Join the thousands of readers who enjoy the savings and convenience offered to Regency Romance subscribers. After your initial introductory shipment, you'll receive 4 brand-new Zebra Regency Romances each month to examine for 10 days. Then, if you decide to keep the books, you pay the preferred subscriber's price, plus shipping and handling.

It's a no-lose proposition, so return the FREE BOOK CERTIFICATE today!

A $19.96 value – **FREE** No obligation to buy anything – ever.
4 **FREE BOOKS** are waiting for you! Just mail in the certificate below!

Say Yes to 4 Free Books!

Complete and return the order card to receive your FREE books, a $19.96 value!

FREE BOOK CERTIFICATE

YES! Please rush me 4 FREE Zebra Regency Romances (I only pay $1.99 for shipping and handling).I understand that each month thereafter I will be able to preview 4 brand-new Regency Romances FREE for 10 days. Then, if I should decide to keep them, I will pay the money-saving preferred subscriber's price for all 4... (that's a savings of 20% off the retail price), plus shipping and handling. I may return any shipment within 10 days and owe nothing, and I may cancel this subscription at any time.

Name _____

Address _____ Apt._____

City _____ State _____ Zip _____

Telephone (_____) _____

Signature _____

(If under 18, parent or guardian must sign)

Offer limited to one per household and not to current subscribers. Terms, offer and prices subject to change. Orders subject to acceptance by Regency Romance Book Club. Offer Valid in the U.S. only.

RN083A

If the certificate is missing below, write to:

Regency Romance Book Club,

P.O. Box 5214,

Clifton, NJ 07015-5214

or call TOLL-FREE
1-800-770-1963

Visit our webstite at
www.kensingtonbooks.com

Treat yourself to 4 FREE Regency Romances!
A \$19.96 VALUE... FREE!
No obligation to buy anything ever!

ll..l...ll.....ll.l.l..l.l...ll..l..ll..ll..l

REGENCY ROMANCE BOOK CLUB
Zebra Home Subscription Service, Inc.
P.O. Box 5214
Clifton NJ 07015-5214

Chapter Eleven

Whilst Serena was opening her residence, refurbishing the living rooms in the first style of elegance (though more tastefully than the dowager's exertions and at half the expense thanks to the silk bazaars), the earl, putting up at Strawberry Hill, was engaged in exertions of his own.

Naturally, he was signed up at Watier's and Boodles and permitted himself to become the nine days' wonder—or *one* day's as the case happened to be, for despite his simplicity of dress and extraordinary style of hair he was immediately recognized as a gentleman and therefore disappointingly unworthy of any further speculation. If there were some among the upper ten thousand who had heard rumors of a certain Robin Red-Ribbon, no one ever said, and certainly it was not reflected in any lack of civility or invitations that happened to flood onto the silver salvers at Strawberry Hill.

Captain McNichols, by extension, was just as popular. This, possibly, because he was not only likeable—not to mention impeccable—but could also spin a fascinating yarn whilst holding his wine with uncommon stoicism. Virtually no invitation that arrived included the one and excluded the other, a fact that both gentlemen considered gratifying and Mrs. McNichols considered a personal triumph.

Whilst Adam rigged himself out in the finest Weston had to offer, and visited with earnestness such legendaries as Lobb and Lobb for boots, Charting and Co. for canes, Willis and McNight for beavers, tricorns and other imperative headgear, Robin sought out, with firm determination, Mr. Gabriel Addington, late of Caraway.

He wrote several missives to Oxford, to Cambridge— for he was certain he must be the younger son of an impoverished lord, so classical was his education—and even more to employment agencies. If Addington had been seeking any work at all, he was bound to show up on these lists.

Once and for all, he was determined to discover the mystery surrounding this man—both his presence at Caraway and his sudden, unheralded departure. Though he had immediately formulated the intention of following this path, the matter now seemed of greater urgency. He was certain there was some mystery concerning the Honorable Lady Serena that needed to be unraveled. His instincts had always served him well in the past and he was perfectly certain they would do so now.

He just hoped that the disclosures he unraveled showed Serena up in the same honorable light as her title. He had misgivings, but these needed to be allayed before he could proceed any further with the romance he fully intended to wholeheartedly indulge. He grinned, a little, at this, then ordered his tiger—still a mischievous lad with the tartest tongue ever heard—to bring his carriage round. This the boy did, for he prided himself on his whip hand, if nothing else—and Robin continued with his thoughts as they headed toward Whitehall.

Why was he suspicious? What mysterious link was

there between Addington and Serena? Chiefest among these links was the fact that Serena curiously seemed to know his mind on all issues relating to Caraway, from the simple matter of stocking fish, to his designs for a new schoolroom closer to the village. Only Addington had known of these plans, for he did not think Adam— or anyone else for that matter—would have the remotest interest.

Serena seemed to understand his reasons for the crop rotation, she approved of the sheep experimentation—indeed, she had given him cause to assume it had been her idea that Addington had taken it up—oh, innumerable curious coincidences and circumstances that forced him to wonder.

Strangest of all was that no one but Serena herself seemed to know anything about the man, although many at Caraway conceded vaguely that there must be a bailiff, but "he don't no-how show 'is face about these parts, awful private he must be."

Then, of course, there was the certainty that the accounts at Caraway were all very neatly recorded, very succinct, and the decisions made accorded wholly and precisely with Robin's own wishes.

The hand used in record keeping was definitely that of Addington's—Robin, thorough in everything, had checked the hand against a magnifying glass for clarification. Definitely Gabriel's—he would recognize it anywhere. Mystifying, for the correspondence to tradesmen had been in the bailiff's hand—not in Lady Serena's, as he might have supposed from stray snippets of her conversation.

The depth of her knowledge puzzled him—also, her resistance to any probing and her preference for him to think her ignorant of estate business. Strange, when he found her very interest so intriguing. But it was a sad fact that whenever he quizzed her on Caraway matters he was positive she knew a good deal more about them than she was prepared to reveal. More than that—the lady actively turned the subject and disappointed him with a sudden flurry of nonsense about bonnets or the weather or some other desultory affair.

"Tea?" she would say. "I know nothing of tea, save for the frightful cost of it. You would think one were drinking gold rather than a few silly little leaves from China or wherever it is that they grow such things!" Or she would *swear* she knew nothing about accounts when Robin had it on perfectly good authority that most of the merchants dealt directly through her, and a hard businesswoman she was, too, if some of them, whom he had diligently tracked down, were to be believed.

"Oh," she would say, when quizzed, "don't *fret* me with such trifles. I have my pin money and whether it is placed on the Royal Exchange or in a private bank I really couldn't say. Ladies, you know, can really not be expected to follow such things."

Despite his disappointment when she uttered such trite—and patently untrue—statements, he was virtually positive he had encountered, in living flesh, the woman of his future—someone to share not just his bed (and he was perfectly certain this was something he wished to share) but also his interests.

He had not thought that his prodigal return to Caraway would prove anything more than an amusing diversion of sorts. Now, he found that his roots tugged at him, his establishment in the Americas receding quite astonishingly in significance. Perhaps when he finally tracked down the mysterious bailiff, he could ask him to manage those vast estates. In the meanwhile, he had several pressing engagements to attend to.

Julia, having been presented at court—an event that the dowager actually *did,* quite properly, manage to attend—was now officially on the marriage mart. Though her birth was not so impeccable as Serena's, it was still excellent, and that, coupled with her friendliness, her natural beauty, and her horror of being a wallflower—which everyone found amusing and bent over backward to ensure would not occur—meant that she was never, ever short of partners and even achieved the dizzy heights of having to mournfully refuse three dances on account of her card's being too full.

Captain McNichols, reproachful, reminded her that he had been the first to secure two dances, at which she offered him a bashful smile and whispered that she had not been so rude as to have forgotten. So, all was perfect bliss with Miss Waring. *More* so because Captain McNichols, who had sworn to court Serena most avidly, forgot his intentions altogether in the delightful mists of mutual passion.

Serena, half miffed, half amused, threw aside her *own* card, which Captain McNichols had dutifully inscribed with his name for the current dance, and supposed, with a sigh, that she had best assume the much feared title of wallflower, for the set was already in progress.

"Stood up, are you?"

Serena refused to allow her heart to leap, though she experienced a sudden startle at the unexpected voice.

"Lord Caraway! I thought you had cried off this festivity!"

"Missed me, did you?" Robin could not suppress a grin.

"Not at all," Serena lied, though she took the precaution of crossing her fingers behind her elegant back as she did so.

The smile she received in turn was quizzical. "When I was a child I used to cross my fingers precisely as *you* are doing. It never worked. I was always found out. Most crushing!"

"How in the world did you know . . . you rotten rascal! You were guessing!"

"Correctly, too. Let me see those pretty little fingers. Come on, they can't hide behind your back all night."

"You make me feel like a child."

"Do I? How terribly disconcerting. I could have sworn I was making you feel the very reverse."

"You are a coxcomb."

The coxcomb simply smiled and drew the errant fingers to his mouth. Serena refused to humor him by appearing in the least bit confused. Instead, she hissed that they were making themselves the spectacle of the ballroom.

"Nonsense! Lady Govender is the spectacle of the ballroom with that plumage she is wearing upon her head."

Serena's face lit up with laughter. So much so, she almost forgot he was committing the dreadful social offense of retaining her hand far too long for comfort and a great deal longer than was proper. After he had pointed out Lady Worthington, with her two lapdogs—heaven only knew how the creatures had been permitted to attend such a function—and several other permutations of the ballroom scene that were equally outrageous, Serena was forced to remind him that they were now—quite definitely—becoming the subject of gossip.

He released her hand, but regretfully. "Do you care so much for gossip?"

"Not a fig, but it would not do, you know, whilst I am chaperoning Julia."

"Ha! The situation is perfectly ridiculous. Chaperon indeed! You are in dire need of one yourself."

"Only thanks to *your* exertions."

"What, kissing your hand? Those are hardly exertions, my dear Serena. Meet me at midnight behind the trellis and I will demonstrate the true meaning of the term exertion."

"I should really cease all conversation with you. You overstep the bounds at every turn. Trellis indeed!"

"You are right. Far too flimsy. Meet me . . . meet me aboard my ship, *The Albatross*. I promise to exert myself to the utmost."

"And *I* promise to stand on your foot if you talk any more absurdities. Listen, the set is ending. I must find Julia."

"Nonsense, she doubtless has a thousand eligibles dancing attendance including my poor Adam. Dance with me instead."

For a moment, Serena was tempted. Then she remembered their pact and that Lord Caraway should have been dancing attendance on Julia, not herself. "No, I do not believe I shall dance with you tonight at all."

My lord's eyes narrowed a fraction. "That is passing rude, if I might comment upon your manners, Lady Serena."

"I did not mean it so, my lord! You pull straws with me! I just do not wish to become an object of speculation. It would be bound to reach the dowager's ears."

"Bother the dowager! I can deal with her in a moment, if need be. There is another reason, is there not?"

There was, but Serena could hardly say she feared desperately that she might be falling hopelessly and foolishly in love with him, and that a dance—especially the type of intimate waltzes that were now permitted—might overset her completely. Just the thought of his hand about her waist reduced her to quivering schoolroom status, and it was *not* a feeling she relished. She liked being in control—always had—and the earl overset her common sense.

"Of course not," she lied. Fibbing was becoming a most appalling habit, it seemed. Robin regarded her closely, noting her high color and her desire to look everywhere about the room, just so long as it wasn't at him. For some reason, the circumstance lightened his forbidding frown and he almost smiled.

"Very well, then, we shall hunt for your charge. I saw Miss Waring only a few moments ago, crushed between a veritable sea of admirers. Poor Adam! It goes hard with him, I fear. But see! *There* she is!"

My lord pointed at a gap that had opened up amidst the crush of people. The candelabra flames seemed multiplied a million times by the crystal all about the hall, but clearly, between two unknown officers, the Viscount of Stanforth, and a determined-looking Captain McNichols, Julia seemed to be holding court perfectly well on her own.

"Rest easy. She is managing perfectly. If you are set on refusing me at every turn I shall ask that perfectly ravishing creature over there to dance. She has been ogling me all evening."

"But naturally. It is the *vogue* to ogle you!" Serena, relieved that he had not pressed her about the dance, returned to form.

"Is it? How terribly quaint! It must be my fortune."

"It is. I shan't *mention* your good looks, for you are quite conceited enough already.'

"Oh! You think they are good?" Robin cocked his head to one side. Serena, who could not avoid his eyes, but refused to concede anything at all that might make that devilish twinkle deepen, nodded offhandedly and pronounced, rather dampeningly, that they were "passable."

He seemed not to mind this offhandedness, for he took her by the elbow and steered her toward a table laden with refreshments that looked like they might possibly be a day old.

"Pile your plate up high."

"I am not in the least bit hungry."

"Neither am I, but see, my plate is already gratifyingly full."

This, as he dished out two sandwiches, a confection of strawberries, three slivers of ham (hardened from an evening's exposure to the currents of a hot fire in the grate behind them) and a purple substance that Serena neither could nor wanted to identify. All this, one might add, was upon her plate, not his own. *His* plate was full of a dozen randomly selected sandwiches. He ignored Lady Marvello's pointed glare as she discovered he had seized every savory upon the serving plate.

"I tell you, I am not hungry!"

"Good, for there is not a damn thing worth eating here. A person could starve, I swear."

"Pardon me for being obtuse, but why are we helping ourselves to a collation we have not the slightest intention of eating? One, moreover, that makes any respectable palate feel squeamish?"

Lord Caraway led Serena out of Lady Marvello's immediate earshot.

"It is elementary, my dear Serena! Elementary! If someone requires you for the next dance, they shall not be so rude as to ask you whilst your plate is full. If they require you for the dance following, you can say no, you are engaged for the supper dance. If they require you after the supper dance, you can say you are either queasy—and one look at your plate will prove the veracity of this—or full. Delightful scheme."

"Simply delightful if I did not *wish* to dance, my lord!" Serena's voice was tart.

"*Do* you wish to dance?"

'Well, of *course* I do!"

"My dear Serena, why *ever* did you not say so?" said Robin, with a grin, as he pushed both dishes into the hands of Lord Alderfoot, who happened to have the misfortune of threading his way through the throng at just that moment.

"Try the ham, Alderfoot! It looks . . . exceptional," called Robin over his shoulder as he placed one guiding arm about the Lady Serena's waist.

"Lord Caraway, I did not mean to dance with you at all!"

"No, but now, having confessed a desire to, you cannot possibly refuse. That *would* be the height of ill manners."

"Your mind is far too cunning."

"Matched only by my body, which is equally so. "

"What in the world do you mean by that?"

"Come, let us take up our positions and I will show you."

Which he did, though so subtly that none but Serena knew the dangerous game he was playing. Trouble was, she could not scold him for it either, for scolding would show him that she had *noticed* his subtle maneuvering, and she was perfectly certain he would be passing pleased that she had.

So, she said nothing, and endured the occasional brush of his muscled thigh in silence (and yes, it must be said, with pleasure, though wild horses would not drag the confession from her.) Also, his soft breath on her neck, the very tips of his fingers imprinted on her waist . . . only sometimes it was the full palm of his hand, and the shock of it almost made her gasp, though quite why it should she did not know, for surely a man's palm was not anything so very shocking? Perhaps it was the way it imprinted itself on her skin. His palm, elegantly gloved, seemed not to notice the garments that so genteelly separated them.

His gloves, her gossamer silks, her petticoats, her soft, pliant undergarments—Serena had never held with corsets. She wriggled a little, for despite all these protections, she *still* felt his hand, searingly warm, upon her. Worse, as she moved out of sight of the crowd, under cover of a huge potted plant, she could have sworn his hand moved just a fraction lower than her waist. Her eyes flashed, for the gall of the man was insane!

No one had ever made free with her derrière before, particularly not in full sight of a thousand people at the crush of the Season. But no! It was *not* in full sight, for as they glided past that plant, so, too, did the hand smoothly rectify its position, so none but she was any the wiser.

She fumed, but Robin only smiled engagingly and cocked that brow of his, so she could hardly remember the words of outrage that she had meant to use upon him. Moreover, far from being unrepentant, he seemed singularly pleased with himself and the effect he was having upon her person.

She wished her heart did not race so revealingly, or that her breathing would steady. She tried to think of Lord Kirkby, who had had all his teeth pulled, but she could not. She could only think of Robin, Lord Caraway, and the worst of it was that he knew it! Yes, he tightened his grip about her just enough to draw her that bit closer, so that the gap between them was far less than the required three inches, and her bodice, tight before, now seemed tighter still.

By the end of the waltz he was brazen enough to be laughing. Serena would very likely have lost her cool demeanor and trod hard upon his toe had she not detected something else—something she could not yet quite divine—beneath the subtle surface of his amusement. She could not dwell upon this, however, for her hand was almost immediately solicited by the Duke of Bedford.

"Can't hog her, Caraway! She should have been mine, you know. Asked her a dozen times but the chit is obstinate as sin."

"Not obstinate, Your Grace, but sensible! You know perfectly well that if I married you we would come to blows within a sennight."

"If I married *anyone* we would come to blows in a sennight. Only natural, stands to reason . . . but if I *must* get leg-shackled, you are the one, my dear girl, and so I shall always say!"

"And so I shall always think you are a dear. But no more talk of this nonsense, I pray you, it fatigues me."

"There you are! I *said* we should be perfect together, for a more tiresome topic I cannot think of myself, but Mama does pester one so. Marriage this and marriage that! It quite gives me the headache."

Serena smiled and cast a laughing glance at the earl, who seemed to share her secret amusement. To the duke, however, she was everything that was soothing.

"Your mama wants only the best for you. She would be a very unnatural parent if she did not, and I must say, Philip, you know perfectly well that you have to marry to secure the succession. It would simply be beastly if your cousin—whom I must tell you I despise— accedes to all your titles."

"Yes, for he is a nasty piece of work and Jenkins has had several complaints about him . . . I declare the whole matter has sent my head into a spin. It would be so much easier if you just let me post the damn banns."

Serena shook her head firmly at this most unromantic of all proposals. "I am most sorry to disoblige you, Your Grace, but I cannot marry simply to save you the headache."

"It is most uncivil of you, and so I shall always say, but you have ever been a stubborn wench. I suppose I shall have to ask that Wicherley chit."

"No! Oh, no! I advise you, sir, in the strongest terms, not to be so foolhardy! She will not give you a moment's peace and if you think *your* mama is bad . . . !" Serena grimaced, the duke nodded, and the earl tried his damnedest not to snort with laughter. Serena frowned at him heavily and turned an engaging smile upon the duke.

His Grace sighed, and applied his monocle to his eye. Then, with diligence, he surveyed every young maiden in the room. This blatant perusal caused several curtsies and giggles and hurried fanning, for he was, after all, a duke, and therefore the most satisfying catch of the Season if not quite the handsomest. None of this curious behavior seemed to please. His Grace's lugubrious sighs grew louder as he adjusted his stiff corsets and appealed hopelessly to Serena for advice.

"Who, then? I tell you, I am defeated at every turn!"

"Nonsense. Brace yourself, Your Grace. You have the pick of this Season's crop. It is not everybody who can boast of that. How about Miss Everley? She is a pretty-natured thing and I happen to know she has a penchant for gentlemen with blond hair such as your own.

"Has she?" The duke was thoughtful. "Will she ride Amberley, do you think?"

"Passably, but you make a mistake, my dear sir, if you are selecting your bride on the basis of your stables."

"I can't see why I shouldn't. *You* would be perfect on Amberley."

"I thought we were agreed we would not suit."

"You are merely being quarrelsome, if I might say so, Lady Serena! Yes, quarrelsome and irksome, for if you would simply accept my offer I would not need to put myself to the trouble of this tedious process of selection. "

"And if you would stop offering, I would not have to put myself to the trouble of pointing out my many unsuitable points! Come, my dear, sir, admit I rest my case. We shall not suit at all if I am as quarrelsome and irksome as you so delightfully point out. Now *do* you, my dear Phillip, still wish me to dance this quadrille or are you really quite at outs with me?"

"Quite at outs but we shall dance, anyway, else my mama will doubtless descend on me with some other hideous prospect."

"See how flattering he is?" Serena turned to the earl. Her heart was still beating erratically from their encounter, but she simply could not resist.

The earl, whatever his own shortcomings (Serena could not immediately think of these but was certain he must have some) shared her delicious sense of the ridiculous. It was delightful to have someone who could understand her thoughts so precisely. Certainly, it enlivened the tedium of functions such as these.

Robin bowed. "Inept, most inept. His Grace should be *whipped* for such a comparison as that. It is the *'other'* that is your undoing, Duke!"

The Duke of Bedford, perfectly splendid in a nipped-in waistcoat of broad candy stripes and two huge golden fobs dangling from their clips, looked bewildered. Serena took pity on him.

"I am sure you did not *mean* to imply I am a hideous prospect, sir," she said, kindly.

"Gracious no! However did you come to think that I did?"

"It was that fateful use of the word 'other,' my dear man, and so I have told you! You know, *'other'* hideous prospects . . ." Robin could not resist a chortle.

Serena frowned at him, but since this had no effect on his amusement whatsoever, she ground his toe into the floor.

"Your Grace, the sets are forming. Shall we?"

"Oh yes, by all means. Yes, let us at once," the Duke of Bedford answered most affably.

And so, to Serena's satisfaction, they did. Her satisfaction, sad to say, was greatly increased by the fact that Lord Robin, by contrast, sat out the dance and did not invite anyone—pretty or otherwise—to nestle in the comfort of his arms. As a matter of fact. he seemed perfectly intent on nursing his sore toe and cursing wrathfully as his cousin—or whatever Serena actually was, she could not quite work it out herself—glided past.

Chapter Twelve

When Lord Caraway and Captain McNichols called the following afternoon, they were forced to be satisfied with merely leaving cards, for Serena had informed the house staff she was not at home to visitors (forgetting that they would consider his lordship a visitor rather than family) and Miss Julia Waring was having a delightful time riding through Hyde Park on a mare bought by Serena specifically for the purpose.

She was accompanied, very properly, by a groom, with a maid walking purposefully alongside her, but these impediments were as nothing, for it stopped not a single gentleman from stopping and admiring the weather—and, quite naturally, her bonnet. London was, quite simply, delightful. She quelled a little voice telling her it would be more delightful yet if a certain captain of the seas should happen to have his horses take exercise here and she should *happen* to see him, for she knew she was being absurd.

That very gentleman was escorting her—or strictly speaking, Serena—to the ridotto that evening. She wondered why, of a sudden, the day seemed to be so slow in passing, and the gentlemen doffing their beavers at her so . . . uninspiring. She would lay a farthing none of them had a shine in their boots *quite* like Captain McNichols. As for their eyes, though she had looked at a dozen or so pairs that morning, it was fair to say that none were as soulful, or as compatible with her moods as his were.

Julia had come, rather guiltily, to understand that despite her very proper upbringing, she preferred an impudent smile to polite admiration. Admiration, though pleasant, did not have that fascinating effect upon her pulses, and though she loved pleasantries in the proper form, there was nothing so pleasant, really, as flirtation in the *improper* form! Captain McNichols had not yet been so bold as to *flirt*, precisely, but she was very certain he would be amenable to encouragement.

And how much more fun it would be than with Lord Blanely, who leered, or Mr. Curruthers, who lisped simperingly, or even Sir Peter Blakeborough, who had picked a delightful posy for her, but somehow did not have the same effect upon her person as dear Captain Adam McNichols.

As for the Earl of Caraway . . . well, he was positively *frightening!* Julia blushed as she recalled—again, for how could one not reflect on such a thing?—how he had tried to kiss her in the conservatory. Bold as brass, yet somehow too mocking and confident for her tastes. No . . . he might have kissed her—shameful behavior!—but he had not meant it to mean a thing. She was positive of it, despite all her mama's hints and hopes. Thank heavens, too, for she was quite certain that they would not suit. Besides being a great age older than herself (to the young at heart two-and-thirty seems very ancient indeed), he was too confident, too careless with his caresses . . . not at *all* like his debonair friend.

A small sigh escaped Julia, as she reined in the mare. Was it unreasonable of her to wish he were a little more forward in his dealings with her? To imagine what might have been had it been *he,* not Lord Caraway, who had come across her sobbing in the conservatory? *He* would not have been so bold as to tease her with a nonchalant kiss and an exasperated shake of her pretty shoulders. No, she was sure of it. *He* would have taken her in his arms, and wiped away her tears and maybe, yes maybe, just brushed his lips across her own . . . .

The mare stumbled over a hawthorne bush, which was not surprising, as Julia had *quite* forgotten where she was. Fortunately, her groom, seeing the danger, had grabbed hold of her lead rein and averted anything more serious. The maid, rushing forward to keep up, however, tripped over her skirts, so between her squeal and Julia's apologies—not to mention embarrassment, for a curious crowd was forming—no one noticed the very object of her speculations approaching until he was right upon them.

"Miss Waring, we meet again!" Julia wanted to sink into her sidesaddle with embarrassment, for she was certain he must have witnessed the spectacle and she was perfectly aware that stumbling over hawthorne bushes did not set one off to advantage.

In this, of course, she was mistaken, for Captain McNichols would have thought her ravishing anywhere, and now found her doubly so owing to her confusion and the rosy glow upon her delicate cheeks.

"Captain McNichols! How fortunate! I did not expect to meet you here at all! This was only half-true, for while she might not have been *expecting,* she had certainly wearied her mare, her groom and her maid with her *hoping.*

These hopes had led her to haunt Hyde Park half the day, for she remembered perfectly clearly that it was the captain's habit to ride out there most afternoons. The captain greeted her with all the enthusiasm she could have dreamed of, much to the amusement of Lord Caraway, who, having been balked of his prey (Serena) now compounded his tedium by accompanying Adam.

"Lord Caraway!"

"Miss Waring, how perfectly delightful." But his eyes were dancing and Julia did not take heed of him one bit. He was teasing, and she was not perfectly certain it was not at her expense. The wind played with the ribbons of my lord's smooth, unpowdered hair as she smiled demurely and permitted her hand to be kissed, though her mare danced with impatience.

"I think we should not tease your mare any longer, Miss Waring. All this formality is fretting her."

"I fear it is *I* who am fretting her by not looking where I am going!"

"Then by all means let us lead you. It is a pity Lady Serena could not accompany you. She is not ill, I trust?"

"Oh, no such thing! She is probably all nestled up with a book, for I very much fear she thinks the pace I set rather giddy. There is the ridotto this evening, and Lady Halbrook's tomorrow . . . I feel guilty, really, for she misses Caraway, and all the things she used to do there."

"She can still do them."

"No! It is different, for she is used to making decisions and having people depend upon her, and . . . oh, a host of things! People are forever telling me of all the complicated wonders Serena gets up to. I am afraid she might need time to adjust, really. Society life must seem very dull by comparison."

"But not to *you*, I trust?"

"No, Captain McNichols, for at the risk of seeming quite horribly shallow, I have dreamed of my Season since I was a little girl!"

"How refreshing! Most debutantes feign fatigue."

"Yes, and I think it is the height of silliness! Why should one pretend to have a bad time when one is having a very good time indeed?"

"To appear sophisticated?"

"To appear *stupid,* more like!"

"Do not change, Julia, your freshness becomes you." This remark from the earl, so unexpected, made sudden tears sting at Julia's wide eyes. Somehow, the comment touched her, especially as it was then rigorously endorsed by the captain, who exceeded *all* her ladylike dreams by expounding upon *all* of her various virtues, real and imagined.

"That will *do!*" came the quelling response of the earl, who had started the whole affair, but Julia did not take it amiss. He was smiling.

Lady Caraway closed the epistle she had been reading thoughtfully and tucked it away in the ornate drawers she'd had installed at hideous expense in the dower house.

By all accounts, the earl was dancing attendance on her daughter at last, but there were still some spiteful old tabbies out there who reported otherwise. Yes, indeed, Lady Baldwin herself seemed to think it was *Serena* he was captivated with, and that, naturally, would not do. Fortunately, these were not the only reports circulating about London. Some, more sinister, were far more intriguing. If rumors had it right, the earl had led a varied life. Yes, varied indeed if certain telltale tidbits were to be believed.

She rummaged through her old pile of *Tatlers* and *Gazettes* (she saved them all, despite Serena's comments that they would make excellent kindling for the castle fires) and scanned at least ten of them with an impatient rustling of highly manicured—but nevertheless slightly gnarled—fingers.

She found only the odd, unhelpful snippet of what she was looking for, but on page five of the *Gazette* of two years before, found at last what she had vaguely remembered. Three paragraphs devoted, rather tongue-in-cheek, to the exploits of Robin Red-Ribbon, a detailed description of the treasures seized from *Le Liberté,* the French vessel waylaid on the Spanish waters of the Iberian coast.

Not full—it fitted any person of medium height and slight, muscular build—but full enough to arouse the dowager's already wakened suspicions. Yes, she remembered now, there had been much talk of the famous Robin Red-Ribbon, just as there had been similar talk, nearly a generation before, of the elusive Scarlet Pimpernel. Romantic drivel, most of it, but a few grains of truth, surely.

There was no doubt, now that she skimmed through the correct dates, that several important ships had not reached their ports. When they had, they had been short of a great deal of cargo, most of it rum and contraband lace.

She, reading, could know nothing of the several French spies who had been foiled in their attempts to reach English shores, or of the English spies who had landed on French shores as *The Albatross*—immune, as an American vessel, to the restraints placed on the British—glided easily in and out of coves known hitherto almost exclusively to smugglers.

Lady Caraway rather hoped that she was correct in

her surmise, for to have a pirate chief in the family was no small thing and a fact she might well use to advantage. Even if he were *not* a pirate—which she very much doubted, now she came to think upon it, for he looked every bit the rogue—he would not wish for a scandal.

Such a little gossip-worthy item this was! She smiled, as she called Redmond to dress her hair. Tomorrow, if her gout permitted—and somehow she was certain it would—she would undertake the journey into London herself.

No, better yet, for really, she could not bear any unnecessary exertion, she would summon the Lady Serena back to Caraway. Doubtless a few judicious words, sprinkled liberally with a few equally judicious threats, would bring her back. Yes, she was perfectly certain they would indeed.

Lady Caraway—for she simply could *not* think of herself as the dowager—life was so unreasonable!—sank back into the comfort of her luxurious, ancient Egyptian-style opulence.

When the sun trickled in through the drapes and finally caught at her expensive, ermine-trimmed skirts, she was daydreaming in a haze of pleasant thoughts, chiefest among these being her *complete* rule over Caraway and her ability to crush any pretender in the palm of her prettily gloved hand.

It was the following day—maybe two or so later—that the silver salver so laden with invitations bore one marked with the familiar green Caraway seal. At first, Serena, recognizing the hand, tossed the letter on to Miss Waring, but Julia, who had already ripped open the missive, thrust it back with a grin.

"For you, my dear Serena, and it is probably a scold! Mama never puts herself to the trouble unless it is to admonish one. I have thankfully not had a letter in days, though I live in dread."

Serena, responding that Julia was becoming an undutiful little varmint and that she had half a mind to send her straight home, now idly extended her hand for the unlooked-for letter, which was bound, she thought uncharitably, to be full of complaints and hints at expenses and artful bemoaning of this and of that.

Serena, who had been in a perfectly pleasant mood—and it was nobody's business of what or of whom she had been thinking!—regarded the letter with distaste. It was, as she feared, a mysterious, heavily underlined and virtually unintelligible load of drivel from her sister-in-law. She very nearly tossed the whole damn thing into the fire before finding her wrap.

She had an engagement at the bank—for she wanted to transfer some of her bonds on the exchange, and cash some for the maintenance of the club at Caraway—then planned on showing Julia the Tower (for Miss Waring had a delightfully vivid imagination and seemed to relish the horrors) and Astley's, compulsory for any visitor to the city sights.

Naturally, they were to have been accompanied by Captain McNichols, who bravely tried to maintain the fiction that his interest was firmly fixed with Serena, and Lord Caraway, who ignored Serena in company and flirted with exasperated enjoyment, (for Julia had none of the spunk of her aunt) with Miss Waring.

Julia, breathless with anticipation—whether for the tower or for the sight of the captain or for Lord Robin's mild attentions, Serena could not quite divine—had tried on several different gowns and combinations of cloaks, hoods, pelisses, and caps until Serena had lost all patience with her and told her that she was in danger of becoming spoiled.

Which naturally had caused the tears to well up in

Julia's fine eyes and Serena to feel like a veritable Miss Mean-Spirit, so after much hugging and kissing and eye-drying, a suitable gown had been chosen—delectable, if slightly cold for the Season—and all had been well, once more, at Number 2, York Crescent.

The clock was just chiming the hour when a linkboy arrived with a message for the ladies, indicating that the outing was to be delayed an hour on account of "Captain McNichols requiring a further fitting of his topboots," an impatiently dashed message that had Serena smiling—clearly, the earl had been the author—and Julia cluck-clucking, hoping that the captain would take his time, for there was nothing worse than boots that did not quite fit, and did Serena remember the time . . . Serena, with a sigh, remembered.

So, being somewhat at a loose end for the moment, Serena picked up Lady Caraway's missive and struggled with it once more. It appeared to be full of dire warnings that Serena did not for a moment give the slightest credence to, but the abuse of Lord Caraway's name annoyed her, and the tone of the dowager's letter seemed far too gleeful for Serena's liking.

The dowager was talking a great deal of balderdash relating to the new earl, but it was the sort of drivel that would delight her contemporaries—not to mention the eager ears of Sally Jersey, who was always on the lookout for a juicy scandal.

Pirate indeed! Serena smiled at the very thought, and wondered how much truth could be in the fabrication.

He did *look* like a pirate, with his roguish air and red-ribboned hair, but Serena had firsthand insight into his business dealings and did not for a moment think that his gains were ill gotten, though possibly a little privateering on *The Albatross* had occurred from time to time. Yes, she would not put a little light-hearted adventure past Robin, but anything dishonorable—as the dowager insisted in many pages of gleeful underlining—was perfectly out of the question.

If Serena had been so diligent as to read and remember every article in the morning mail, she might have made the same connections Lady Caraway had made. As it happened, she was far too busy to cast her mind so far back, though the name Robin Red-Ribbon, had she but recalled it, might have intrigued her a little. As it happened, she had not a scrap of romance in her backbone and therefore did not immediately suffer the trembling heart and spasms of shock one might have expected.

Still, such rumors should be scotched at the source and Serena felt it her duty to do so. Also, she rather thought that a last missive from the mysterious Mr. Addington might be in order, to allay the earl's suspicions.

If it was fine early on Thursday, she would have a chance to return quietly to Caraway, for Julia had engaged herself not only for several fittings, but also for a picnic in the company of two of her oldest friends, Miss Chartwell and Miss Lila Weatherby, both of whom were unexceptional young ladies whom Serena liked very much indeed. If she found their company just a trifle tedious—especially Miss Weatherby's high-pitched giggles, she was far too good-natured to say so, for the girls were kindhearted and perfectly well mannered in their own way. So Thursday would be ideal for a return to Caraway, a firm chat with the dowager, and a letter-writing session that would hopefully put an end to the wretched affair of Mr. Gabriel Addington.

As it was, it was quite a few days later that Serena set out, for the picnic was postponed on account of Miss Weatherby's aunt taking a chill. The seamstresses had also been postponed, for Lord Caraway had been persuaded to drive them the forty miles or so to show them the interior of *The Albatross,* a sight quite worthy of their interest, though Serena's maid had felt seasick and Julia herself had turned a trifle pale at the high winds that had caused the anchored vessel to tug at its moorings.

Still, it had been a sight to behold, with the brightly bannered flag flying full mast (though not the flag of the notorious Robin Red-Ribbon, which Lord Caraway had circumspectly exchanged for the green Caraway crest upon landing). If indeed Lord Caraway had ever been a pirate, his demeanor did not reveal as such, for he was the perfect gentleman as he helped the ladies onboard, instructed the maids on the stowage of such items as cloaks and reticules and pelisses, and guided them through the cabins—though not, curiously, his own—Serena found him more scrupulous with their honor than she would have suspected.

When Lord Robin commented on Serena's new periwinkle blue gown with matching fur tippet, kid gloves, and feathered bonnet, Serena blushed like a child and stammered rather foolishly that they were only bought so as not to shame Julia.

It was a remark that quite set his eyebrows on edge and caused that damnably quirkish smile to appear on his handsome face so that she had to clench her fingers not to hit him, for it was as though he were reading her very thoughts, and really, those thoughts were highly embarrassing and entirely her own, after all. Gracious, did not every young maiden not in their dotage wish to look passable? It was not as though she were committing some heinous offense, or wearing dampened skirts or rouging her cheeks, which she knew perfectly well was common practice among even the most genteel of ladies!

But Robin had not challenged her remark except by the appreciation in his eyes, so she was not so gauche as to fault him for it, but accepted her compliments at face value; and, after her embarrassment had worn off, felt rather pleased, for after all, she *had* gone to some considerable trouble and at least he'd had the civility to notice.

She had to take off and hold the delicious feathered bonnet, for though it was tied with ribbons it was not to be trusted in the strong northerly breeze that was now tossing the ship upon little crested waves, and causing some stress upon the landing ropes. Still, she rather liked the sea scent and the rush of wind through her hair, which was more than could be said for poor Davina, her trusty maid, who was looking green but determined.

Serena, eyeing her sympathetically, suggested they move inside, for though the breeze was refreshing, the sight of the waves was a trifle giddying for anyone of weak constitution.

Inside was Spartan but on the grand scale, if such could be imagined. There was not a stick of unnecessary furniture, and virtually no drapes at all, but everything that there was, was of the finest, and the floors were contrived of dark ebony and polished so highly that they shone. In the center of the room was a nautical chest, ornately carved in rosewood, and inlaid with ivory and gold. It had huge, heavy piano hinges and locks that gleamed in the light shining through the portholes. Serena noted that it, like everything else, was firmly bolted to the floor. Captain McNichols explained, with a smile, that in stormy weather the furniture could often do more damage than the cannons. Which led Julia, of course, to excitedly ask to examine these and whether the vessel had ever been boarded by pirates.

A peculiar smile crossed the captain's features as he answered in the affirmative, and shot a laughing glance over to Robin, who frowned and shook his head ever so slightly. But not slightly enough for Serena, who already had a thousand questions in her head. Her sharp eyes had not missed a few vital points like the ship's stowing capacity, its crew—a motley lot, quite unlike the sailors she had encountered in her past—and one or two other things that unsettled her slightly. Perhaps it was the presence of the dowager's missive in her pocket that made her more aware than she should have been. Perhaps, *au contraire,* it was something more. There was an air of mystery about this vessel, and anticipation.

Even as *The Albatross* tugged at its restraints, it seemed almost alive, and certainly more than a pleasure craft. But she was simply being fanciful—she needed more than strange daydreams to convince her anything was amiss.

She reserved her judgment—for if my lord proved to be a pirate—or in league with pirates—she could not think that the matter would be any more serious than the smuggling of French wine, or the contravention of some trading right or other. Her correspondence with Robin had convinced her of this, for in everything, he had been guided by principle, had been rational beyond rationality. Even *she* had balked at the high costs the dowager had set against the estate while *he* had not murmured so much as a word against it.

The ladies examined the nautical viewpoints, the upper and lower decks, the large lounges with their woody leather furnishings, and exclaimed over the cannons—well, Julia had, Serena had merely regarded them with interest and inquired how often they needed maintenance, how many hands were required in their loading, and so on. Then lunch was served on deck, a surreal experience considering they were still docked and could easily hear the bustle of porters and pie carts and sedan chairs busy upon the pier.

An interesting afternoon, altogether. Serena was glad of the experience and suddenly overset with the longing to tell Lord Caraway to cast off anchor and carry her disreputably away, Something of her private thoughts must have been revealed, for she was startled to find the earl at her elbow, a deeply amused smile upon his annoyingly inviting lips.

"Feeling adventurous?" he asked softly.

Serena did not know how to respond, for once again her heart was beating so wildly she was certain Davina, her maid, would hear it. But Davina was either deaf or magnificently dumb, for she appeared not to notice the exchange. Moreover, after several agonizing seconds in which Serena could only respond with a nod, she curtsied and announced that "what wiv these chill winds an' all she 'ad better go see about them pelisses" and she quite conveniently disappeared. Captain McNichols, on the other end of the deck, staring soulfully into Julia's eyes, was no great chaperon either. And Julia's maid was sticking to her like glue, a fact that Serena could only be thankful for.

"Relax, your chicken is really quite safe," assured Lord Caraway.

"Captain McNichols is the soul of propriety. I was not really worried, only Julia is just out and a little impulsive at times . . ."

"You think she might try to ravish my Adam?"

Serena laughed. "Now you are talking balderdash, but since I have undertaken to keep her from harm's way . . ."

"I thought we were agreed Captain McNichols is no harm? As a matter of fact, if I had chosen a suitable guard for her it would have been he."

"Maybe so, but she could probably twist him around her little finger."

"A woman's prerogative, I believe. It will do him no harm."

"Oh, you think so?" Serena's tone was demure, but her eyes sparkled just a little.

"I said it would do *him* no harm. Me, well, that is another matter entirely."

"I could not twist your arm?"

"Certainly not, but I could twist you *in* my arms!"

"An idle threat, for we are in full sight of the shore."

"What care I for that? Beware how you tempt me, Mistress Serena! It is a simple thing to transform desires into action."

"I am not tempting, merely arguing." But Serena's color was high at the thought of Lord Robin's desires. She was not foolish enough to deny there was a strong attraction between them . . . a *dangerous* attraction, for it grew stronger every moment and there seemed no natural conclusion for such a thing . . . Serena was virtually positive, from certain comments he had made during their strange correspondence, that matrimony was not chiefest on his list of priorities.

She, on the other hand, was not brazen enough to throw caution to the wind and contemplate a connection with him on any other terms, despite such modern examples as Lady Caroline Lamb and even, more recently, the Countess of Trubrook.

But Lord Caraway was not listening, his eyes were too fixed on Serena's lips. If she noticed, she said nothing, merely moistening them slightly, for they were unaccountably dry.

"You should not do that unless you wish to see the inside of my cabin."

"Beg pardon?"

"You heard me, my lady."

"You insult me!"

"Do I? Curse my wretched tongue. I never meant to, you know. I am simply not used to desiring well-bred young ladies. It is really very inconvenient."

"I am glad I am well-bred, then, for I must shudder

to think what becomes of the *other* young ladies you desire."

A slow smile crossed Robin's face. "They have not, to my knowledge, ever complained of their treatment."

"This is a most improper conversation!"

"I am *not* very proper, you know."

"I know." This was almost a whisper, for Serena could not help wondering, in the midst of her own maidenly confusion, how much was truth and how much fiction in the dowager countess's outpourings. Somehow, in this environment, on this deck, the notion of Lord Caraway as pirate chief did not feel quite as far-fetched as in the cozy comfort of York Crescent.

He touched her chin. "Tell me what you are thinking."

"My thoughts are absurd, sir."

"Don't distance yourself from me. I am not 'sir,' I am Robin."

"It is a lovely name."

"Indeed, though unusual in a man. My mama was being whimsical. You would have liked her."

"I would, if she had been like you."

This, almost a whisper, for Serena was feeling unaccountably shy, though moved beyond words. She hardly knew why, unless it was the extreme intimacy that they were permitting each other. Not physically, for there was still the proper distance between them from anyone glancing from the bird's eye, but emotionally.

"That is quite the nicest thing anyone has ever said to me."

"Nonsense! You must be used to a *thousand* pretty compliments! I have heard them myself!"

"All brazen flattery, I despise it—or use it." Serena did not miss the sudden hard inflexion in his tone.

"You are harder than you seem. I should be afraid, but I am not."

"You are braver than you seem. If anyone should be afraid, it is I."

"What a strange thing to say! What can you possibly be afraid of? When I am not slapping your face—and that, you must admit, is a rare occurrence—I am all that is charming!"

"Baggage! And that, my dear, is precisely what I am afraid of. Your rare charm."

Serena wanted to press him to explain himself, but somehow, she could not. Maybe she was not as brave as he gave her credit for, or maybe she already knew the answer. It leapt at her from his eyes and left her quite speechless to reply.

She had never considered herself above the ordinary in looks—though she knew she was not an antidote—and she really *had* stopped thinking of herself as marriageable. She had a damnably fiery temper and impossibly high standards, and truly, the exchange of her independence for a spouse had never seemed quite as attractive a notion as everyone put about.

But when Robin, Lord Caraway, looked at her thus, all her well-ordered thoughts flew from her copper-stranded head and she felt like the most beautiful girl on earth, and yes, the most powerful.

"So tell me . . . what were you thinking?"

"There are rumors . . ."

"Yes?"

Serena swallowed. It was not as easy as one might think to ask a gentleman, with whom one is privately very much enamored, whether he was a pirate. One might be less dramatic and use the more genteel term "privateer," but the notion was still the same and perfectly bizarre.

"Robin, I do not think you would ever do anything dishonorable."

"Your confidence in me is gratifying. No, do not look

like that, I am not snubbing you! I mean what I say. It *is* gratifying!"

"Then the rumors . . . they are untrue?"

"I would have to hear the rumors to give you my reasoned opinion!"

"Oh! It is a nonsense, really. I intend to scotch it at once."

"What is nonsense?"

"That . . . oh, it sounds absurd, now, in the light of day, with all this fine furniture about us and *The Albatross* bobbing so respectably on its mooring!"

"My dear Serena, at the risk of shaking your very lovely shoulders—and yes, I realize I am putting you to the blush but bluntness is a peculiar fault of mine— what in the name of heavens are you alluding to? There are *lots* of rumors about me."

"Are there?"

"Indeed, and some are true and some, most decidedly, are not."

"There are whispers . . . My lord, there are whispers that you have been a pirate!" Serena blurted it out for all the world as though she were *not* five-and-twenty and well past her first blushes of youth.

He laughed. "Would it be so very bad if I have?"

"Have you?"

The moment grew intense. Slowly, without his gaze leaving her own for a moment, Lord Caraway withdrew from his hair a single red ribbon. Serena was too entranced by the manner in which his dark, silken locks fell to his shoulders and spilled beyond even these to realize, at once, the significance.

He put his hands to his lips then took her own hand, kissed her palm, and crushed his ribbon into the fist he had slowly created. A strange smile crossed his features, but still he said nothing. It was well, for Serena had forgotten all about her question. His eyes were devouring her and her demure bodice seemed to grow tighter with the intensity of his gaze.

He leaned forward a little, just slightly to cover that small distance between them. When his lips touched her own, it was like a smouldering ember. A mere brush of flame, but promising of much, so much more.

The contact was bittersweet in its duration, for Robin was aware of reputations and Serena—gracious, she was aware of nothing but his fresh scent, and the silken strands that just brushed across her cheek. The moment was so short, in fact, that Serena could not even swear it had occurred at all, save for the sweet taste on her lips and the sudden racing of her recalcitrant pulse.

"You are a danger to our sex, my lord."

"No, Serena, I am a danger to *you.*"

"You say it simply to tease me."

"I have never been more serious."

"You are a rake!"

"I am not inexperienced, but neither am I a rake."

"What, then?" The words were barely a whisper, for Captain McNichols approached.

"When I have solved all your mysteries, Serena, I shall tell you."

Serena was about to deny she *had* any mysteries, then felt hot and flushed, remembering the fictional Mr. Addington who stood between them. She opened her mouth to confess—for after all, it was not so very great a crime writing to a gentleman, directing him how to spend his inheritance, joking about the neighbors, teasing about one's family . . . Serena swallowed. Not so bad, surely, that she had continued with a correspondence she should not have undertaken, meddled in affairs that were no longer hers—worse, treasured each letter, relished each one she had clandestinely penned, wondered for night after lonely night what the response, from miles over the sea would be . . . oh! It was mortifying. And she could only guess at his lazy, knowing smile if she confessed . . . oh, she couldn't! Really, even for the sake of honesty between them, she really couldn't!

She would hurry back to Caraway, pen him one more absurd letter, and hope and pray that *that* would be the end of it. Robin seemed to be waiting for something, for his regard never wavered from her, though he had stepped back a little, to preserve the customary space between them. He, more than she, was aware of certain grinning deckhands gazing down from the uppermost masts of his ship. He would have his revenge later, but for now, it was imperative that the lady's reputation be properly preserved.

The silence between them was a little too long. Serena had struggled with her conscience to tell him, but somehow could not. She was sure she was imagining his slight withdrawal, the tightening of his handsome jaw as if in disappointment. She was so anxious about it, she quite forgot to press him with her own questions, or to ask him about the significance of the ribbon that now lay crushed in her palm.

Davina, far too late, reappeared from below deck with the promised mantles and pelisses. He selected Serena's cloak from the pile and drew it snugly over her shoulders. The moment had passed. Serena could not help feeling relieved and anxious and ever so slightly miserable. How fanciful she was becoming!

As Julia approached, color high and a delightful smile upon her lips, the ribbon was slipped into a certain periwinkle blue pocket and laid to rest in the velvet folds. She had not been able to resist the purchase of such a cloak, so chic and smart, and perfectly blue, the precise color my lord admired.

The remainder of the breezy afternoon was spent in

pleasant chitchat. If no one noticed that Julia's maid
had defected, on account of a very handsome member
of the crew and a wink from Julia herself, it was all to
the good. Captain McNichols had something of a serious nature to confess to Julia, for how, he wondered,
could he sustain a proposal when she knew nothing of
his colorful past?

If Miss Waring were to accept his heartfelt proposal
of marriage, it must be with her beautiful eyes widely
open, both to the dangers and to the reasons behind
his youthful escapades. He was dreadfully nervous, and
hardly knew how to broach such a topic. There was
nothing about confessing to piracy in any of the common books on etiquette, and he had only his instincts
to guide him.

His instincts, as it happened, were unerring, for Miss
Julia, far from raising her hands in horror, really seemed
quite deliciously pleased. Shocking, really, for a closeted
schoolroom miss of tender years, but Captain McNichols,
apparently, was a rogue beyond all shock. If he could
have kissed her he would have, but the wretched maid
seemed to be reappearing out of the thin air, and he
had no wish to incur Lady Serena's wrath. He contented
himself, instead, with innocent sweet nothings that left
Miss Waring prettily pink and himself a little breathless.

After a few minutes of this pleasant discourse, Captain
McNichols remembered it was *Serena* he was meant to
court. He wrenched himself from Julia and walked across
the deck to her ladyship, where he tried, for a few valiant
moments, to make convivial small talk. *Not* that he did a
particularly good job of it, for despite his excellent
manners, his eyes kept trailing to Miss Waring, who was
now leaning dreamily over the railings and throwing
crumbs to the seagulls.

"She is lovely, is she not?" Serena took pity on him.

"Miss Waring? She is delight itself. You do not mind if I say so, Lady Serena? It is just that I can think of little else."

"I have heard love attacks the brain in that peculiar manner." Serena did not say she knew firsthand, for try though she might, her thoughts kept flying to Lord Caraway, who was treading lightly on the other side of the deck, and murmuring orders to two of his staff. She did not know that they were discussing her and her various amiable features until Lord Robin threatened to draw their blood if they so much as uttered another word, never mind cast another appreciative eye in her direction.

"Yes, it is passing strange, I had not expected to be affected so. Lady Serena, do you think the dowager can be brought round to accept my suit? I am not wealthy, but I own a great deal of land in the Americas, and I have made several worthy investments on the exchange . . ."

"My dear Captain McNichols, you do not have to justify yourself to me! I am perfectly certain that you are all that is acceptable, and Julia appears positively giddy with happiness. She is wearing that dreamy look I know very well indeed, so I must suspect that maid or no, something intriguing has taken place between the two of you. I make a very poor chaperon, I am afraid."

As usual, Serena was blunt and forthcoming, a fact that startled Adam, but would have made Robin chuckle had he but heard it. Serena waved her white-gloved hand dramatically into the air.

"No, do not begin making excuses! I must applaud your taste, for truly Julia is the most delightfully good-natured young lady you could ever desire. What is more, she is good and dutiful and biddable, all qualities I am afraid I lack, but which *she* has in abundance."

"Yes, but Miss Waring's mama . . ."

"Captain McNichols, Julia's mama does not despise you particularly, but rather anyone who stands in the way of a union between her daughter and the earl."

"Robin?" Adam, for once, looked stupid.

"Of course, Robin."

"But Robin has no interest . . . that is to say . . ."

"Robin shall make his *own* declarations, Adam." This from the Earl of Caraway himself, who had finished his discourse on the starboard side, and had returned in time to hear Adam's musings. Hands behind his back, his expression was unreadable. Serena, unsure, hoped it was not forbidding.

Julia, having supplied every last crumb to her feathered friends, now returned—with her maid following faithfully behind—to the circle. She squeezed Serena's hand meaningfully, then, quite unable to contain herself any longer, blurted out that she had just accepted Captain McNichols's proposal of marriage.

Adam shot a guilty look at his greatest friend. "I did not intend . . . that is . . ."

"Gracious, Captain! First you did not intend with me, and now you do not intend with Julia! I am beginning to think you unchivalrous in the extreme!"

"You tease, Lady Serena! You know perfectly well that I *do* intend . . . that is . . ."

"Oh, Serena, he is being all stuffy because Mama has taken him in dislike!"

"I should not have asked *you* before gaining consent from your parent. It was very poor form . . ."

"Oh, *bother* form . . ." came the combined voices of both an unusually disobedient Julia, and a forthright Lady Serena, who had very little patience left for the dowager countess's wishes.

"I wish you very happy, Julia . . ."

"And I," came an amused voice from behind—oh,

subtly, slightly behind—the nape of Serena's neck. She tried to ignore the presence, but it was hopeless, and she thus hardly heard Robin claim his right as head of family to deliver all necessary permissions. Adam, as a matter of form, insisted that the dowager be consulted, and Julia, perfectly certain that her mama could be brought round, allowed her happiness to overshadow all qualms.

Serena had many qualms of her own, not least of these being the necessity to lie about her plans for the next day, a lie that had Lord Caraway regarding her too closely for her liking—it was so inconvenient how he could read her thoughts! To make up for the blunder, she was almost certain he knew she was telling a Banbury tale—she began almost to chatter.

Then she drew out her journal from the fold of her cloak, and began to inscribe quite randomly any thought in her head, so that Robin would take the hint and walk away. He did not; he stood watching her, noting with amusement that the little book was upside down. Something about it arrested his attention, but before he could quite place the notion, Serena had obviously changed her mind about her activity and now slammed the book shut almost as if it were guilty of some hideous crime.

Then she stared up to see if he was watching her, flushed up when he was, and began, once again, with her silly chatter on such topics as the sugary ices at Gunther's to matters of such extreme frippery my lord could not recall the half of them, save perhaps the classic where she bemoaned the loss of a peacock feather.

Lord Caraway, watching her, decided firmly that if ever he was going to uncover her mysteries, it was now, before he positively went mad. This would either be from her small talk, or from her sensuality, which he tried very hard to ignore, but which caused him to struggle against his piratical urges for many long and tormenting hours.

He held his tongue, though, restrained his carnal desires, and mildly commented that the change in winds made the carriage journey look more favorable. "Perhaps," he suggested, "if they were all ready, they should begin to make their departure?"

Serena, already wrapped in her mantle, had nothing more to do than follow sedately down the gangplank, and make several adjustments to her modish bonnet. This had been tossed mercilessly in the breeze, but thanks to some exquisite stitchery remained miraculously intact, feathered plume and all.

As Lord Caraway gave his orders to the coachman, she wondered whether she had imagined their private interlude of earlier, for he was paying her less attention now than his horses. Whilst he was extremely solicitous of Julia, he threw *her* up into the chaise without so much as a pretty compliment. If he glanced at her, it was so speedily she felt sure it had been the merest of chance.

What with both the maids, the picnic basket, and both gentlemen, the carriage was rather cramped. Save for feeling slightly crowded—and more than a little breathless, for Serena was seated just opposite the earl and their knees *did* keep bumping, despite her best efforts—they all made do.

Was Robin a pirate, or was it just her silly imagination? *Had* he winked at her, or had she just wished it? What did the fabulous red ribbon mean, save that he looked so sensuous without it, so utterly debonair *with* it? She wished she knew and wished she was not behaving as foolishly as every heroine she had read of in the Minerva press.

She shook herself, charmed Captain McNichols di-

agonally opposite her with her repartee, clasped Julia's hand, and made perfectly certain not to catch Lord Caraway's eye more than she could help it. In this, naturally, she was highly—and perfectly adorably, if only she knew it—unsuccessful.

Chapter Thirteen

It was perhaps a couple of days after this unnerving outing that Serena received a posy of flowers from the earl. This, in itself, was not unusual, for it had been his custom to send around a nosegay of flowers each morning, but it was usually a simple one for Julia.

This particular one, however, was sent directly up to Serena's rooms, with a shilling to the maidservant to sneak it past before she woke. It smelt heavenly, and consisted of blooms and buds all in red. Upon each long stem was a ribbon, bright, crimson red; and attached to the whole, a poem, or more accurately, a riddle, which made no sense to Serena's sleepy brain.

What *did* touch her, however, was that the earl had been at the flower markets before dawn, else he would not have been able to assemble such a bouquet. Further, though she could not quite fathom why, she suspected that its sentiments were hardly proper—a floral arrangement for the boudoir rather than for the drawing room.

She could hardly tell why she thought that, or why that now-familiar frisson of excitement flooded through

her as she handled each bud and examined the velvet ribbons carefully. They were cheerful and exotic, and told her something she had been really too stupid this morning to perceive. She grappled with the puzzle, a classical quotation scrawled carelessly across the card.

"Cum finis est licitus, etium media sunt licita." Definitely not Homer, or Aristotle. She rather thought it might be something more seventeenth century in tenor ... It certainly sounded familiar .... *The Medulla Theologiae Moralis* perhaps?

Possibly, although at this time of the morning she could not be certain. She would have to peruse the library to decipher whatever message the earl had wickedly contrived. How much easier if he had just used simple English ... or quoted from someone contemporary like Byron. But no! Nothing simple for Robin, Earl of Caraway. *He,* of course, must dredge up hideous quotations from her past and force her to puzzle them out. Wicked, wicked, wicked! But Serena was smiling as she clambered out of bed.

She waved away Davina, with her chocolate, and ordered up coffee, instead. She needed her wits about her today and clearly, so far, they had all gone begging. And all because a damnably handsome man, with an irresistible smile and a wicked mind, was playing havoc with her thoughts.

"Serena Addington Winthrop Caraway," she admonished herself, "use your wits!" But she had little chance to do any such thing, for soon after she was dressed—in something a little drabber, today, for she was journeying to Caraway and did not think she would bump into any stray laughing earls who might tell her to wear periwinkle blue—there was a knock upon her chamber door.

The upper maidservant, with a message for her to see Royce, the butler, with some urgency. Curious, for she had never received such a summons before—Royce always managed Number 2 York Crescent, with silent grace—she sought out the manservant at once.

"My lady," said the butler portentously, "I am afraid there is a . . . *person* waiting for you in the servants' quarters of the Crescent."

"A person? Whoever can that be?"

"A Mrs. Hitchens, ma'am, should that mean anything whatsoever to you. For," said the butler with a distinct frown upon his forehead and heavy disapproval in his tone, "the person—I shall not say lady, ma'am—was insistent I speak with you. Very strange, I am sure and you must forgive my impertinence in bringing the small matter to your attention . . ." His voice trailed off but returned with renewed vigor at a nod of encouragement from Serena.

"The person, as I say, was adamant that she speak with you, my lady. I naturally referred her instantly to Mrs. Higgs, but she said she would wait!"

Serena's eyes twinkled at his outrage. "Then I suppose I had better see her, for I cannot think you would wish her to do all this waiting in your kitchens."

"No, ma'am, not with her crying and all, and sniffing pitifully into her handkerchief, and with Jenkins laughing, you know what scullery hands can be like . . ."

"It sounds like you are earning your wage!"

The butler allowed himself a small smile. "Oh, I can deal with the likes of Jenkins. He now has all of the silver plate to polish, and very sorry he is too. Shall I tell this Mrs. Hitchens that you will see her presently?"

"Please do. I shall set down these tiresome draperies and come at once."

"Not to the kitchens, ma'am!"

"Why ever not?"

"It is not fitting. No, not fitting at all. Let me rather deposit the, ah . . . person . . ."

"Mrs. Hitchens," Serena interposed gently, for she

was tired of dear Mrs. Hitchens, whom she had known all her life at Caraway, being described in such disparaging terms.

"Precisely. Let me deposit her in the blue salon. It won't take a moment to light a fire, for there is already kindling in the grate."

"Very well. Tell her I shall be down directly." The butler bowed and seemed satisfied with this arrangement.

After just a moment, a slight pause for puzzled reflection, and for the promised fire to soothe away the inclement chill, Lady Serena Caraway found herself in the aging blue salon she had hardly paid much attention to up until now. It was very pleasant in style, with high ceilings and fluted cornice work, but it was the one room that had not yet undergone her tasteful transformation. Some of the heavier pieces of furniture had been removed to storage, but not much had as yet been purchased to replace them, save for a mantel clock, two mahogany chairs by Thomas Chippendale, and a Louis XIV writing desk complete with quills and a few pots of dried ink.

"Mrs. Hitchens!"

"Lady Serena, bless yer lovely 'eart! I do go beggin' yer pardin' but Joseph, wot is Tommy's son an all, 'e be coming up to Lunnon-like and it seemed a blessing, you see, for it saved me the cost of the stage. Very comfortable it were too, save for all them bobbin' apples wot kept rollin' onto my side of the seat. But the weather 'eld off, it did, for it would 'ave been an almighty wetting what with the leaking roof an' all, not but that I have not fared worse in me time . . ."

Serena smiled, knowing that if she waited patiently, the point would gradually reveal itself. "Take a seat, Mrs. Hitchens."

"No, bless me soul, I would rather stand as wot's proper."

Nothing Serena could say would convince her that it would not be the most grievous breach of decorum to sit with the lady of the house, so she ceased trying but managed to coax some sense, at last, from the lady.

"It is about me son, like. Stanforth, wot has returned from the war but 'as 'alf 'is foot blown off, 'e 'as."

"I am so sorry."

"Ah, it is right glad I am to see 'im alive and that is the truth of the matter, but the silly old fool 'as gone an' taken it into 'is 'ead that 'e be a burden an' all, an' . . . oh, me lady, I am right fearful for him!"

"Mrs. Hitchens, how simply dreadful! Is there anything I can do? May I fetch him a doctor . . . ?"

"No, for the wound is merciful right and tight, but 'e 'as no work, me lady, no one seein' no call for a one-legged farm 'and, like, and the army ain't wantin' 'is services no more wot with the war an' all finished-like . . . oh, me lady, it's regular hopeless, 'e feels!"

"Nonsense, Mrs. Hitchens, he is a hero! If it were not for the likes of him, Lord Wellington might not have been so fortunate at Waterloo. He shall naturally always be provided for at Caraway."

"He'll not take charity, he won't! Right stubborn 'e is and that I be telling 'im, don't you worry your 'ead! 'E won't take nothink that don't rightfully belong to 'im, 'e won't." Serena tried to interrupt the flow but failed. Mrs. Hitchens continued. "But wiv a gammy leg like that . . . They won't even try 'im out for them newfangled steam engines and don't you go thinkin' 'e 'asn't tried!"

"I shall think nothing of the sort, Mrs. Hitchens! But I still say you need not worry so. He shall be well provided for at Caraway." But even as Serena said it, she had that nasty knot in the pit of her stomach that told her she could no longer set about ordering things at Caraway as she had in the past.

Mrs. Hitchens, fussing about the fire, set down the

poker she had taken up and repeated her point miserably. "There ain't no 'oping 'e is goin' to sit back an' take your kindness. Don't 'old with no charity, does Stanforth, 'e don't!"

"Who is talking about charity? I am certain there are a hundred useful things that require work about the place, but not necessarily the use of one's legs. Can he get about at all?"

" 'E can 'obble about on crutches, 'e can, and 'e can mount a 'orse wiv a little 'elp from Barnaby . . ."

"Excellent! Then he will serve very well as a steward for Caraway. He can report back to the bailiff on what roofs need mending, he can negotiate with merchants, he can . . . Mrs. Hitchens, can Stanforth write?"

"No, but it's a quick learner 'e be, and that's a fact!"

'Well, then I am certain he will be much in demand. He shall be the bailiff's apprentice, when appointed, and earn every cent of his wage, I assure you!"

"Oh, Lady Serena! You are goodness itself and so I 'ave always said! But what of the new lord, that is wot is worryin' me and I won't nohow deny it! It ain't up to you anymore, is it?"

"It never was, really."

"But the late lord, bless 'im, 'e never paid much attention to these matters. It was always you, Lady Serena."

"With his lordship's approval, Mrs. Hitchens. I shall have to gain the new earl's approval, too."

"It's wot I thought, and him not being born of Caraway, 'e'll not look at it in the same way!"

Out came the handkerchief again and Serena, guilty aware that she had no right to be promising jobs for his lordship's tenants, waited as the lady blew long and hard. When Mrs. Hitchens had returned her handkerchief to her commodious apronlike pocket, Serena put her arms about the old lady impulsively and received for her kindness much clutching of her hand and blessings and the occasional extra sob.

"I am returning to Caraway today, Mrs. Hitchens. Would you like to accompany me?"

"Oh, Lord, luv yer, I couldn't! But I 'ave the cost of the stage in me reticule, I 'ave, and if I am sharp I could still find me a place on today's coach."

"Nonsense. It is very uncomfortable on the stage and I am sure those pennies could be put to better use. Mrs. Higgs, my housekeeper, will find you a strong cup of coffee and you can weigh out some tobacco for your Stanforth, for I am certain he can do with such a luxury right now. No, don't protest, for I am quite firm on this point and I always get my own way, you know."

This said with such a kindly smile that Mrs. Hitchens could do nothing more than draw out her handkerchief again and mutter that it were "a right shame my lady were no more at Caraway, for she was sore missed and that was a fact." Which nearly made *Serena* want to cry, so she merely paced about the room, turned the key of her clock, which did not actually *need* winding thanks to her efficient staff, and swallowed softly.

"In an hour, then?"

"Yes, if you be certain . . ."

"I am, and what is more, it is a help to me, for my maid, Davina, is feeling poorly and if *you* are so kind as to accompany me, I shall not have to require her to travel again. She is recovering from the sad effect of a bout of seasickness."

Serena did not add that she wished it were possible to recover as quickly from the effects of a certain Lord Caraway, but *that* matter she felt perfectly entitled to keep to herself. So she rang the bell for Mrs. Higgs, and when all was made perfectly clear, and Mrs. Hitchens had been ushered from the room with great efficiency and kindly murmuring from Mrs. Higgs, who was glad of the company, Serena damped the fire and made her escape thankfully back to the second floor.

There, she climbed a carpeted stairwell to reach the library with its many tomes, some still in bandboxes, barely unpacked. The vellum volumes she sought, however, were not amongst this sad lot, but already upon the uppermost shelf. She bore them down and read hurriedly, until she came to a certain chapter of interest. She smiled, though no one was about to see the transformation in her face.

A small time later, Miss Waring, wavering between anxiety and ecstasy, begged Serena to break the news of her engagement to the dowager. "For," she said, "I have never known anyone who can wheedle Mama as you can!"

"I do not wheedle, Julia!"

"Yes, you do! You know you do, and you are a dear, for if you did not have the knack of managing Mama I would never have gone to the Nottingham fair, nor been allowed to keep my kitten because of mama's aversion to pets, and then there was Flotsam, and the maypole dancing and . . ."

"Stop! You are making my head spin."

"But you *will* speak with Mama?"

"Oh, I will speak with your mama all right!'

"But about the captain? Please? Please, please?"

"Oh, very well, and do not tell me you do not know how to cut a perfectly good wheedle yourself! You are twisting me all about your little finger!"

Julia grinned. "It is in such a good cause, Serena! Shall you be back tonight?"

"I do not know, it depends on what the weather does and what the roads are like. I will try, but do not hold out much hope. Can you bear an evening in London without a ball?"

"You make me sound utterly spoiled! Of course I can! Truth to tell, now I am engaged I have lost all interest in balls, for Adam"—Julia blushed as she pronounced his first name and found it fitted very nicely round her tongue indeed—"Adam can only dance with me twice and the rest of the time it is really quite dreary."

"Surely not when Lord Caraway dances with you?"

"Lord Caraway has his eyes cast elsewhere, I will have you know, and very disconcerting it is to find my toes are being trodden on just because he loses sight of you for a moment!"

"Oh, what . . . what poppycock!"

"Poppycock *yourself,* my dear Aunt! And I tell you what, the sooner you will have him, the sooner I can get my slippers mended, for there is simply no point when I know they shall suffer the same fate, night after night, until you do! You forget he is meant to be courting me, so I spend longer with him than is strictly comfortable. He is beginning to grow tedious."

"He has not tried to kiss you again, has he?"

"No, he only threatens with that enormous, big, lazy grin on his face."

"He *does,* does he?"

"Indeed, but I cannot think he means a thing by it. He is just like the earl, who used to *threaten* to spank me a dozen times a week, but never did. Very thankful I always was, too, though I gave him a thousand opportunities!"

Serena laughed. "I wish *I* had been as fortunate! But do not be so sanguine, my Julia. If Lord Caraway threatens to kiss you, he might just take it in his head to make good his pledge."

"To *you,* maybe! Not to *me.*"

Serena, praying Julia was correct, nevertheless pushed the question a little further. Not from the strange, unfamiliar tingle of jealousy, she told herself firmly, but from interest. Julia *was*, after all, her charge.

Miss Waring answered the question thoughtfully. "If he meant to kiss me, he would have by now. His lordship could have made good his threat many times, for we are often together, you know, and my maid is so timid she stammers whenever the earl is about, and besides, she would very likely like to be kissed herself."

"Very likely." Serena's tone was wry. "He appears to have that effect rather universally, I fear."

"Well, not upon *me*, he hasn't, and he knows it! That is why he uses kissing as a *threat* rather than a reward."

"But why should he need to threaten?"

'Why, indeed!" Julia's voice was indignant. "But he seems to relish the fact that he is the head of the family. Just because I wanted to waltz with Adam . . ."

"But you are just out!"

"So is Lady Tryon, but *she* got to waltz with Lord Fizherbert and hardly a scandal it caused!"

"Only because Lady Jersey is a close friend of her mama's and scotched all breath of a scandal instantly. But Lady Tryon was whisked off to Bath, after that."

"Was she? I *wondered* why I had not come across her again. I like her."

"So do I, but you are veering dangerously from the point."

"Well, the point is, Lord Caraway threatened to cause more scandal than even that if I dared to set foot on the dance floor! Adam refused, anyway, so I could not test him out."

"I should *hope* not!" Serena sounded shocked. "You had better marry your Captain McNichols as soon as you are able, Julia, for you are more of a handful than I would have expected."

"Well! If that does not beat all, after *you* waltzed, and

very shocking it was too, though I contrived not to let that spiteful Miss Wicherly peek at you from behind the potted palms."

Serena colored, for she recalled precisely what had occurred behind that palm and her derrière still tingled when she thought on it.

"Good God! I shall be the talk of the *Tatler!*"

"No, for I trod on her gown and it ripped at the frill—hideous. My adjustment was a vast improvement, though Miss Wicherly did not seem to think so, for she called me a very rude name, squealed, and rushed for the powder rooms."

"Julia, I do believe you have more spunk in you than I give you credit for!"

Miss Waring's mischievous eyes sparkled. She *did*, but she would not be saying so to her aunt. *Nor* would she be staying home that morning, as Serena seemed to expect. But she answered Serena's compliment with one of her own.

"We are even then, for *you* have more spunk, Serena, than *I* give you credit for!"

Her ladyship forced the humor from her face. It would not do to be setting Julia such a poor example. So she said, rather depressingly, that "Lord Caraway's behavior is not always quite proper and I have told him so!"

Julia just laughed.

"You are blushing!'

"Nonsense! It is merely hot."

"Hot but heavenly . . . no! I shall not tease you so! But you *will* speak with Mama?"

Serena, her traditional defenses thoroughly assaulted, relented. If it was the quickest way to change the subject, then so be it.

"Oh, very well, you little baggage, I shall leave at once. Now, for all that wheedling and teasing, *you* may stay and oversee the delivery of the harp—I want it in the top gallery, next to the other instruments. Also, the chaise longue is arriving and some man about a stable of horses for sale. I have his card somewhere."

"Hear him out, will you? I am interested in a pair of matched bays, but nothing above two hundred pounds, however persuasive he may be. No, don't pull such a dreary face, the wind might change."

Miss Waring muttered something about "boring and tedious," but beyond a rebellious murmur, agreed quite placidly. If only Serena could spare her one of the dowager's famous spasms, she would be perfectly content. She did not mention, of course, that the harp could be overseen by Royce, the chaise longue deposited in the hall, and the salesman . . . well, there would always be another time . . . . Naughty thoughts, for Miss Julia had *other* plans for the day. If truth be told, she was developing a disobedient, and just a trifle willful, streak—all quite normal in a young lady of her tender—and lovelorn—years.

Lady Serena, unaware of her charge's mad impulses, penned a prim note to Lord Caraway, informing him that she would be away from London for a spell, (with no further explanation, though she dreamed up a thousand and crumpled a minimum of ten crisp wafers into the basket, so intent was she on the perfect wording). In the event, she left it crisp and cryptic, and asked both Captain McNichols and the earl to excuse the ladies their evening engagements. Serena rather thought it was to have been the theater, but her senses were so disordered she could not perfectly recall.

She also thanked his lordship politely for his posy and ended with a quotation of her own, *"L'amitié de la connaissance."* Yes, the Comte de Bussy-Rabutin, though quoted slightly out of context, seemed apt enough on such short notice to think cleverly. "Friendship from knowledge." Knowledge of Lord Robin's secret pursuits, friendship . . . well, she rather hoped she would act always as the earl's friend. She also suspected, at last, that she understood the meaning of the red ribbon, and its cryptic clue.

"Cum finis est licitus, etium media sunt licita." The *Medulla Theologiae Moralis* had been correct. Translated? "The end justifies the means."

If Robin *was* a pirate—and Serena rather thought he was, for she had suddenly remembered a certain piece she had read in the *Gazette,* and the coincidence of the red ribbon just seemed to be too providential to conveniently ignore—then he was a very honorable one indeed.

The more she thought on it, the more positive she was that Robin was exactly who he said he was. A devoted peer of the realm, and a British courier besides. It was with a light heart, therefore, that she set off that very morning, in the company of Mrs. Hitchens. Also, a four-horse coachman recommended most highly from the employment agency, a baize-covered portmanteau, a picnic basket and a single perfect bloom, ribboned all over in red.

She was followed from the house, some thirty minutes later, by Miss Waring, very properly accompanied by her maid. Unfortunately, while Serena's coach took the main road south, Miss Waring's took another route entirely. Indeed, as she approached Strawberry Hill, she decided, on a sudden spur of the moment, that it was an excellent time to provide her maid with a day's leave of absence. This she did, with blithe disregard for the conventions, but with a strange, tumultuous beating of the heart. There would be no turning back, she knew, if her sudden thirst for adventure went all too horribly wrong.

Chapter Fourteen

The Earl of Caraway was searching in earnest. He had to suppose, given all the time and energy he had expended in finding this Gabriel Addington, that he had either changed his name, vanished entirely from the face of this earth, or did not exist at all.

Despite the offer of a reward—and yes, he had had to receive *several* tedious people all claiming to be Addington but none of them, of course, fitting the bill—he was still no closer to the truth.

He read and reread the last missive he had had from Gabriel, for the remainder were still safely stowed away in his desk on *The Albatross*. Nothing in it seemed to indicate a sudden, anticipated departure. Nothing in it revealed anything more than Addington's usual neat handwriting, witty comments and sound, somewhat tentative advice. He had written about several of the tenants, but none—not one of these—remembered him personally. It was so odd it was almost surreal.

What was worse, was that the earl was daily becoming more certain of a connection between Serena and the bailiff of Caraway. The more he teasingly quizzed her, the more shuttered she became. Not only shuttered, positively witless! Yes, it was an extraordinary thing, but the only time he had ever been at odds with Serena, or felt her shallow, or was somehow, illusively, disappointed, was when the bailiff or her role at Caraway was being highlighted.

She was a master at turning subjects, but not so deft that the earl did not notice. What was more, when she *did* alter the subject, it was always to something mundane or inane. Why did she do this? Was she protecting Gabriel? Robin preferred to assign a nobler cause to her motives than the more obvious base one, that she was having some sort of illicit relationship with the fellow. After all, she seemed to be intimately acquainted with matters she could not possibly know about . . . . she was perfectly open about the fact that she was no longer a green girl, had seemed comfortable, even with his kiss . . . . Robin stopped short.

No, *"comfortable"* was not how he would have described her reactions, but certainly, she was not shocked or missish. *Should* she have been? Robin's fingers unwittingly clenched at the question. He surprised himself, for he had not thought, in all of his thirty-odd years or more, to care that much.

Despite his best efforts—and a little bout of personal torture—he could not imagine Serena brazenly comporting herself with the bailiff, then being complicit in extracting funds from him, no matter how worthy the cause. But it remained a puzzle and one that was not just intriguing, it was damn well irritating! He was going to solve it with or without Serena's help.

He strode over to the mantel, grabbed the sword skillfully concealed in a scabbard crafted to look precisely like an elaborate walking cane, and came very close to shocking the poor servants of Strawberry Hill by slamming the door behind him. He had no sooner taken five steps toward his waiting chaise, than he was arrested by the sight of a familiar face staring at him from one of the stucco columns on the terrace.

The man was not skulking, precisely, for his bearing was as erect as any gentleman's, but he was waiting, and in a recess which ensured he would not be noticed before he desired to be. Now, however, he obviously so desired, for he stepped out from the shadows and stared meaningfully at the earl.

"James! It is a long way you come to seek me out, for that, I infer is what you do?"

The tall man nodded. "Yes, and I am sorry it is in this dramatic manner, but I fear I am being watched at the clubs."

"Not now, surely?"

"Yes, and there is never a better time to be on your guard than when you think the enemy is defeated."

"Gracious, James! That upstart has not escaped again?"

"The Little Emperor? No, but there is a faction . . . listen, Robin, how would you like to raise the brave flag of Robin Red-Ribbon again?"

"Last week I was yearning for the excitement. Today I am more sober."

"You are not refusing us?"

"Not precisely, but you must have a superlative reason, for I am hot on investigations of my own."

"We *always* have a good reason."

"In truth, you are right, and there is always the odd treasure in it to make it worth my while, but right now, I tell you, you need to find another man!"

"Not many men I know have a perfectly good ship, kitted out with all the tricks, bobbing handily on the North Sea!"

"I could name you a few!"

"Bona fide pirates, you mean."

"Precisely. Or smugglers, to be more precise. By the

by, what in the word do you *mean*, bona fide? I should call you out for that!"

"Stop playacting, Robin, you are no more a bona fide pirate than *I* am!"

"Spoilsport! And to think I wasted my time teaching you to fence. I should rather have made you walk the plank."

"We will *all* be walking the plank if a certain letter from the Regent is not overtaken by the next packet."

"The next packet only leaves on Tuesday."

"Precisely. And it is not in the habit of intercepting foreign schooners at the barrel of a gun."

"Cannons, actually."

"There you go, then! I knew you were eminently qualified!"

Robin sobered a little. "What sort of letter is it?"

The man called James looked keenly at the earl. "I am not at liberty to say, you know that."

"Political or personal?"

"It is not one of the Prince's affairs of the heart, if that is what you mean!"

"I grow too old for this, my dear James!"

"Nonsense! You were observed at Gentleman Jack's yesterday. You are, if anything, in better shape than ever before. Landed a crushing bruiser to poor Alvaney if half of what is muttered is true!"

"London has not changed a *thing* since I left! The gossips are still wagging their busy little tongues."

"Give their chatter substance, Robin."

"I am on half crews."

"A pity, but they're an experienced lot. It is only the Channel, after all, and you have a few days before you leave. I have reason to believe the schooner is moored at Upper Leith and will only depart when certain other vital links have been coordinated."

"Upper Leith is a stone's throw from Caraway!"

"Yes, though the coincidence is not really relevant to the case. You should not, I think, need to go ashore."

"Can't you reclaim whatever you need to by land? You can cut through my fields."

"Thanks, but the matter is not so straightforward. Theft would be riskier, for the schooner belongs to the Prince Valmont. Yes, I see that that name rings a bell with you. He is supposedly in England to take the waters, but he has been sighted nowhere near Bath, and rather too close to . . . ah, I see you understand! I shall say no more. Naturally, he is officially under the protection of the Regent himself. A burglary, under the circumstances, would be both suspicious and embarrassing."

His lordship looked speculative. "If I do it, can you track down some information for me? Speedily? I urgently need to find out about a person I suspect does not exist at all."

"Intriguing, but not entirely beyond our scope! Give us details and I will see what can be arranged."

So James—Major James Rittledon, formerly of the Fifth Hussars—was duly invited inside. There he was greeted by all of Captain McNichols's sisters and pressed to stay for tea that he definitely did not want, but he could not possibly bear to hurt dear Mrs. McNichols, who had helped him out of many a scrape when he was a boy. Finally he was given a chance to have a private exchange with the earl, in which certain papers were transferred, certain key aspects discussed, and the problem of Addington dismissed, for the present, from the earl's mind.

It was not that he had given up on his mission, but merely that he had delegated it with extraordinary panache. For now, he was certain, the combined strengths of Whitehall and Bow Street were working on his task. Gabriel Addington, if he existed at all, would be discovered within the day.

* * *

Captain McNichols cursed when he realized he had missed out on all the fun. Yes, he complained, he had missed all Robin's careful preparations, his purchase of gunpowder, his directives to chandlers—for what use was a pitch black night without the use of lanterns and the finest wax tapers? The moon was against them, on the wane, and the tides, at this time of the year, were more unpredictable than most. Reed matting was ordered for the decks, and food, mostly fresh, for Robin could not abide salted and they were not to be at sea so very long.

Out of great chests at Strawberry Hill came Captain McNichols's most cherished pirate outfit, a gaudy confection in reds and blacks and ice white stripes, something he had not thought to wear again. The doublet had a hole, but that enhanced the theme, rather than posed any real problem.

In truth, Robin was more concerned about the mission than his clothes, which he was certain, in any event, were stowed safely aboard *The Albatross*. Patch and powder, wigs and buckled shoes, all awaited him, but only after the ropes were tested, the crew assembled and sober—no mean feat, considering the close proximity of the wharf to the Fox and Hound, selling ale to all seamen—and the blacksmith called in to see about certain odd patches of wear. Then there was the matter of compasses, the analysis of currents, the sail selection for the crosswinds, the stowing of a second pair of sails—procured from Abernathy's at enormous cost, considering the lack of notice—and a dozen different details one would never associate with a pirate, or privateer, or smuggler, or any of these combinations that Robin adopted with such mischievous poise.

Captain McNichols traveled by road to London— and what an adventure he had along the way, for Miss

Waring, perceiving that some mischief was afoot, had blithely decided to surprise him by stowing away in the depths of his badly sprung chaise. That, however, is a tale for later, as Lord Caraway had been entrusted with a very dangerous and delicate mission.

Robin, leaving far later, traveled the whole way by horseback. He stopped only at Linklater, to resaddle and water the dappled stallion he had chosen for the purpose, but otherwise rode like the wind and abandoned his mount at a nearby port posting house, with enough oats and hay to keep him happy for a fortnight.

It was well into nightfall that the anchor was finally raised, and only seven leagues into the purple waters of the North Sea did the Caraway flag, green-crested and proud, give way to another, more flamboyant banner. Not the traditional skull and crossbones—but something bold, and bright, and crossed with gold, the crimson crest of Robin Red-Ribbon, fluttering high in the firm crosswinds from the south. There was a bold salute, and not a few tears in the eyes of a loyal crew who had not expected to see this flag flown again—and a whoop of joy from Adam, and an indulgent chuckle from the captain. Yes, high upon the seas, hair once again bound by a single red ribbon, Robin, Earl of Caraway, breathed life into his role.

The cabin smelled of leather and sandalwood as he completed his ablutions and sank into the comfortable winged chair that he had purchased specifically for the purpose. It was small enough for the confined space, but just roomy enough to feel luxurious. The taper flickered, affording far too little light, so he lit a lantern, took a long, reflective pinch of snuff, and drew a leather pouch from his bag.

It had been thrown up at him just as they cast off, and with his usual outstanding reflexes he had caught it without so much as a backward glance. From the jetty,

Major Rittledon only smiled as he made a small, mocking salute. It had been no more, after all, than what he had come to expect.

The contents were disappointing, a carefully folded piece of paper, in James's own hand, stating that Gabriel Addington had neither been born in England, nor died in England, that there was no record of his existence in any registry, employment or otherwise. As a mild addendum, and to show his diligence, Major Rittledon commented that the name Addington itself had a convoluted link to Caraway, originally through the line of one of the previous countesses. Naturally, though, that information was immaterial, for there were other scions of Addingtons with no such connection. A dead end.

Robin sighed as he burned the little wisp of paper on the candle flame and returned the empty pouch to his greatcoat pocket. It rustled. Something made him remove it again, and check that he had not missed a page. He had, though it had obviously been stuffed into the pouch prior to the later missive then forgotten. A familiar hand, Lord Robin thought, though it was overwritten at the top by Major Rittledon's hasty scrawl.

> *A note left for you by your cousin, Lady Serena Caraway. I took the liberty of receiving it from the linkboy this morning, in case it was urgent. I knew you would not have a chance to read it, else.*
> *Yours,*
> *James etc.*

Robin stared at it for a very long time, then a peculiar smile lightened his features. It was well they had cast off and he had had no chance to respond to Major Rittledon's question. He rather thought that if anyone should respond, it should be he.

He had never had a letter from Serena before—why

should he? Even this one was most improper from a well-bred young lady—but now he could not think why he had not sought out, at least, a sample of her handwriting. A simple matter of peering at her dance card, perhaps, or at the table settings of her quite fashionable soirées. Oh, what a fool he was!

If he had only been a little more observant he would have known at once that the smooth, calligraphic hand of Lady Serena Caraway's was identical in every way to that of Mr. Gabriel Addington. Yes, a fool, for here were the delicate strokes, and the stylized twirls over the C's and E's he had come to know and look for.

Gabriel Addington could not be found because he did not exist. It made perfect sense. Serena was intimate with Addington as he had feared, but *only* because Gabriel was her alter ego. A wide smile curled his lips. It held none of its usual laziness, and the deckhand trying to offer him a mug of black coffee was bemused to find the earl chuckling out loud.

When Robin finally focused on the poor lad, he waved the freshly ground brew away in favor of a bottle of vintage champagne, an essential item for all sea trips. Adam, watching him, could only surmise that Robin, bless his lordly soul, was up to something. He would have inquired further had he not—very guiltily—been up to something himself.

The breeze was high and gulls still circled the topmast despite the lateness of the hour. Robin changed into the familiar attire of gentleman pirate, adjusted his patch—for what kind of pirate could he be without the ubiquitous patch?—and stepped back up into the open, noting with satisfaction that the lanterns had been efficiently lit, the sails were lashed in place, and the hard wood decks quite literally shone.

There was time enough, he felt, to lurk on the ready for Prince Valmont and his precious cargo. The schooner would only leave on the morrow at the earliest, for His Highness—that is, His Royal Highness, the Prince Valmont—had several key engagements in the city he would *certainly* not curtail for a short sea venture, no matter how interesting the cargo.

Leaving now had been for two reasons—to satisfy James, who was restless, and to satisfy his own suspicions. *The Albatross* would be closer to Caraway than Robin would be in London. He would row out with the short boat, leaving Adam in charge and undertake some urgent investigations of his own.

Chapter Fifteen

Serena, perfectly oblivious to the excitements of the gentleman, arrived timeously at Castle Caraway. Despite Mrs. Hitchens's protests, she ordered the carriage to bypass the avenue of oaks that lined the grand entrance. Instead, they pulled to a halt outside Mrs. Hitchens's own dwelling and although Serena did not meet Stanforth, her son, she *did* have time to wave to several of the tenants, and to catch up on some of the gossip, some of the troubles, and a great many of the opinions of the people who had colored her life for so long. Only, they were not her dependents any longer. She had a very difficult time remembering that, and cursed once again the system where inheritance was by the male line only.

Not that she grudged Robin his inheritance—certainly, a more worthy master for Caraway she could not imagine. It was only that the place was not hers, anymore, and whilst she could listen sympathetically, she could not actually do anything. Serena was a doing sort of person, and this naturally went hard with her. So it was with a slightly heavy heart that she ordered the carriage to move on this time, but again, not to the castle, but to the bailiff's quarters, which stood locked, for-lorn, and looking rather hollow some fifty yards from the meeting house she'd had erected.

It took some moments to fiddle with the lock, for her key was slightly rusty with age, but she managed, and cast aside her cloak immediately to begin work. It felt strange, for usually she worked from Castle Caraway, and replaced the ledgers when she had done, but this time, of course, she had no wish to run into the dowa-ger before she had conducted her business.

Lady Caraway might have moved to the dower house, but there was no reason to suppose she did not still have the running of the castle! Especially, of course, now that the present owner was conveniently domiciled in London. Serena tried not to think of the present owner, but in vain, for his image just seemed to creep into her consciousness at the most inconvenient of times. Robin Red-Ribbon . . . She smiled. It rolled off the tongue whimsically, not at all the fearsome appellation one might expect, though, reading more intensively (and this time consulting both *Hookham's,* the *Times* and her own ex-tensive library) she heard several gruesome tales of extravagant exploits. Lord Robin, it seemed, was the very devil with a rapier.

But enough of such thoughts. There had been time enough on the carriage trip down, and if she were to make a return journey by nightfall she must make haste. There would be time enough to take up the idle pursuit of daydreaming half her life away when the mat-ters she had come for had been properly concluded.

She took up a quill pen—quaint and old-fashioned—then dipped it into the inkhorn. The letters, when they formed, were a familiar deep indigo on parchment.

"My lord," wrote Gabriel Addington, for the very last time, "forgive me my hasty departure. The business was

personal and therefore requires no real explanation—I have trespassed on your good nature enough.

"However, I would be failing in my duty to the estate—for such I perceive it—were I not to mention a few last points requiring your attention. The first is the matter of Mr. Stanforth Hitchens, lately returned from the war, but unfortunately without the use of his right leg.

"Do not, I pray you, pension him, for he is a man of character and loathes charity, no matter how well meant. In your position, I would appoint him as assistant bailiff, for he has a quick wit- and give him every chance to prove himself. I feel sure you will not be disappointed in this investment, no matter how expensive to your pocket at the outset.

"Now, the dowager . . . I shall say no more, for by now you will have met her yourself, a thousand pities to you, sir! Please, I pray you, do not allow yourself to be taken in by her turns and starts and do not open your purse to her any more than you already have .

"Miss Waring, however, is another matter, and will probably require a dowry of sorts when the time arises. I leave the matter to your capable judgment—it behooves me not to overstep the mark now that you have returned to your rightful position.

"Finally, dear sir, to a matter I cannot help acknowledging I feel uncomfortable about, but which must, I suppose, be addressed. You will notice I have not allocated any funds to myself this year past, being in the comfortable position of living off a legacy inherited through my uncle. Whilst I have very much enjoyed the task assigned to me, I nevertheless feel that a small annual stipend for the work done should be allocated.

"I am certain you will pardon my forthrightness in suggesting a sum of eighty pounds—this, though high, being in keeping with the salary of the bailiffs of County Moors, Darrington, and Upper Leith, though I cannot

*confirm the latter. At all events, I shall leave the precise
sum entirely to your judgment and ask that you forward
it to me care of the Dowager Marchioness of Penreith,
with whom I am now employed."*

Serena had long mused over this further lie, but considered it unlikely that the dowager marchioness (who was a dear, but sadly deaf) would deny that her bailiff's name was Addington. This because she, being in her dotage very likely had no notion that she had a bailiff at all.

As for the eighty pounds, Robin would not miss it and it would molder away for ever more under the pile of my lady's correspondence. Serena hoped that one way or another, it would be set to a good cause, but she could muse on the matter no further. A reckoning had to be made to allay Lord Caraway's suspicions and set his far too active conscience at rest. As for her, she must sign off, for the last time, as Gabriel, and stop being such a *damned* watering pot about it.

Serena sniffed. Yes, she actually sniffed, for as she folded the wafer, she knew for a certainty that she was closing a very special chapter in her life forever. She only hoped that the letter would serve its purpose. Both for Stanforth Hitchens's sake, and for her own.

She found the familiar tinderbox under a pile of papers, and lit herself a taper. Then, very carefully, using the flame and the traditional green sealing wax of Caraway, she sealed her missive, placed it in the out tray. One of the house staff habitually cleared the mail from the bailiff's quarters and she had no wish to be associated with that particular missive. Then, and only then, she rose to leave.

Not far behind her, my lord had berthed close to the cove known, amusingly, as "smuggler's cove." He should really have waited for nightfall, but felt the urgency of his mission upon him. If the prince's vessel left a night early, he would feel a fool to have missed it. Best, he thought, anchor closer to Upper Leith to get ahead of Valmont. This meant conducting his personal business by day, but Robin, weighing the odds with a slight, mischievous curve to his indecently handsome lips, did not seem to care.

He approached the bailiff's quarters almost at the same time as Serena approached Castle Caraway. He was not unseen, for the gamekeeper, who was still cherishing his half sovereign, doffed his cap knowingly and pointed toward the castle with a great—and very impudent—wink.

Torn between depressing the man's pretensions and casting him at least a florin for the welcome news, Robin restrained himself and did neither. In the event, he merely nodded slightly in greeting, then spoiled this noble effect by winking ever so slightly.

This unprecedented action set his gamekeeper to guffawing, so that very soon the whole of Caraway knew of the lord's presence, save Serena herself, who was closeted with the dowager in a hideous room swathed in purple silks. The dowager was reclining smugly on an ottoman reminiscent of either a Chinese dragon or a werewolf, Serena could not quite tell, save for the bill, which she remembered quite distinctly. This had itemized—at preposterous expense—one ottoman, Ming dragon, gilt on cherry oak, and a figure that had made her gasp for air and write at once to the earl.

Lord Caraway had paid for it without a murmur—or rather, with a caustic comment that had made Serena laugh. Now, however, she was not laughing as she confronted her sister-in-law, who seemed to want to do nothing more than smirk horribly and threaten to call in the watch.

"For I can tell you, Serena, there is something smoky going on with Lord Caraway, and I won't stand for it, and that's a fact! If I weren't so furious with the Princess Valmont, I'd speak to her myself, for her husband is forever going on about spies and pirates and what have you, though why he should worry I really cannot say."

Neither could Serena, but the news, under the circumstances, was not welcome. Lady Fanny continued. "He has the ear of Prinny, after all, and I cannot imagine anyone wishing to attack his schooner, which is positively overflowing with guards, all in a hideous mustard uniform—no taste at all, these foreigners . . ."

Serena stemmed the tide. "I thought you *liked* the Princess Valmont? I could *swear* the last missive you sent Julia was full of nothing but her praises."

"She is a tedious woman. I do not wish to discuss her at all."

"Very well, then, we shall not. But tell me, will you still wish to inform on the earl if he agrees to marry your Julia?"

"Ah, now that puts a different complexion on the matter, and I would have to see the banns first to believe it!"

"And if you do not?"

"And if I do not," the dowager uttered slowly, "if I do not, Serena, then I do believe I might enjoy being at the center of a delicious little scandal! Lord Robin Caraway is not what he seems. He is a villain and a scoundrel, not to mention an impostor and he should be taken from Caraway in chains."

"I thought you wanted to see the banns?"

"Well, of *course* I do! If he marries Julia, the whole situation is really quite different."

"He will no longer be a villain and a scoundrel?"

"Certainly not, for who shall dare to call into question someone *I* have endorsed?"

Serena very nearly said "half of London," but bit her pretty little tongue smartly. If Robin *was,* as she suspected, acting as an English agent, he would not want his activities to be examined too closely.

"My lady, you are wrong. Lord Caraway is no pirate, though I believe it is sometimes an effect he hopes to achieve. Any close examination will show as such, and I am very much afraid that if you are identified as the informer, you shall look a fool, besides risking his wrath."

"What care I for his wrath?"

"You live at the dower house by his grace."

"Nonsense! By entitlement! I am, after all, your brother's widow."

"Then I shall say it again, it is by his grace. It was my brother's first countess and her progeny who are entitled. Spencer added that as an addendum to his will upon his marriage, never thinking he would not have sons. He was thinking of the entail, you see."

The dowager's eyes were cold, but Serena, pitying her slightly, noticed that her fingers were trembling and the stick of her fan was about to be snapped into two. "You shall have to prove that."

"*I* don't have to prove anything! Prove it *yourself.* I am sure it is an open secret at Caraway. Consult the records if it pleases you, or call in Mr. Wickens, who handled my brother's affairs."

"It is a passing strange arrangement."

"Indeed, I thought so at the time, but *I* am not at fault for that."

Lady Caraway glared. "What do you want, Serena?"

"Nothing at all, save the preservation of the good name of Caraway. If you accuse the earl you will become the laughing stock, my lady, and whilst we might have our differences, I do not wish that for you. Take my advice and not only *drop* these scurrilous claims, but make an effort to scotch them yourself!"

"And what if this doesn't suit me?"

Serena shrugged her shoulders. "If it doesn't, you take a great risk, Fanny."

"You threaten!"

"Nonsense, I merely suggest, I have not the power to threaten."

"Yes, you do! I have seen the way he looks at you!"

"I do not know what you are talking about!"

Serena's words were hot, but her heart had begun beating slightly faster. *Did* he look at her differently? Julia had said as much, but oh, he was just a flirtatious rake. He looked at *everyone* so! She could refine nothing on the matter.

The dowager rapped the table with her fan. "I think you do, but I shall not quibble. It is obvious from the first you have had designs to become the next Countess of Caraway! A snake I have nurtured in my very bosom!"

"Do not talk such fustian, ma'am! If you must swoon, please do so after I have spoken with you. I have a very bitter pill for you to swallow, and I want you to swallow it with grace, for truly there is no turning from the matter."

"Now you are going to tell me that my beloved—my one true delight, the angel of my heart, my little baby, is attached to some loathsome creature without a penny to his name!"

"It is not so bad as that, Lady Caraway. Julia is betrothed to Captain McNichols, who, as you know, is of very good family and I have it on the best of authority that he is quite wealthy in his own right."

"Wealthy, wealthy, that is not the question. Is he *rich?* And what do you *mean* he is betrothed? He has not my permission!"

'No, but he has the *earl's* permission, which is perfectly proper as the male head of family."

"I won't have it! You are all conspiring against me. I always *knew* Julia was an ungrateful little wench!"

"Nonsense, when you have recovered from the shock you will realize that she is . . . well, she is the angel of your heart, your true delight, your . . . what was it you said? Your little baby . . ."

"Oh, don't try and flummox me! I feel very out of sorts and if I get the sick ache, I shall have you to thank!"

"I am very sorry for it indeed, and can concoct you a potion directly."

"Can you? For really, after today's shocks . . ."

"Yes, very troubling. I have a mint and juniper balm that Redmond can rub into your forehead. It will revive you instantly."

"Oh, nothing can revive me, Lady Serena, nothing at all, but I shall take your balm all the same . . ."

"Then you will consent to the match?"

"What *more* can I do when I am positively being bullied at every turn? I am not a well woman, you know."

Serena suppressed her smile—for the dowager countess was in the very pink of health, if she could just, for a moment, forget her grizzles—and pushed home her advantage.

"And the earl? You will do all that you can to scotch those silly rumors? I cannot think where they came from—pirate indeed!—but you can be sure it will drag the Caraway name—including our own—through the mud. You cannot, I am certain, wish for that."

"No, indeed, though the earl is far enough removed for the scandal not to reflect on *me* . . ."

"Can you take that risk? Think of poor Lady Amelia Watford, who was forced to withdraw from the Season when her cousin—just her *cousin*, mind you, was big with child."

"Scandalous! It was the underbutler, you know, though she tried to pass it off as one of the Marquis of Fane's many brats . . . !"

Serena groaned, for Lady Caraway was dangerously missing the point. "Yes," she replied as patiently as she could, "but that is another story altogether. What I am saying is, the matter was *not* Lady Amelia's fault, yet it was *she* who suffered."

"You mean . . . yes, I see. If the earl is hanged for a pirate or a smuggler or whatever the damn hell he might be, I might not get invited to court."

Serena privately thought the chances of the dowager countess ever being invited to court were minuscule, pirate or no pirate, especially if she used such offensive language, but she kept the thought to herself.

"Precisely, madam. It would not look good for Queen Charlotte or the Prince Regent to greet the family of so dire a rogue. He could be sent to Newgate, you know, or even as you say, hanged." This was not possible, Robin being a peer of the realm, but Serena saw no need to mention this.

"They say they rot in Newgate."

Serena tried not to shudder at the thought, and to focus firmly on her belief that Robin was a risk-taking, rakish, altogether too handsome king's agent, *not* the villain the dowager countess tried to portray. She had only her judgment and a small Latin verse to confirm this notion, but it seemed not to falter, even in the face of Fanny's obvious belief in the worst.

"They shall sell off the estate, first. All the furniture, the fittings, the tables, the carriages . . ."

"Enough!" The countess, cornered, relented. She was not a stupid woman, despite her foolish airs and graces, and she knew very well where her bread was buttered. If she could be evicted from the dower house at any moment, and if there was the smallest grain of truth in Serena's comments, that changed the gravity and complexion of things greatly.

Truth to tell, in the month she had lived at the

dower house, she had rather enjoyed the place, for there she was undoubtedly mistress of all she surveyed, and everything she surveyed was of the finest and the most expensive, thanks to her quick-witted foresight in removing most of the earl's prized marbles to the dower house, and in ordering a *complete* refurbishment whilst the incumbent earl was absent. Which reminded her, she still had a few bills stuffed in her bureau drawer and they must be attended to.

"I have some bills and notes of hand . . ."

Serena sighed.

"Give them to me. I shall see that they are attended to."

"And my stipend?"

"That shall remain, naturally, while you are at the dower house, though it is not me you should be conversing with, but the earl."

"Hmph!" The dowager narrowed her eyes and opened a new vial of sal volatile while she thought.

Serena coughed and stepped back, for Fanny was absentmindedly wafting it under not only her own nose, but under Serena's, too.

The dowager looked blank, but under that vacant stare was a mind of steel. If Julia—silly chit that she was—was going to throw herself away on a mere handsome face, no title, then she must wash her hands of her—pointless crying over spilt milk; one must, after all, observe appearances. So then! Her initial scheme had to be revised.

The earl was *not* going to marry Julia and he was *not* going to marry *her*. Though why not, she couldn't tell, for at five-and-forty she really had scarcely a wrinkle to her name, and though she would never *dream* of boasting of such a thing, even the Prince Regent, to whom she'd been presented, had said she was a fine figure of a woman. But she did not think she could live with his lordship's unfortunate sense of humor and strange, unsympathetic manners. Besides, it was obvious to all but a blockhead that his sentiments were engaged elsewhere.

She had had dozens of letters from Lady Bradbury and Lady Bowbeck, all very annoying, and all alerting her to the very same thing. After she had hinted there would be a match between Julia and the earl! Oh, it was all very irksome. Well, Serena could *have* the castle! It was sorely in need of a mason, the plaster was peeling in places, and nothing short of a small fortune would really save it from becoming yet another ruin.

Not that she doubted, of course, that the earl had the means, for his clothes, by all accounts were very fine, and he was far too generous with the servants. Still, it was not her problem any longer. She would cut her losses while she could and ingratiate herself with Serena, who was about to become the future Countess Caraway.

Serena would have been astonished to know the convoluted workings of the dowager's mind. As it was, she slipped below stairs and skillfully blended the promised mint and juniper whilst the Lady Fanny reflected on the pros and cons of turning informer. All in all, despite the lure of a reward, there was really no contest if she were to live out her days at Caraway. The rumors must be scotched directly! She would go right to Ermentrude Bowbeck at once, and even to Lady Howe, who owed her several favors.

Serena never knew whether it was the healing effects of the balm, or the curious effect of Fanny coming, at once, to her senses, but whatever the cause, she was docility itself when Redmond brought in the tea service.

As a matter of fact, she seemed to have rallied, for it was with a good deal of vigor that she decided to make a few social calls around the neighborhood, and answer an affirmative to Lady Middleton's ball in London. After all, as she said, there was no need to stay with that meddlesome Lady Bowbeck, when a hotel was perfectly comfortable, and she was *quite* certain the earl would not wish her to stint on expenses. She called for her writing implements and declared her intention to write an eloquently nasty letter back to Lady Cavendish, who'd had the gall to first allude to the privateer business in the first place.

Serena could not help noticing that even Fanny's vocabulary had undergone a transformation, for what once was "pirate" and "villain" was now "privateer" and "gentleman." Whatever the reasons for this miraculous change of heart, she was glad, at all events, to have wheedled the dowager over. When she departed, clutching a fist of bills and swallowing hard on some vile orgeat the dowager had insisted she drink, she was well satisfied with her day's work.

Chapter Sixteen

It was a trifling matter for a man of Robin's diverse skills to break into the bailiff's quarters. If he had stopped for a moment to consider, he would have realized he carried a key, for one of Lady Serena Caraway's first acts upon his return to the estate—apart from slapping him, of course—had been to hand him a ring of keys he could hardly get his head around, so vast were they in their content. All in all, it was easier to break in, and this he did, with supreme ease, and with none the wiser, for he had approached from the sea rather than from the usual avenue of trees to the south.

His eyes rested almost immediately on the letter, neatly inscribed in Addington's hand. It no longer bothered him that his heart leapt at the very sight, or that certain other passions were aroused by the vision of that neat, calligraphied script. All that mattered was that his own name be visible upon the wafer.

He turned it over, almost caressingly, and stared at the seal. To rip it open, or *not* to rip it open? That was *hardly* the question, for my lord did not hesitate, other than to smooth over the folds. He did not *rip*, precisely, but his customarily languid air had all but vanished.

The letter did not take long to read, but was also not dated, leaving him ignorant of the fact that Serena was but a stone's throw away, at the dower house. He smiled. How like her to practically *order* him to employ some unknown tenant in the very letter she was tendering her resignation! And how like her to care enough to do so, and to warn him yet again about the dowager's greed, and to care enough for Julia to ensure her a decent dowry.

But the Dowager Marchioness of *Penreith?* Lord Robin, who had had dealings with this aging denizen in the past, could only laugh out loud. He wondered where Serena had dreamed her up from, and what she anticipated happening with his eighty pounds. Naughty scamp! But when could she have written this?

She had, to his certain knowledge, never had a single day to slip from his watchful eye. Well, certainly not long enough to undertake a day excursion like this. When was this note written? The ink looked fresh, but one could never tell with these things. He opened a drawer. No clue, there, either. Just neat ledgers—ledgers he had familiarized himself with during his first week at Caraway. He looked more closely. Yes, the self-same hand as the script he had come to know as Addington's.

Serena must have been single-handedly running his affairs for at least a year. But why had she been so secretive about the matter? Why had she shied away from him, turned every subject, purposefully made herself seem a fool? The only time she had ever disappointed him was when she was feigning a silly ignorance to match Lady Caraway's or even, to some extent, Miss Waring's. Why persist in disappointing him? *Why?*

Robin, still dressed in slightly theatrical clothing, for

he had cast off his role of the Earl of Caraway on boarding *The Albatross,* cast his mind about for the answer. He was inordinately glad it was *Serena* who was Addington, and not some upstart second son who had somehow beguiled her, stolen her heart, and then circumspectly left when threatened with the incumbent earl's return. Such a scenario had haunted many a thought, especially when Serena was at her most annoying.

He couldn't bear her lying to him, but did her the justice of believing there must be good cause. Her motives were obviously not base. He had thankfully established that they were not driven from matters of the heart, or worse, to cover some tawdry, ill-fated love affair.

What then? What, what, what? He had given her every opportunity—ample opportunity—to be straight with him. Why had she *not* been? He fingered one of the ledgers and stared at one of the bills of sale. The indigo ink was long dried, but it was not the ink he was looking at, but the hand. How could he have missed such an obvious clue? He was more of a fool than he thought!

For there, as clear as day—had he but taken the time to peruse it—was *not* the signature of one Gabriel Addington, as he had supposed, but of a certain Serena Addington Winthrop Caraway. He had seen the same signature a dozen times, upon a dozen slips of notes of hand, promissory notes, and bills of sales. He had seen it, and noticed only the Addington. True, this was emphasized, the Caraway being merely a scrawl in comparison, but curious, nonetheless. Strange how the mind picked out only what it expected to see.

His thoughts now flew back to the day Serena had been disturbed writing her journal. He had noted something strange at the time, but had been too enthralled by her presence to pursue the matter carefully enough. It had been that same careful lettering on the journal cover. *Serena Addington Winthrop Caraway. She* must have remembered, for he recalled the breathless way in which she had slammed the diary into her cloak. He had been foolish enough to hope there was *another* reason she hadn't wanted him to see that journal. . . .

And by God, unless his mind had *really* turned to jelly, there was the cloak! The very cloak he remembered, carelessly thrown on the back of the hard, ornately carved oak chair. He could not mistake it, for he had privately laughed at her flirtatious impudence in purchasing precisely one of the shades he admired. Gone were her muted colors of mourning, and he had watched her transformation with whimsical interest and a half suspicion, half hope that *he* had been the cause.

He loved her all the more for it, of course, notwithstanding the perfectly feminine wiles she was using to keep him riveted. For she *was,* he was perfectly certain of it, though Adam might tease him for a coxcomb. Whatever the attraction between them, it was a mutual blaze, not a fire all on his side and a miserable taper on hers. He could feel it, beneath her intelligence, and her laughter, and her teasing manner, and yes, even beneath all the little indiscretions and the strange urge to veil all her cleverness and her incredible achievements at Caraway beneath a garrulous guise of silliness.

She was just fortunate that he had not, for a moment, been fooled! The only thing that perplexed him was why she found it necessary to go to all the trouble of this subterfuge. Why could she not have straight out written to him as Lady Serena? He checked himself. The answer to that was obvious enough—society prohibited it. It would have been extremely unfitting, not to mention unpardonably forward of her to have approached him, even by correspondence.

He would have regarded her as an interfering little

wench with designs on himself and his title. Her motives would have been called into question, not to mention her judgment, for who would have imagined a
young lady of her birth and breeding could prove so capable on matters so traditionally of the male sphere?

He would probably have written her a polite but dismissive note and thus ended an unsuitable communica-
tion. But having *continued* with the subterfuge, even
after he had returned to his inheritance, *that* was quite
another affair!

He remembered how Serena had said she disliked
even the whitest of lies. Oh ho ho, how she must have
disliked *this*, then! So why had she done it? He would
not have punished her for telling him the truth. As a
matter of fact, he would surely have kissed her most
thoroughly but since he was set on making an honest
woman of her anyway, she could hardly have objected
to this outcome. Or *could* she have? My lord was now
unusually beset with self-doubt.

He had seen, firsthand, after all, how she had shrugged
off the Duke of Bedford—the Season's most glittering
catch—like a fly. Could she—would she—do the same
to him? Trifle with his affections, his obvious attraction,
then let him suffer the fate of a score of men before
him? The very thought was intolerable!

Robin snatched at the cloak. Where was she? She
must have left at first light if she'd traveled by road. She
had worn the cloak yesterday, which meant that even
now she must be on the estate. What could have brought
her here, with such speed? Surely not the edifying letter, which could have been written from London just as
easily. He slipped out of the small, low-ceilinged room,
decorated with gilded beading and painted all about in
a tasteful cherry red. A few portraits adorned the walls,
one of them of a child with a dappled pony. He rather

thought it might have been Serena, but the rendition was poor, which was why the portrait was probably consigned to these quarters. Such were his fleeting impressions, as Robin slipped out from these quarters and made his soft way to the stables.

When he saw the chaise, rather mournful-looking on three wheels with the fourth removed for the attentions of a wheelwright, his suspicions—fantasies really—were confirmed. Serena, for reasons he could not yet quite fathom, had traveled up from York Crescent. Whether her charge was with her, or whether Adam suspected a thing about it, he could not say. By the look of the wheel, though, it would be nightfall before she could make the return journey.

Robin remembered that the moon was not at its zenith, and that there were very few lamplighters or outriders currently employed at Caraway. He wondered whether she would be fool enough to take the risk. Knowing Serena, he rather thought she would. He walked back to the bailiff's quarters, his stride slightly brisker than before. The moment had almost come, he thought, to take matters into his own hands. He had hours, yet, before the coach would be ready to travel. Plenty of time to hatch a plan and wait.

"It's a broken spoke, ma'am! It will be all on four hours before the wheelwright can be called in from Upper Leith, where 'e is just doin' a spot of work for the Prince's party, which wiv fifty coaches an' all, all cabriolets and them fancy high-perch phaetons and wotnot, the ladies are restless-like, and there are a few repairs and the 'orses all needing shoeing and stablin'—well, it's a busy time it is and that's a fact."

Serena looked tired and crestfallen. The last thing

she wished to do was return to the dowager, for she did not trust her fluctuating mood to last more than an hour or so at best, and she was too tired for any more explanations or recriminations. She was just congratulating herself on using no stronger term than "bother"— for bother it was, undoubtedly—when the sound of hooves and carriage wheels crunching up the long, tree-lined drive drove all annoyance from her lips.

Who could this be? This was not a morning caller, but a positive entourage! There were five carriages at least that rolled up, all of them very smart and furbished with squabs of purple and silver, colors Serena could not immediately place. Her sister-in-law upstairs obviously could, however, for it seemed no time at all before she had leapt from her writing table—where she had been engaged in writing a particularly spiteful letter to one of her dearest bosom friends—and glided her way down the stairs of the dower house. Serena knew she never would be so indecorous as to run.

Then, seeing the fanfare stop at the grand entrance to Castle Caraway, which was empty, she sent out staff to redirect the throng to her elegant new establishment. The coachmen clambered up once more and doors were hastily closed almost before they were opened. It was not a great distance, really, a mere matter of a few yards, but it was unthinkable for such visitors to have to walk, or to muddy their boots and slippers in any unnecessary way. Not that there were any boots to speak of, in this instance, for it seemed to be a visit comprised almost entirely of young *ladies* in day dresses of taffeta and lace and little seed pearls carefully stitched into corseted bodices.

Serena blinked, for not since His Majesty had made a brief stopover at Caraway ten years or more ago, could she remember such a fanfare, or such unsuitable clothes for the country—all plumes and the highest poke bonnets she had ever seen.

She chuckled, for it must be taking all Lady Fanny's strength to wait for the butler rather than to rush out herself. In this, she was entirely mistaken, for Lady Fanny was too busy squealing for her emerald-studded Spanish comb and declaring she could not be seen dead in her attire, which, while elegant and preposterously expensive as Serena knew, for she had to deal with the bills, nevertheless was cast into the shade by her visitors.

Serena thanked the coachman, who was eyeing the new carriages with misgiving, and ordered her own conveyance to be set aside until such time as the wheelwright could be located. Then, resigning herself to a night's stay at Caraway, she walked toward the throng of people, trying to work out who in the world they might be. They seemed to have foreign accents, and were all talking at once, which did not help Serena make any sort of sense in the least.

Stranger yet, Lady Fanny was curtsying, which made the matter more intriguing still. Serena hastened toward her. She was caught out in a drab gown. If only she had her new, delectable cloak, but of course, like a silly jackanapes she must have left it at the bailiff's lodge.

"Serena!" Lady Fanny rather maliciously looked over Serena's attire, which must have been a sad trial to her.

"May I present to you her Royal Highness, the Princess Valmont, and her ladies in waiting . . . gracious, I can't remember you all!' She laughed in a high-pitched, ingratiating kind of way. "There is the countess, of course, and Lady Gracia De Salvo and Lady Du Barrie, and— oh, come inside, and we shall make our introductions in the comforts of the dower house, which I have naturally just refurbished. The castle, you know, was too vast for my tastes. I simply *had* to have something cozier, but not inelegant, I am sure you will think, Oh, do come in. Yes, yes, pelisses and cloaks . . . I am sure the butler and a few of our liveried staff will see to it . . . . see to it, will you, Stevens?"

Lady Fanny was in a high fever, for though she aspired to the highest of circles, it was *such* a coup to have royalty drop in on one! It would have been better, of course, had it been *English* royalty, but what with the King so . . . disabled, and the Prince without a suitable consort—for really, one could hardly count that Caroline creature, it was all very trying . . . . Still, royalty was royalty. . . . She must write to Lady Bowbeck at *once*. She would be green, positively green with envy!

"I am so glad you could come! When you did not answer my invitation I feared you had other, more pressing engagements."

"No, my dear, we are all so bored, bored, bored. This England, it can be so boring . . . no? I look at my maids and I say, "Ladies, what can we do? What can we do on this dull English day? Then Lavinia, here, she remembers your oh, so sweeeeet invitation, which really I thought I had thrown away, for I am vairy vairy naughty that way, but see!

"She had it still. It does not matter, *n'est pas,* that the day 'as passed? We think, Oh, that Lady Fanny, it will not matter, this day, that day . . . all days are the same when the skies are dull and we are stuck at the coast—sea air is *vairy* bad for me—when we could be in London."

"No," said Lady Fanny faintly, "no, the day does not matter at all. I *did* have a banquet prepared, and fresh strawberries and ices ordered up from London, and a confection known as an ice castle, which I am positively *certain* you would all have been entranced by . . ."

"What 'as 'appened to thees ice castle? Can we see it?"

"No, for sadly it melted into a puddle of pink sugar. The confectioner warned it would be so."

The princess pouted. "But 'ow vexing!"

"Yes." Lady Fanny ground her teeth and said no more, for "vexing" was hardly the word for her fury at being publicly snubbed but two weeks before by the princess.

The dowager had invited several of the surrounding neighbors, and she was certain—though naturally they had said nothing to her face—that they sniggered still. The ice castle—for only the tiniest sliver had actually been eaten—had long been consigned to the pigs. It seemed a very poor exchange, really, for no one of Fanny's social standing would be seen dead eating bacon, or salted pork, so the only people to gain by this tragedy were the cottagers, who would kill half a dozen pigs as Christmas drew close. It was no wonder Lady Fanny had said unkind things about the princess! Serena concentrated on the Gothic eaves—hideous— so as to hide her smile. It was cold. She wished, once again, she had her cloak.

Chapter Seventeen

At the same time as Lady Serena Addington Winthrop Caraway was making that wish, Robin was discovering something interesting lying hidden deep within that same cloak's folds. He drew it out, and with it, a deep breath.

It was not the custom of a gentleman to read the diary of a lady, however hopeful or besotted he might be. He told himself this, and a great deal more, in extremely stern terms, but the book seemed to beckon to him like a siren. Here, he thought, lay the answers to all the secrets he wished to unravel. He did not need to employ the Bow Street runners or anyone at all to find out what he most needed to know.

How easy it would be to simply glance at the entries—*glance*, mind you, no more—and understand, at last, the very secrets of Serena's heart.

It was a moral question, and a hard one. He, travel-stained, conscious of some greater danger before him, yet smitten by that terrible disease he had long scorned and taken pains to avoid, set the little book down with a sigh. How he detested love! It removed from him all his

resolve, for surely, the most trifling of peeks could harm
no one and save him a great deal of time? But no! He
had to honor Serena and her secrets and leave the
tempting little book be.

He shuffled some papers, consulted his pocket
watch—practically the only adornment he permitted
himself—and stared steadfastly out the window. Inactivity,
he was certain, was a penance.

Serena, who had just heard the dowager describe the
princess as "tedious" was now bemused to find that
Lady Fanny was practically apologizing for her own existence, begging—no *pleading*—with that personage to
stay for tea.

"If you will be so kind as to overlook the paucity of
our table, Highness, I will be glad to have a collation
served outside. Nothing grand, you understand, merely
a few roast pheasants, some chilled blackberries, mulled
wine, oh . . . I don't know, I always leave these details to
the servants, so much more efficient, is it not? Ah, Mrs.
Dumpley, there you are at last! I rang the bell this age, it
seems! We have been honored by a visit from the
princess and all these delightful young ladies, only see
how elegant they are! See to it that a table is prepared
outside at once, with a suitable collation. You know the
sort of thing. Soufflé, a little of that tureen of turtle we
dined upon last night for dinner . . ."

Serena had to valiantly suppress a chortle at this, for
she knew perfectly well that Lady Fanny was *far* too
much of a skinflint to dine on boiled *chicken,* never
mind the outrageously expensive turtle she boasted of.
Housekeeping came from her own purse, generously
endowed by Robin, but since she was a nipfarthing beyond compare, not much of it ever saw the light of day.
The only person more bemused than the princess

(who spoke only a smattering of English and had no notion of what "turtle" might be, never mind "soufflé" which Lady Fanny pronounced "so–flea") was poor Mrs. Dumpley, who could *not,* for the life of her, recall anything but jugged hare being on the previous night's lamentable menu.

She curtsied, however, and shot an imploring glance at Serena, who excused herself and hurried after her to once again save the day. "Some of your freshly iced cupcakes, several loaves of bread, and an assortment of cheeses, Mrs. Dumpley. Many thanks, and if you could ask one of the scullery hands to pick some wild grapes and some cherries from the hothouse, that will do very nicely indeed with a serving of your famous clotted cream."

She returned to find the ladies exclaiming about this and about that, and her sister-in-law gushing on about the heraldic crest of Caraway, and mentioning that there had been Earls of Caraway almost since William the Conqueror had landed from Normandy in 1066. *None* of which the ladies were at all interested in, being more partial to the *current* earl, who they were disappointed to hear was still away from home.

As Serena, still in her drab gown, ushered the ladies to the outside pavilion, she could hear the princess still bemoaning her boredom with Lady Fanny, who was practically groveling in sympathy.

"For I cannot see why, *ma chèr,* zee prince—my 'usband, you understand—'e cannot leave me in London while 'e catches these very great rogues. I ask 'eem, this ees what I say: Why, *why* your 'Ignees, must you choose this cold damp rrrrrainy part of England to catch your corsair? If you want to catch zee buccaneers you should do so in Spain, or Malaga, or somewhere there ees sunshine for your *très belle* Sancha. But does 'eee listen? No, no, I may just as well not spik! But come, Lady . . . Carlaway?"

"Caraway."

"Zat is wot I said. Lady Carlaway, we must not grumble, you and I. It is our lot, our sad, sad lot. Tell me, what in zee virld . . ." But Serena had stopped listening to the spate of ceaseless chatter. Lord Valmont was wanting to trap a pirate and truly, it stretched imagination a little too far to think there might be two lurking in the calm waters of Caraway. But Robin was safe in London . . . *The Albatross* was berthed and anchored, she had seen as much with her very eyes; there could be no possible connection . . .

"Princess, did you say *pirate?* How utterly terrifying!"

"Yes, but it ees all *vairy* boring. No treasair, no gold, no twinkling jewels . . . just papair . . . bits of old papair . . . just because this *très* fat English prince—wot you call 'im? Zee prinny—just because 'c goes and 'e signs with 'eez own hand . . . what eez all zee fuss? I ask 'im. 'Ighness, I say, wot eez all zees fret, fret, fret? *Mon Dieu,* I say! Boring, boring."

"And what did the prince answer you?" Serena, now riveted, was fascinated.

"Oh, 'e only snaps 'eez fingers, so! You know! Then 'ee say, wait, *mon amie,* there is much reward for such slugs, and 'e will buy me zee emerald necklace I see in Venice. Ah, it eez a little beauty, so I say yes, yes, we wait in zis rrrainy side of zee earth."

Serena did not object that it was not raining at all, but really rather fine, if a little crisp for this time of year. She was more interested in extracting as much information as she could from the princess, without seeming overly curious.

"You are very long-suffering, Your Highness, but it must be for a worthy cause! How long are you waiting?"

The lady shrugged her shoulders, bored with the topic. "Zee prince, 'e promise, not more than four days. Not tonight, 'e say, for zee vessel is anchored and 'ee 'as *quelle* important duties, but mebbe tomorrow, mebbe next day . . . . we shall see. It is zee tiresome, is it not?"

Lady Fanny agreed effusively, but secretly rejoiced, making plans in her head for a lawn party on the next day, for what use, she thought, was being visited by royalty if none of the surrounding neighbors were available to witness her triumph?

Oh, doubtless the news would spread—she would make perfectly certain of that—but it would not be the same as playing hostess and being seen to be on terms with the princess, and ushering people here and there . . . thank goodness the roses were in full bloom!

Serena, less serene than her name would imply, was seriously disturbed. Was Robin planning some action in the next few days? If he was an agent for Whitehall, as she suspected, and the Prince Valmont never a political friend to the Regent, despite all his glittering receptions, had some damning piece of . . . *goodness* knew, it could be anything!

Valmont was reported to be very cozy with the Czar, and there was a faction in France dissatisfied with the Bourbon reinstatement . . . then there was the issue of the Prince's appalling behaviour toward Caroline of Brunswick, whispers of a morganatic marriage with his mistress—a political disaster . . . all of these could have serious ramifications for the England still coming to terms with a troubled peace.

So Valmont could very well be holding something he knew perfectly well was politically sensitive. He was planning to leave England through Upper Leith, rather than through more usual channels. But worse, he was expecting to capture pirates. Did that mean he knew that Robin was going to act, or was it just that he had had trouble, in the past, with unscrupulous knaves who had boarded his vessel and made off with the pickings? Why was he so certain he was to be boarded this time?

And why was he so sanguine about it when he had a sensitive document in his possession?

Because, as the princess seemed to believe, he was after the reward, or was it something more sinister? A plot, perhaps, to expose the best of England's spies? Serena shuddered. It could be worse, still. He might choose *not* to expose him, just to run him through with his sword and claim he had rid the shores of one more villain.

The latter, though the most horrible, seemed the most likely. The Prince Valmont was a man of cunning and strategy. He would not like a scandal any more than the next man, and dragging Robin through the courts would undoubtedly be that.

She wondered if he suspected the earl's identity and had to assume that he did. Already, thanks to the dowager and her cronies' ready tongues, rumors, once quashed, were once again rife. Gracious, she had even overheard Lady Claremont rather archly remark that she should hold a masked ball, for then it would give *everyone* the opportunity to fashionably attire themselves as pirates, and what a stir that would cause!

There was *nothing*, Lady Claremont dramatically claimed, so invigorating as the sight of a gentleman in skin tight breeches with a powdered wig (for she seemed to think that this unfashionable frippery was a necessary accoutrement to being a corsair of the first stare) and a patch.

She seemed to know nothing of the grime, and the blackening from cannon powder, and the strong scent of rum and candle wax, and the congealing of blood — or that privateers, intent on their loot, fought among themselves almost as much as against their victims, who were often ruthlessly cast overboard.

Serena knew not much of the matter either, but her views were less romantic, and she was inclined to disregard Lady Claremont as just another bubbleheaded fool. Be that as it may, her romanticization of the trade did little for Robin, who everyone now looked to with ill-concealed interest.

Rumors that had faded were now remembered and circulated, so much so that they could *easily* have come to the ready ears of the likes of His Royal Highness, Prince Valmont of . . . where was he from again? Some little European state, she could not precisely recall. It mattered little.

If *he* put the pieces together, it could be extremely dangerous for the earl, for the prince, playing a double game, would be excessively careful not to let *himself* be duped. Serena did not for a moment imagine that Robin was simply after gold, as was the case with most of the pirates off the coasts of England and Spain. Even if he proved to be involved in smuggling, rather than the more nefarious piracy, she *still* did not think that profit drove him particularly.

Not when he had at his disposal all of the rents of Caraway and his American plantations besides. She did not know the sum of these, but the Caraway yields were excellent, despite the ruinous state of the castle itself. No, she did not think Lord Robin would risk his neck and his reputation for mere pecuniary gain.

What, then? "The end justifies the means." The words were so obvious they *flew* into this context. The unscrupulous means must surely be justified by the intended outcome. That meant that the end was worth more than the villainous acts of robbing, dueling, and sinking ships laden with cargo. There could only be one end to which this could be applicable—the service of King and country, and the treatment of the boarded ships as enemy vessels. Prince Valmont, supposedly neutral, was known, in most inner circles, to be conspiring against the Regent.

The Prince of Wales, whether held in the thrall of blackmail, or in the thrall of Valmont's intriguing personality, seemed an easy target in these times. It was left to the likes of the Earl of Caraway to see that justice prevailed and that the good name of the Regent remained unbesmirched. More importantly, it was his task, along with those of Major Rittledon, and his aides, to maintain the security of the nation. If the Prince had secretly signed an alignment treaty against Russia, or contrary to the Versailles agreement . . . Serena's eyes widened. Robin, if he was adopting the pose of pirate, would surely—*must* surely, act in haste.

Something told her he would not object in the least, for those lazy, smiling eyes always hinted he relished the chase. For some time, she suspected *she* had been the chase.

This time, unfortunately, the victim was going to be a thousandfold less susceptible to his wiles. No contest, really, for even *thinking* of him made her pulses faster and her breathing ever so slightly shallower.

But there was no time to reflect, or to dream, or to even demur about setting her horses to at this late hour. By now, the wheelwright was to have solved the problem of her carriage, and if he hadn't, she would just have to borrow Lady Fanny's barouche, for she needed to reach London—and my lord the earl—as soon as was humanly possible. She had the grace of this evening, but after that, Prince Valmont's men would be posted.

She wondered how much this intelligence would upset Robin's plans. But he needed to be warned if he was to do the stalking, rather than become the stalked. Serena felt physically sick at the thought of Prince Valmont, who had once languidly inclined his superior, Brutus-style head in her direction, but had made no push to offer her his hand, though a slight leer, as the evening advanced, had apparently been in order. She did not like the man, she could not say she liked him at all!

As for the princess, she was still talking rapidly in

that unique blend of English, French, and her native tongue which caused Lady Fanny to listen closely, and to nod intently to half a dozen different assertions that made no sense in any language at all. Serena did not stop to pity her. The dowager had made her own bed and must now lie in it. The entire party now seemed to expect entertainment, and the only instrument in the dower house had all its Holland covers on and had not been tuned for a sennight at least.

"Lady Fanny, you must excuse me, but I am already late returning to London."

"Late? What nonsense is this, Serena, when I depend on you to open the madrigals!"

"I am sorry, madam, but I cannot leave your daughter unchaperoned for this evening. We are to be escorted to the theater and to Vauxhall if it is fine . . ."

"What care I? It is not as if she is making the *slightest* effort to contract a suitable alliance—she is already betrothed, is she not?" This in a whispered hiss, with Lady Fanny's fingers firmly digging into Serena's arm. Even through the sleeve of her sensible serge traveling dress, it hurt.

"Yes, but that does not mean she can attend theatres unchaperoned, let alone Vauxhall!"

"Well, if she has any sense she will claim the headache and stay home. Serena, you simply *must* stay! I cannot be expected to hostess eleven—yes, it is eleven, I counted—foreigners and the princess!"

"Then *tell* them so!."

'Oh, *must* you joke even at a time like this?"

"I am never more serious."

"Then you have far less wits than I give you credit for. You do not tell a princess of the blood to go home!"

Serena tried to check her exasperation, but failed. "Then do *not!* Fanny, you invited them. You entertain them!"

"I invited them for a garden party two weeks ago, not for *today!* You are a wicked, hardhearted wench. I always knew it. And what, pray, shall they eat? My stocks are limited."

"Call on the castle kitchens and alert the gamekeeper to provide you with all the pheasant and partridge you need. Keep a tally so I may inform the earl and reimburse him his loss."

"Well, that is something, at least. " The tone was grudging, but a little more mollified.

"I must go . . . , it is more than the theater. Fanny, did you hear that reference to pirates?"

"Yes, and I do not like it at all! Something smoky is going on and if we are involved in a scandal I shall hold you personally accountable."

"Well, this *was* a turnaround!"

"Then you will not expose the earl?"

"No, for it will give Lady Bowbeck *far* too much pleasure!"

Serena was relieved, but did not place too much weight on the dowager's words. Fanny might mean what she said now, but if she was flattered by the prince . . ."

"*Swear* you will say nothing to Valmont!"

"So dramatic! Yes, yes, I swear!"

"And keep the ladies at Caraway as long as you can. As long as they are here, Valmont cannot cast off."

There was nothing further Serena could say, for it would look passing strange for the lady of the house to be speaking any length of time in hushed whispers when there were exalted guests to be attended to.

So, as Serena smiled and backed through a French door, doubling back on the other side and racing across the cobbles in her slippered feet to the stables, Lady Fanny rapped the knuckles of a certain lady-in-waiting and rather archly announced that since it was such a pleasant day—poetic license, for it had now become drearily overcast and promising of rain—they should all take a stroll through the gardens and try their hands at the famous Caraway maze that had been cultivated for the amusement of visitors.

Three hours later, stuck in the center of the labyrinth with no map as Fanny had not thought to bring one, the guests were not quite so enchanted as they *had* been. Fortunately, rain still only threatened, but several ladies were shivering in their delicate muslins and the princess was indulging in a strong fit of the hysterics, rivaled only by Fanny's own. All this, however, is another story entirely and one that Serena, engrossed in conversation with her coachman, knew nothing about at all.

Chapter Eighteen

"It be threatening rain, me lady. The roads will be no-but a series of puddles from 'ere to Essex."

"Can you do it?"

"I could do it wiv me bleeding eyes shut, saving me language, me lady, but it won't nohow be an easy ride for yer, and as for the maid . . . well, she'll be bawlin' 'er eyes out after the first turn!"

"Davina is not with me, remember? I brought Mrs. Hitchens from the cottages in her stead. So you see, it is only *me* you have to worry about, and I promise not to disgrace myself!"

The coachman grinned, for though he had only just been placed in Serena's employ, he thought he knew a game pullet when he saw one.

" 'Oy, miss, but savin' yer pardon, loik, you canna be driving without so much as a lady's maid! 'Av no-but 'eard the loiks, I 'aven't!"

"Well, you hear the likes *now*, Mr. Wilks! I need to return urgently to London and if you hurry, we need not stop at any of the posting houses along the way. The horses are well fed and watered, I checked them myself. Not a soul shall know I travel without a maid."

"Oi oi, me lady!" The coachman grinned. "I 'ave a blunderbuss at the ready, and a tin horn, too, so if them 'ighwaymen try to cross yer path, they shall 'ave Aldus Wilks to deal wiv, that they will!"

Serena smiled at his verve, and found herself staring, in turn, at two black holes, where teeth once graced his noble noggin, as she laughingly, though very improperly, thought in cant.

"Thank you, Mr. Wilks, and you may be very sure a large tankard of the finest brew awaits you at York Terrace! Can we first just tool around to the bailif's quarters, just a wee way beyond those trees? I have left my cloak and would not wish to travel without it." *Would not like it to be discovered in so incriminating a spot,* she revised in her head, but only smiled charmingly at Wilks, who was at once her slave.

It was a mere matter of fifty yards before the moment Robin had been *impatiently* waiting for—occurred at last. Serena, unsuspecting, did not wait for the coach step to be laid out for her, but rather leapt from the chaise, muddying the rim of her gown as she did so. Then, motioning Mr. Wilks to wait—and what *else* could he do, with four horses to manage?—she inserted her key in the lock.

It turned at once, almost as though it had been oiled—which it *had* been, for Robin was now practically dead with boredom—and Serena soon found herself in the room that was now almost familiar. She looked about her for her cloak, but it was not laid out on the chair where she could swear she had left it.

"This is yours, I believe?"

She swung round, her heart beating more wildly than ever she thought possible. There, facing her, looking more impossibly attractive than ever, but rather forbidding in his high starched points and shining buckles, was the very man Serena was flying to London to warn.

"Robin!" She said his name, even as she knew "My lord," or "Lord Caraway!" would have been the more appropriate greeting.

"Your cloak, Serena *Addington* Winthrop Caraway? I have been a fool."

"I am sorry." The words were a whisper, for Serena realized that there was no turning back, no faking one last letter, no turning, anymore, from the truth.

"Why did you do it?"

"It is not so very great a crime!"

"It is when you compound it with lie after lie!"

"That is better, surely, than pretending to be a gentleman when you really are no more than a pirate!"

"Do you believe that?" The words were suddenly sharp, and slightly bitter.

"I do not know *what* to believe!"

"I think you *do,* though we are wasting time in the argument." Robin leaned forward and swift as a dart drew something out from the folds of her cloak. It was not the diary that had tormented him, but another, more pleasant, more alluring, more exquisite discovery. It was the ribbon, the single red ribbon that had tied up his hair.

Serena flushed. "Give that back, it is mine!"

"Do you want it?"

"Yes."

"Why?"

"*Why?*"

"You are not an exotic parrot, do not repeat every scintillating word I utter! Answer the question."

"I do not have to."

"Yes, Serena, you do. I am tired of games." Robin's voice was suddenly very low as he drew her toward him. His grip was nothing like the teasing caress of the waltz. It was tight, and unyielding, and really rather stern. His lips were but inches from her own, but they did not look like they were going to kiss her. They looked forbidding.

Startled, Serena relented, but not without one pert arrow of her own. "And *I* am tired of fearing for your life, Robin Red-Ribbon!"

"So you know?"

"Of *course* I know! The whole of London knows, by the sound of it, though I have worked like the very devil to scotch any breath of whispers. I fear for you, Robin, because it is not only *I* who knows, but also the Prince Valmont. It can be no coincidence that he is berthed at upper Leith when you are here, at Caraway."

"No coincidence, just good fortune." The grip upon her sleeve released almost to a feather-light touch. It might just as well have remained as a grip, however, for the simple touch once more burned into her skin like the veriest brand.

"Why are you scotching the scandal rather than sending me hair and hide to Newgate?"

"Why are you smiling at me when I have deceived you?"

"*Touché,* question for question, but unless I kiss you I fear neither of us will have the answers we seek."

"You cannot kiss me *here!*"

"Why not? It is a very pleasantly furbished room and I have been looking forward to doing so, with agonizing intensity, ever since I discovered your cloak here this morning."

"You have been here all *day?*"

"You have employed a lazy wheelwright, I fear. Mine could have managed in half the time."

"He was in Upper Leith, at Prince Valmont's . . ." Serena dodged the mouth that was hovering tantalizingly close and was playing havoc with all her good sense, not to mention teasing the most wicked of her senses. She ducked from his grasp, but not without a sigh that my lord heard and found profoundly enjoyable.

"Good God, Robin! You cannot stay here! They are preparing a trap for you! I came to warn you, which is why poor Wilks is tooling the horses outside!"

"Send him away."

"Beg pardon?"

"Send him back to Caraway. We have no need of him, for *The Albatross* is berthed just a few leagues offshore and I am about to abduct you."

Serena took a few moments to understand. "You mean . . . my lord, you must be out of your senses!"

"No more than *you* were when you pretended to be my bailiff!"

"It is a whole different matter!"

". . . and one we shall quite forcibly pursue in the comfort of my cabin."

"Over my dead body, my lord."

"I am very much afraid it might have to be, ma'am. I am known to be an excellent shot, you know."

"You are behaving precisely as a pirate!"

"Why so indignant? I *am* one!"

"Nonsense! You do not fool me for a moment, my lord courier, and if you are not acting for the Regent I shall eat the stuffing from my bonnet! Now, if you persist in putting your arms about me I shall have to scream."

"And have Mr. Wilks rush in to rescue you?"

Serena, in a daze of happiness, for while the earl sounded very fierce indeed, he was commencing his promised activity really very gently, and she found the strange butterfly kisses across her throat quite entrancing, never mind impossible to resist . . . .

"You are a rogue."

" Indeed, but I cannot *tell* you how gratified I am that I do not have to return the compliment and call you a bailiff! It is a very salutary thing, you know, to find oneself in love with one's manservant. I have suffered most severely for it, for after the second of your letters, in which you had me in a fit of hysterics, I was a condemned man."

"I am sorry. There seemed no other way . . ."

"It has been . . . intriguing for me, Serena."

"Then you are not angry?"

"Oh, I am very angry indeed. I shall have to punish you aboard my ship."

"Are you making improper advances?"

"Very improper, though I might as well also mention that I fully intend to make you my lady wife. "

"Then you shan't dally with me in your cabin, my lord, for I will surely then be compromised beyond redemption."

"You are right. So young but so wise. I shall save that pleasure, and tease you, rather, in full sight of my crew!'

"You couldn't!"

"Do not look so shocked, you know perfectly well I can!"

Serena remembered the waltz and the last time she had been aboard *The Albatross* and tried very hard not to flush. It was almost impossible not to, however, for though one can hide a smile or cast one's eyes in a different direction, or flutter lashes to hide an expression, one cannot, really, stop the color rising to one's cheeks. My lord, seeing this dilemma, laughed, almost as though he had not a care in the world rather than a fleet of mustard-garbed guards gathering in a hundred different shadows to trap him.

"You will marry me, then? You have no doubts?"

"Why *should* I?"

Robin laughed rather wryly. "You have not yet seen me sporting my wig!"

"I look forward, with anticipation, to the honor!"

"You are a remarkable girl, Serena. You do not question me at all."

"*Cum finis est licitus, etium media sunt licita.* You have already said it eloquently, Robin, though why you should condemn me to a revision of the *The Medulla Theologiae Moralis,* I cannot fathom! I must plot a suitable revenge."

The earl laughed. "I *thought* that might keep you busy! You understood my meaning from the very start?"

"It was not hard. Having corresponded with you for nearly a year I knew perfectly well that it must be a very honorable end that justified your particular means. A very little research and it was as nothing to discover that your victims always had an enemy alignment and that, though you may have sunk their ships, you always took prisoners."

"I may not have killed my men, Serena, but do not look at me *too* closely through rose-colored glasses. I always took their cargo for my trouble."

"You would be a fool if you did not. That is the nature of privateering, and I'd wager my last groat that not all of it was spent on debauchery."

The earl smiled. "Not all, but a good few pennies."

"I can live with that."

Robin did not answer, for he was very much engaged in kissing the nape of Lady Serena's neck, and thus did not hear the door creak slowly open.

"Hmph! Hmph!"

Serena was the first to notice Wilks, beaver in hand, staring fixedly at her youthful portrait.

"Mr. Wilks! I am so sorry! I quite forgot . . ."

The earl grinned and reached into the depths of his elegant, if rather piratical, silver-buttoned doublet. "Take that, my good man," he said, grandly pressing a guinea into Wilks's hand. "Turn the horses round, if you please, and the coach back to Castle Caraway. My lady has had a change of plan, as ladies, you know, are accustomed to do—most trying, but there it is!" Then, with a most unlordly broad wink, he waved the coachman back outside, and firmly shut the door.

Serena dodged my lord's excessively pleasant advances. *Not* through inclination—she positively *loved* everything he had dreamed up to tease her with, and would have actively encouraged him in this rakish behaviour—but through fear.

"Robin, you are not taking the danger seriously enough. I *tell* you, they are set to spring a trap!"

Robin only snapped his fingers. "Faugh! What care I when I have my lovely bailiff to pleasure?"

"You have not, for I am *not* your bailiff, whatever I may have pretended in the past, and a thousand apologies for that but there is no time to grovel for your forgiveness, we have to go!"

"Go where?"

"Back to the ship."

"You would have me return to London?" His lordship looked quizzical and slightly—just slightly—disappointed.

"Certainly not! You are obviously briefed with a mission, my lord, and the sooner you accomplish it, the sooner I can have dinner in peace. I am positively famished, for I swear Lady Fanny counts every lump of sugar and I had no time to raid your castle kitchens."

The tension evaporated from Robin's lean, but nevertheless muscular shoulders. "I think I love you more than I did a moment ago."

"Good, for there is always the possibility the feeling is reciprocated. Now! What exactly are we stealing, and shall we depart at once, for we have not a moment to lose?"

"*We?* I'll see you safely stowed aboard *The Albatross* and that is all!"

"Not a chance!"

"Let us argue about it as we row, for the tides are still in our favor. If we dally, we shall lose our chance and be caught in a moonless night."

Serena nodded. "Very well, we shall argue at sea but I warn you, sir, I am determined!"

Robin sighed. "Such a shrew I have found for myself! I will carry you to the shore, for your slippers are quite unsuitable and you will cut your feet."

"But . . ."

"No buts, Serena, as of now, I am acting as captain of *The Albatross*. There are men depending on me. It is not all a joke, you see." Serena nodded. "You shall have to sit at my feet, I am afraid, for the silhouette of a man in a boat across the evening sky will draw no comment, but one of a lady—especially one as recognizable as you in these parts—most surely will."

Which is precisely how the sensible Lady Serena Addington Winthrop Caraway found herself stowed at the bottom of a rowboat, wrapped in a perfectly splendid (but now decidedly fishy-smelling) cloak. It was periwinkle blue, but black night was overtaking them, so she could enjoy nothing of its color. As for its scent, she did not mind at all, for it was superseded, quite completely, by the delicious smell of polish and beeswax. Robin sported a most impeccable gloss on those silver-buckled boots. Serena, stowed safely out of sight, closed her eyes dreamily and sniffed.

Chapter Nineteen

The road to the port was not far, so Captain McNichols settled back with a sherry of excellent vintage and cared not at all for the bumpiness of the road, which in truth was less at fault than his own rather antiquated chaise.

Miss Waring, hiding at the back, was not so fortunate, for she was accustomed to delightful pink squabs and a less demanding call on her derrière than the hard, badly sprung floor. It was not, then, so very long into the trip that she made her grand appearance and nearly startled Adam into fits. His drink, fortunately, was finished, else it would have ruined the fine velvet trim of his interior.

"Miss Waring! What on earth . . . good gracious, you startled the life out of me!"

But Julia only smiled naughtily and dimpled and asked, as she seated her posterior on a much more comfortable surface, if he was pleased to see her.

"But naturally! I am always pleased! Julia, we need to turn back at once!"

"Why?" asked Miss Innocent dreamily.

"Because it is not proper, that is why! Julia, your maid is not stowed at the back, is she?"

"Gracious, there was hardly place enough even for *me,* and to creep in without your coachman noticing . . . Polly could *not* have done it, I assure you!"

"Then you are entirely alone?"

"No, silly, *you* are with me!"

"That is not what I meant and you *know* it!" Adam tried to sound severe, but truly he failed, for Miss Julia, though mischievous in the extreme, was also enchanting, and she looked particularly glorious today with her little curls all tangled and her bonnet wholly squashed.

"Fusty, fusty! You shall have me all to yourself for an hour or so, then return me to York Crescent. No one will be any the wiser, for Serena has gone off jauntering for the day."

"*You* have gone off jauntering, my girl, for I am not returning to London tonight."

"Beg pardon?"

"So you *should.* I would turn the chaise around and deposit you safely home, only I shall miss the sailing."

"*The Albatross?* "

Captain McNichols nodded, thinking of his strange costume, waiting for him at the bottom of the very bandbox that had flattened Miss Waring's hat.

"How perfectly exciting!"

"How perfectly *dangerous!* Our sailing is not a joke, Julia."

"I did not say it was. You explained it all to me. I *do* understand, you know."

"Then you will let me set you down at port? We shall have to procure some kind of abigail for you. There is an inn at Tibald Street . . ."

"Adam, you cannot abandon me at an *inn!*"

"I cannot take you aboard *The Albatross* either. It is too dangerous."

"I snap my *fingers* at danger! If *you* can undertake these missions, so can I. I am *also* a patriot, you know."

"If we are caught, it will be as pirates, not patriots. There would be no mercy shown."

"I will take that chance, for why should *you* engage in such exploits and leave *me* at home to worry?"

"It is not proper. There is no berth . . . No chamber . . . you have no maid, there is the crew . . . Julia, unless you were my wife you would be ruined!"

Miss Waring colored. "Then *make* me your wife, Captain McNichols!"

Adam drew his breath. There was nothing, he thought, he wanted so much in his life. It was impossible, ridiculous, utterly unthinkable . . . Robin would roast him upon a skewer.

At Balder's end, just before the fork in the road, he consulted his fob. Yes, there was time. And yes, he thought, it would be a shame to waste all his mama's hard-earned pin money. He drew a deep breath and drew from the elegant folds of his greatcoat an almost forgotten piece of parchment. Handy things, special licenses. He motioned the coachman to stop.

Night had approached swifter than Serena expected. It seemed to envelop the little rowboat, as its oars splashed softly and steadily through the water. There was no question of her rowing, my lord had vetoed the very suggestion with scorn, and added that she was to say no more on that subject—or any other—until they had reached the relative safety of the ship anchored just beyond sight of the horizon.

Serena nestled closer to those boots. There was nothing to do, then, but to watch the thin sliver of the waning moon and the clouds that drifted southward, leaving a glorious patch of startlingly clear sky, with a cluster of crystal stars, the chiefest amongst these Polaris, the northern beacon of the celestial world.

Robin was rowing effortlessly through the waves, so confidently that she had not the smallest qualm that she would be splashed, let alone capsized. She could hear the lapping of the water and the odd country sound of a dog barking, or a twig breaking, or a nightingale beginning its song. Once or twice she heard a chorus of chirrups that were the beating of cricket wings but sounded, to her enchanted ears, like the very twinkling of stars.

It was dark now, so suddenly dark that Serena could no longer make out even the shadow of Robin's face, or the dark silhouettes of her familiar shoreline. Presently, she gasped, for seemingly out of nowhere came the twinkling of light, like tiny candelabras flickering softly in the night. They grew larger, until Serena could see they were not candelabras at all, but lanterns, glowing with kerosene oil and slightly reddish from the oil-soaked rope and the tincture of the glass.

"The Albatross?" she muttered in a low voice. Robin nodded, and pointed to the outline of the vessel, now more visible as Serena's eyes adjusted to the light. Also, they were drawing closer now, so Robin drew out a tinderbox and lit his own flame, which he covered carefully with the edge of a cloth and flashed twice in succession, then once slowly, so the wick was revealed to Serena's wondering eyes. Then came an answering flicker, and a rope drifted down the side of *The Albatross,* which seemed enormous now, looming up from the sea.

My lord set down the oars and proceeded with several incomprehensible, but obviously deft, motions before securing the boat, and nodding to Serena to ascend.

"I can't!"

"You can, I will be just behind you! You shan't fall, I can promise you."

"I am not worried about *falling!*" Serena hissed.

"What then?" Robin was anxious, for they had come

so far, he could not brook a possible hitch now, in the eleventh hour.

"It is my skirts! They shall tangle in the rope!"

His countenance relaxed. "So small a matter, my little Miss Brave! Hook them up over your arms, they will be fine."

"I *can't!*"

Serena, who had not quailed at the thought of pirates, who had not shivered at the prospect of Valmont, now faltered under the stern gaze of Lord Caraway.

"*Why* can you not? I have seen you climb like a monkey when you were a child!"

"I am not a child anymore," Serena wailed, aware that interested eyes were peering down upon them.

"I have noticed. What ails you, Serena? Modesty?"

There was a moment's silence. "Yes," she finally whispered.

Robin, expecting the worst, emitted a low, thoroughly amused, highly masculine laugh. "Let that be a lesson to you, Lady Serena! It shall be a penance for deceiving me so grossly and making me believe I was in love with my bailiff, of all hideous and horrible thoughts!

"Up you go, and if I am afforded a view of your splendid ankles and delectable calves, all the happier I will be! Now don't look so glum, for I promise you, after this work is over I am going to marry you out of hand and *then* very penitent—not to mention immodest—you will be!"

So, cheeks aflame—for Serena, though she prided herself on being *quite* the woman of the world and was rapidly discovering that she really *was* just a greenhorn, ascended the ropes. My lord, chivalrous to a fault, averted his gaze and cursed himself for a fool.

The Albatross, once again in full possession of its cargo, the small rowboat having been dutifully hauled in, glided quickly away from the waters of Caraway toward the more stormy ones of the Upper Leith. Belowdecks—for there she had been firmly deposited with a stern warning from her perfectly piratical husband—the newly married Mrs. Julia McNichols waited with as much patience as a very young bride ever could.

Well, she had *promised* not to get in the way, and she meant to be good, for she knew perfectly well that up until now she had been very naughty indeed. But oh, what a delightful outcome it was to have Adam's signet upon her finger. It was a little large, but she cared not a whit for that and would, besides, have it sized in London.

As *The Albatross* sailed off once more, she had no idea at all that her aunt was above deck. If she had, she would naturally have forgotten all about her promise and rushed to throw her arms about her. As a matter of fact, being beset, slightly, by the motion of the ship and the day's excitements, she allowed herself to curl up in a tidy ball—in so much as her petticoats would allow— and drift off into a kind of seminap, semifearful mind state that would have had other less complex people baffled.

"All's well?" Robin grinned.

"All's well. Thanks, Adam! You may congratulate me, but we shall speak of that later."

Serena smiled and looked about her with interest. The vessel seemed familiar, yet it was strange to be standing above deck, so close to Caraway, with the wind at her back and darkness all around.

Captain McNichols, eyeing Serena, grinned.

"As a matter of fact, you might congratulate *me,* too . . ."

"Adam, I shall be delighted, but let us save these social pleasantries for later, when the work is done."

"But . . ."

"No buts, let us cast off at once. Slight alteration in plans. We are headed for the Leith tonight."

"But I thought tomorrow . . ."

"So did I, but by all accounts a trap has been sprung for us. We have Serena here to thank for the intelligence. Valmont expects us tomorrow, and a regular sea battle it would be. Our only chance, if we wish to do this quickly, is tonight."

"Do you know precisely what it is we seek?"

"I do."

"Where is it?"

"I have a very good idea. The Prince's writing bureau, behind the library door on the west side. I have been supplied, most providentially, with a key. Rittledon has been thorough as usual."

"Good. Then we seize the ship?"

"No, they are expecting that. It shall be stealth this time."

Captain McNichols looked so disappointed Serena would have laughed had the matter not been so serious. Robin grinned.

"Do not, I pray you, look so crestfallen! It is you, my friend, who will provide me with the diversion I need."

Adam brightened. "Cutlass?"

"Not unless they board, but we will need cannon fire and trumpets and a great deal of noise, perhaps even a sea approach. They will be anchored, but it will send their captains into a regular tailspin."

"Valmont is away?"

"Precisely. They will not be acting on his directions, so we should witness a fine spectacle of tail chasing!"

Adam grinned. "I think I can manage that!"

"Good. The full flag flying, of course, and a heraldic march might be in order. I want all Valmont's hands on the foredeck."

"So you can climb the aft?"

"Of course. I can deal with any lone sentry."

"After that?"

"After that, nightfall will help shield me back to *The Albatross*. If I am wounded, send some men down in the longboat."

Serena did not wait to hear more. She was being uncommonly quiet, for the very thought of the earl wounded appalled her. She knew she would be no help whatsoever as a wailing watering pot, so she excused herself quietly as the gentleman spoke in low tones.

"I hope to God you are all right."

"So do I. I leave Serena in your charge, of course, if anything should go amiss."

"I shall not fail you. But, Robin . . ."

"What?"

"It is a long and complicated tale, but I was wed today."

"What?"

"I married Miss Waring . . . that is to say, my *wife*, this morning."

Robin's stare was both wry, ironical, and vastly amused. "I collect I am in *truth* to congratulate you, then. I look forward to the tale! I'll wager my pretty silver buckles this was not *your* brilliant notion or timing!"

"No, but I wish it were. I could not be happier."

"I'll sympathize with your madness only because I am midsummer's mad myself! We shall talk on my return, but in the meanwhile it is rather providential, I suppose. Your wife shall chaperone Serena."

"Now *that* is a strange turn!"

"Life is full of strange turns, Adam."

Serena was just discovering *how* strange, as she bumped into a huge-eyed Julia, belowstairs. She restrained herself admirably, however, did *not* yell for Lady Caraway's famous vinaigrettes, though she felt so inclined, and finally heard Julia out, as *The Albatross* drew ever closer to its berth at sea.

A scolding would have been rather like the pot calling the kettle black, so after a few heartfelt expostulations and a little tears, for both felt the dangers their men faced keenly, the ladies forgot their grievances—which were really very few, and in great, wondering whispers, laughed a little at each other's tangled tales of love discovered.

It was all too soon that the silhouetted image of Valmont's vessel, alight with royal banners and a thousand brilliant tapers, drew parallel with but still apart from *The Albatross*. Tension markedly returned to the features of both ladies, still caught belowstairs, but facilitated by two well-placed portholes, from which they ventured to peek. It was too dark to see a thing.

Neither would own to fear, but Serena bit her nails as she had not done since childhood and Julia seemed to clutch convulsively at the strange ring of gold upon her finger, twisting it round and round again as though it were a talisman to ward off evil.

Adam, single-mindedly conscious of Robin's commands, had taken up his position at the helm and was giving orders for the cannons to be positioned, cleared and loaded. Robin, exchanging his dramatic costume shoes for more sensible but less romantic footwear, had just time to thrash out the last details of the revised Whitehall plan. He was casting his mind about for what he would need, when Serena appeared, more subdued than he had seen her in the past.

"You should be belowdecks." He tried to keep his voice gruff, but failed. Even the sight of her gave him vigor.

"I know. I am sorry. I came to say good-bye."

"Not good-bye, you goose: Farewell."

"Farewell then, my Lord Robin Red-Ribbon."

He smiled that old roguish smile that completely transformed his stern features.

"It was the ribbon, you know, that was your undoing. I found it in your cloak."

"I shall wear it in my hair as a talisman. I love you, Robin."

"And I you. Now be gone before I have to start worrying about more than just my back."

Serena nodded and turned back to the lonely stairwell from whence she had come.

"Wait!"

"Yes?"

"Do you have a piece of paper, my lady? I will need one, if I am to effect a switch. If I switch the prince's papers, the theft of his precious document might go unnoticed awhile. It is a chance I think we should take."

Serena did not ask questions. She reached into her cloak and caused a great deal of promising crinkling.

"Will this do?" She held out a sheet.

"Perfectly. Even the color is right. Pass me that lantern, my love, and disappear, once more, belowstairs. Promise me you will remain there. If we are boarded, I cannot wish Prince Valmont to know there are lady prisoners."

"No, indeed." Serena agreed all too heartily, though her throat was suddenly as dry as ash. "I will be very good, my lord, you have my oath."

Robin, never doubting it, nodded with satisfaction. Then he disappeared into the dark blackness of the night, and all Serena could hear of him was the soft lapping of oars on the waves and the high-pitched calls of his men.

The cannons of *The Albatross* went berserk on that quiet, dark evening. Serena and Julia huddled belowdecks and wished, for once, they were men. Inaction seemed so paltry! They held hands, however, and braced themselves against the ship's shaking. Then came the trumpets, and the flames, lit by the helmsmen and the frenzied sounds of sails being rigged to topmast and the rushing of wind against tarpaulin. Serena told herself that this was the diversion, the mad moment that Robin, far on the other side of the cove, most needed to effect his switch.

The Valmont was completely unprepared for an assault on the shore, though it had been stockpiling gunpowder for months in preparation for an assault by sea. His Royal Highness, away on certain strategic last-minute affairs, was not at hand to give the guidance required, and his crew, practically frantic with shock and indecision, were effectively paralyzed on shore. Only a volley of cannons, wildly fired into the blackness, proclaimed a readiness for battle. On all other fronts, the sea seemed as calm and as quiet as Robin could wish.

Julia heard her husband's voice. It was deeper than usual—authoritative, yet strangely hushed. There were footsteps and the clinking of metal chains and again, a great sense of pandemonium above decks and loud, piratical oaths quite unfit for the tender ears of gentlewomen. It was hard to know, cramped in their small quarters, whether the ship was being boarded or not—harder still to sit passively and let the action happen above decks, without their willing aid. But both ladies were bound by promises, and both sat on their hems rather than betray that trust.

All at once—it seemed like an eon—there was silence once more, save for a few murmured voices and a great jerk as the anchor was raised in earnest.

It was a simple thing for Robin to accomplish his mission—child's play, really, for a man of his vast experience and daring. He avoided the steps that were guarded by dark, silhouetted sentries and shimmied up mast posts as stealthily as he had done a dozen times or more.

Silencing the guard at the bridge was a mere matter of some quick fisticuffs, though not, unfortunately, before an alarm was shouted that caused Robin to have to spin around at top speed and employ some exceedingly light footwork to avoid a rapier sharp blade presented to his back.

It ripped at his side and tore at his splendid silver buttons, causing a slight flesh wound that sharpened his wits, and he had his *own* sword drawn in a slightly longer time than he would have wished but nevertheless fast enough to throw his attacker off balance. Before a further alarm could then be raised, the redoubtable pirate apologetically—but efficiently—gagged his assailant while complimenting him in whispers on his swordplay.

"It is not everyone," he consoled the furious man, "who lives to draw the blood of the famous Robin Red-Ribbon! Allow me to offer you a memento." And he shook the crimson ribbon from his hair so his locks fell in streams about his face, bowed silently, sheathed his sword, and was gone, deep into the hidden corridor the man had been attending.

Thanks to the information so thoughtfully provided by Major Rittledon, the matter was accomplished speedily, with only the most trifling of hitches. None of these are really worth mentioning, save to let it be known that Robin did *not* fly through this whole encounter without his heart beating wildly once or twice, nor did he find what he was looking for immediately—it took some agonizing few minutes, in which the Earl of Caraway both cursed and prayed rather furiously.

Through it all, however, his eyes sparkled with an intensity that was both enjoyment and heightened awareness bordering on fear. It was a game—naturally it was a game—but it was also something more, and my lord did not lose sight of that something, even when, his work complete, he came face-to-face with the man he most wished to avoid.

Yes, Prince Valmont, slightly uneasy, had returned early from his festivities. It was *he* who found the gagged guard, and *he* who had sprinted with a speed not usually anticipated in a man who wore mincing ballroom pumps with highly polished pointed toes. Almost too feminine for a man, yet no one could deny Prince Valmont his virility.

No, indeed. He emanated a menacing power that women found entrancing and that Robin found a most particular challenge. Valmont's mistake had been not to sound the alarm, but rather to deal with the intruder on his own terms. He was rather famous for preferring the private duel. Especially the unconventional types, where seconds were not to be found and if a man drew blood no one—least of all the authorities—was any the wiser.

Robin was just emerging into the cool air above decks when he came face-to-face with the prince. Valmont's sword was already drawn, but a mercurial smile hung upon his rather handsome features. He bowed, mockingly, beckoning Robin to step further into the light. Not moonlight, for the night was black, but lamplight, burning low and a dull yellow from the gas glow.

Robin's feet never faltered, and his bow—for he would never undertake such a venture without first bowing to his enemy—was as carefree as his fame. Valmont never suspected the unaccustomed doubt, and the extraordinary wave of anxiety that overtook Robin, now that it was not just himself and his own flesh that he cared for, but Serena's.

A quick clash of steel, and a flash of swords locked,

then unlocked, twined then untwining, lunging, feinting, rapier quick, ever with an ear for the crew, who might come to their master's aid at Robin's deathly peril. Indeed, one *did*, throwing a lit taper straight at the famed pirate, until Valmont roared at the poor fellow to mark what he did, for he would very likely set the whole damn ship ablaze.

Which was *precisely* the distraction Robin needed. With a light jab at Valmont, whose attention had momentarily lapsed, he apologized that he could not stay to actually kill him, which would naturally be the more polite and definitive thing to do, but would instead seize a glorious ruby button—which he greatly admired—as a memento of their interesting bout.

This he did, with Valmont seething and the guard dousing the flames from the taper, which were just licking at the hardwood decks.

Robin did not dally to see if he thought coming to the prince's aid was wiser than averting a small fire. He shimmied down the rope he had prepared for himself and down into the cool, black waters almost as swiftly as he had come.

It was several minutes before cannon fire was shot in his direction, and though he found the consequent waves a great pother and nuisance, he was not overly alarmed. After all, it was too dark to be any real target, and the twinkling lights of *The Albatross* beckoned enticingly to the east.

It was Serena who first heard the whistles of the crew. Yes, whistles and some rather bracing obscenities, but so cheerful she felt her heart would lurch into her slippers from sheer, unmitigated relief. *These* were not the sounds to be expected from a boarded vessel! These were the cheers of a hale crew, greeting their leader in triumph.

"Come on, Julia, let us go see!"

Julia, cooped up and cramped, needed no further bidding. She pulled up her skirts just a trifle (so as not to trip) and rushed after Serena, who was already halfway across the starboard deck.

"Oy! 'And me down a rope! The master is ready, right and tight!"

"Oi threw it into the longboat, along of 'is oars. There is only the spare, and that is a tad short an' all."

"Then 'urry up and fetch one from the stern, will ya? Can't keep our Robin Red-Ribbon awaitin', we can't!"

"Give me a mo!"

Serena permitted herself a peek at the waterline. The earl, a triumphant shadow, was standing in the boat, bobbing up and down like a cork with a balance she found perfectly remarkable, and a physique she found, despite the darkness, more than a little satisfactory.

She could swear, as she peered in a most curious and unladylike manner that she saw the flash of white below. Yes, she was almost certain of it: Robin's teeth were flashing in the half light. A crazy grin, and far too daredevil for her sedate and delicate tastes, but marvelous nonetheless.

"Julia!" But Julia had caught sight of Captain McNichols, on the half deck, and had already deserted her with a little giggle of delight.

Serena, beset with a most uncharacteristic impatience, turned from the view of the men and ripped up several of her sparkling white petticoats. Hurrying, for she wanted to be swifter than the crew returning with the heavy ropes, she knotted piece after piece until she had a length that was wavy and frayed in places, but definitely, as rope went, rather charming.

She tied it to the existing rope to lengthen the piece, then threw the whole overboard, petticoat side first, and held her breath. Robin, catching it, drew in his own sharply. Then, never one to ignore a challenge, he made the slow ascent up and decided that if his lady love did not cause him to actually *fall* to his death, he would strangle her for his pains.

He prayed that she was proficient at tying knots—which she was, for estate management was a varied affair and Serena was nothing if not thorough—and a third of the way up his unusual cord, he was actually enjoying himself and the supreme, crisp freshness of the underwear. Better yet, he was allowing himself to wonder how much of her linen she had spared for herself, and rather hoped the answer was not much.

He also hoped that his men were standing at a discreet distance and that they were minding their very shocking manners. Which naturally caused Robin to climb all the quicker, until he reached the more traditional coil and positively *flew* to the vessel's polished oak banister.

As he clambered nimbly on deck, there was a rousing—nay, a *deafening* cheer, and he signaled for the boat below to be abandoned to its fate upon the seas. *The Albatross* sailed within minutes, but for once my lord was not at the helm.

He was being duly—and perfectly justly—rewarded for his troubles. The only small matter to disturb his *complete* satisfaction was that Lady Serena still had a plethora of petticoats to spare.

Valmont, dowsing the flames upon his blackened decks, cursed. He had miscalculated this infamous Robin Red-Ribbon, bane of the high seas, but his cargo, at least, was safe.

He checked this, for his high style of living depended on the good favors of the gentleman to whom this was being so carefully conveyed. Yes, it was there, safe in his bureau drawer. A telltale little piece of parchment tucked into the gilded picture frame of the Princess Sancha. Really, she was most striking—if only she were not so terribly trying.

Well! The prince counted his blessings. He may not have captured the arrogant Robin Red-Ribbon, but he had, at least, the last laugh. He had his little document and nothing to show for being boarded save the loss of a single red ruby and the aching skull of one of his lesser guards. Stupid fool! Serve him right for permitting *The Valmont* to be boarded in such a humiliating manner.

The prince nodded, and ordered the anchor to be raised.

"You have the document?" Serena, still breathless, hardly needed to ask. Robin was looking far too jaunty to have failed. She ducked one of his kisses—for truly, the men were all grinning quite unreservedly and a lady had to draw the line *somewhere*—and begged him to be serious. My lord bowed. Prince Valmont had been mistaken. The cargo he had smugly cherished—indeed checked upon—was *not*, as he thought, stowed safely away in its hiding place. It was, even now, snug in the doublet of his great arch rival, Robin Red-Ribbon. The Princess Valmont, sadly, was never to receive the emerald necklace she had so prized.

Epilogue

Caraway was in order, the tenants all perfectly content, save for a few grumbles about the sudden hot weather, and the first crop of tea was peeking through merrily. Stanforth Hitchens had been promoted, *not* to assistant bailiff, as Serena had tacitly suggested, but to bailiff itself. In this capacity, he was exceeding all expectations.

Julia McNichols was big with child, and her husband, a certain Captain Adam McNichols, had hung up his side-sword and packed away certain eye-catching garments in the great sandalwood chests at Strawberry Hill. He had been given command of *The Albatross* and was looking decidedly more sober—though no less dapper—in his seafaring clothes.

The Marchioness of Penreith was brandishing a note of hand for eighty pounds. She seemed surprisingly pleased with it, though she had no idea of its origins. In the end, it was tucked into an ancient sketchbook of hers, there to be lost forever except to the endless speculation (and laughter!) of Serena and the incorrigible Lord Caraway.

As for Prince Valmont? He was still cursing horribly and clutching, with disgust, a tattered old piece of parchment. Useless, useless, *utterly* useless! Beautifully inscribed, in letters of gold, was a bill from Gunther's of London. Yes, indeed, the prohibitive cost of cake, no less. One sugared ice castle, though who would squander such a hideous sum on such a sickly confection, he really could not say.

A mistake, of course, for the direction of the bill was Lady Fanny something or other—he could not quite make it out. He wondered, with annoyance, who in the dashed world she was, and how in heaven's name that infernal nuisance of the seas, Robin Red-Ribbon, had effected the switch.

He was never to know, of course, for that selfsame Robin had transformed meekly into a dashing but not at all piratical peer of the realm and was even now partaking of a pleasant morning tea of delicate sandwiches and fresh, slightly burnt smoked trout from his lakes.

Any rumors that might have floated about on a tide of nonsensical gossip had been scotched long since. Lord Robin was positively too languid—not to mention too sublimely rich and handsome—to stoop to common criminality. The very idea was absurd, though people *would* try to puff themselves up by rumormongering! *Not comme il faut, not comme il faut* at all. And such was the verdict of anyone who was *anyone* in the polite world.

My lord licked his fingers—yes, his gloves were off, for they were dining outside and there was really no need for extreme formality. Certainly not now, in the shade of the willow tree, well hidden from the interested eyes of their cottagers.

"I think you are forgetting something." Serena, her mouth filled with hothouse grapes, meekly handed over his share of the plate—but quite spoiled the effect by batting her eyelashes as she did so.

Robin, amused, would not have a bar of her offering, telling her quite sternly that it was not *grapes* he was after, but something sweeter by far.

So, with a great swallow, then a sigh—not as mournful as the lady wished to pretend—the newest Countess of Caraway—perfectly content—allowed him to adjust her ribbons. They were, of course, a perfect crimson red.

Historical Romance from
Jo Ann Ferguson